THE WRONG BROTHER

A PERFECT FOR YOU NOVEL
BOOK 1

AMANDA SIEGRIST

Cover Designer: Amanda Siegrist
Photos Provided by: Conrado/Shutterstock.com
Edited by: Mitzi Carroll and Marisa Nichols

McCord Family Novel

Protecting You

Trust in Love

Deserving You

Always Kind of Love

Finding You

Dare You to Love

Mona & Mason

The Paranormal Chronicles, Volume 1

Perfect For You Novel

The Wrong Brother

The Right Time

The Easy Part

The Hard Choice

Psychic Love Novel

Exploding Love

Captured Love

Slaying Love Novel

Won't Let You Go

Doomed Love

Deadly Crazy

Evidence of Sin

Finding Redemption

Obsessed Hope

1

She brushed a hand across her forehead, trying to hold in her patience. "Run that by me again. You want me to do what?"

Mia rolled her eyes. "Aren't you listening, Gabs? You never listen to me."

"I always listen to you, just not when you're talking nonsense." Gabby stood up from the couch, swiping her empty wine glass from the coffee table. She needed a refill, especially after what Mia asked her.

"I think he's cheating on me." Mia pouted as she followed Gabby to the kitchen.

"You haven't been dating that long. I haven't even met him." Gabby stopped midway as she reached for the wine bottle. "I take that back. I rarely meet a guy you're dating because you go through them so fast. There's always something wrong with them. *He snores. He spits too much. He uses the bathroom for too long. He likes to read instead of having sex. He's a momma's boy.* Should I keep going?"

Mia grabbed a strand of hair and started to twirl it. "If you're saying those are silly reasons to break up with a man, they're not. Snoring is annoying. I could never get any sleep. That baseball player I dated *did* spit too much. And what possesses a man to sit in the bathroom for more than thirty minutes? I have needs, you know."

"Please, I don't want to hear about the reading part. Reading is good. I like to read."

"You like reading when you're about to have sex?" Mia planted a hand on her hip, her lips pursed, her eyebrows raised in defiance as she waited for an answer.

"I don't have sex as often as I'd like. That reminds me, I should put that on my to-do list." Gabby grabbed the pen and pad near her phone. "Have some sex. Soon." She made sure to underline the word soon several times.

She pushed the paper toward Mia. "I even underlined 'soon.' Then I'll pull out a book and read before I do the deed. You know, if you read an erotica book together, it would add to the mood. Did you ever think about that?"

"You're incorrigible. I get nowhere with you. Absolutely nowhere." Mia rolled her eyes once again.

Gabby pulled the cork from the wine bottle, pouring herself a glass to the rim. Sometimes dealing with Mia involved much-needed consumption of alcohol. "Why do you think he's cheating? And if you think he's cheating, dump his ass. Move on. You do it so well."

"Can you, for once in your life, not be so honest?" Then Mia glared at the jar filled with quarters on the counter. "You owe a quarter for swearing."

Damn it, she did. "I'll add it later. You knew what you were getting into when you started up a friendship with me. Remember the day we met, and I told you that green shirt looked horrible with that beautiful red hair you have? Never wear green. You make me think of Christmas." Gabby took a sip of wine.

"But you love Christmas," Mia pointed out. "I like bringing the Christmas spirit right to your door."

"You're right, I love Christmas. But not when I look at you and see a brightly lit Christmas tree."

Mia laughed, covering her mouth with her hand. "I did look pretty bad that day. But not all green looks bad on me these days. I now have a great fashion sense. You, on the other hand, need help sometimes."

"That's why we balance each other out. That's why we're best friends."

"And that's why I need you to apply for my boyfriend's vacant secretary position and see if he's cheating on me."

Gabby took a long sip of wine, letting the warm liquid soothe her. "I have a job, you know. A real job."

Mia snapped her fingers with vigor, pointing at Gabby. "You also have vacation time. Didn't you say you had so much time built up that you might start losing it if you don't use it? I'm helping you with that little problem."

"Mia, come on, talk to him. See if he's cheating on you. You're obviously getting a feeling that he's doing something wrong if you're asking me to do this. It's a little extreme for me to go 'undercover,'" Gabby said, using quotations with her fingers on the word undercover, "to see if your boyfriend is cheating on you."

"Since when are cheaters honest? Like he's going to say, 'Yeah, Mia baby, I'm not cheating on you.' He'd never admit it."

She rolled her eyes. "Oh, God, does he call you baby? That's so...so...disgusting."

"It's sweet. It rolls off his tongue like butter melting on a piece of warm bread. I love it when he calls me that."

"If you say so. Look, Mia, I can't take a week off work to go incognito at his work. There's no way in hell I could lie on the application about prior employment. It's not in me to lie like that."

"You don't have to lie. You were a secretary before." Mia smirked. "That's another quarter."

Gabby raised her eyebrows in disbelief, almost spitting out the small gulp she had consumed. Then she rolled her eyes. "Stop making me swear. I'm blaming you. And I was a secretary when I was nineteen. I'm twenty-nine now. We're a little too old to be playing these games. Talk to him."

"I can't. I don't want to see him lie to my face."

"If you think he's cheating, I repeat—dump. His. Ass."

"You're almost up to a dollar."

"Mia!" Gabby knew she was trying to irritate her.

"I need solid proof before I confront him." Mia produced another pouty face that was hard to resist. "I need you to do this. His secretary is on maternity leave. It's only a temp position, so it's not like you'd be lying that much when you leave after a week. He's been talking about how all the applicants have been horrible. He'll hire you on the spot. I know it. Like you said, one week. That's all I'm asking. I need to know. Then I can dump the lying, cheating, scumbag for sleeping around on me."

Gabby gulped the rest of her drink, wiping her hand across her lips as if she gained a mustache from the sweet red wine. "How do I let you talk me into shit like this?" She groaned. "Yes, I know, I now owe a dollar."

Mia screamed in delight, grabbing Gabby around the waist. "You're the best bestie ever."

"Fine, bestie. One week. No more."

"Yes! I knew I could count on you. His name is Champ Holloway."

"I can't believe I'm agreeing to this."

GABBY SAT on a nice plush black couch, bouncing her leg out of tune to the mellow music playing overhead. Something you'd hear at a symphony. Not that she ever would attend that sort of concert. She'd fall asleep from boredom. She'd take a rock concert over a symphony any day.

A new song, just as light and melodious as the last, started to play. It was annoying music. If she did get the job —a big if—she sure in the hell didn't want to listen to this crap all week. She'd go out of her ever-lovin' mind. Give her a crazy upbeat song, and she'd be good to go. It'd get her in the mood to work and do the best damn job she could.

She still didn't know why she caved into Mia's pleading. This was insane. This problem could be rectified by simply talking to the man.

Mia and men. Problem? Of course. There was always a problem when it came to Mia and men. She didn't know how to talk to them, how to have a normal, "let's have a nice relationship" sort of talk. Although Gabby shouldn't judge. She didn't know how to have that talk either. Her relationships were fleeting, at best. Nonexistent, at worst.

When it came to the man department, she and Mia swung out every time.

She met Mia in the hallway of their elementary school. Third grade rearing its ugly head—in her eyes, anyway. She was new to the school. Not the best way to make friends by insulting her choice of dress, but Mia hadn't seemed to care. She shyly smiled, pushed up her glasses that were too big for her face, and said, "Do you want to sit by me at lunch?" And as they say, the rest is history. Twenty years later, Mia's suckering her into going undercover to see if her boyfriend was cheating on her.

Well, hoping to go undercover. There was no guarantee she would get the job. She'd have to use her wily skills of negotiation. She could do this. She *would* do this. Mia was depending on her to find the truth. That was her job. Finding out the truth. When it came to Mia, if she asked, she always came through for her. That's just the kind of friend she was.

"Ms. Stileano, this way, please. Mr. Holloway will see you now," an older lady with black as night hair—Gabby knew for sure she colored it recently to cover the gray, it was so bold—said with a nasally voice.

"It's Stileano. Like Still-ano. Not Style-ano." Gabby stood up with a bright smile. She hated it when people said her last name wrong. She always corrected them. Most people screwed it up, making her have to correct a lot of people. She always said it with a smile. It usually didn't matter. People always took offense. It was her last name for good-ness sake. She should be the one taking offense. Not the other way around.

Of course, in good order like it normally happened, the older woman took offense and pursed her lips in a thin line. "This way. Mr. Holloway is a busy man. He doesn't have a lot of time."

"Of course."

They walked down a long hallway where they came to a set of double doors. The older woman pulled one open, walked through, and didn't bother to hold the door open for her. She had to rush ahead a few steps to grab the door before it slammed in her face.

The fast movement made her stumble in her high heels. The damn things. She hated wearing high heels. Yet, she managed to stay upright and not fall flat on her ass. The last thing she needed to do was embarrass herself or sprain an ankle.

She told herself to let it go, to not let the woman get to her. If this didn't matter so much to Mia, she would've marched right back out of this place. Judgmental bitch. What did she have to judge about her?

Was her outfit not professional enough? Did her pants have wrinkles from sitting so long? She swore she waited longer than she should've. She arrived ten minutes early because she hated being late for anything. Or maybe Miss I-dye-my-hair-terrible was having a bad day.

She would never work at a place where she'd have to deal with someone like this. Sure, she dealt with some unruly, uncaring coworkers at her other job, but she loved that job. She knew she wouldn't love being a secretary. This would test her patience. She hated being a secretary at nine-teen, and she didn't think her opinion had changed at twenty-nine.

Think of Mia. This is all for Mia.

A desk sat to the left, clutter-free, except for a small computer on the corner and a container full of pens and pencils right next to it. Another plush black couch sat kitty-corner to the desk. A small table filled with several magazines and a nice orchid plant sat next to the couch. A few paintings adorned the walls that captivated her attention. She wasn't into art, but she could appreciate fine art when she saw it. Most were of buildings at unique angles. One really caught her attention. Splashes of color, like someone took a brush, whip-ping an array of colors onto the canvas. It spoke to her. It felt like her life sometimes. Different colors, different directions. The splashes indicating the many derails life held for her.

God, when did she get so deep?

She smiled brightly when she saw the older woman standing by another set of double doors, her hands on her hips and the impatience clear on her face.

"As I said, Mr. Holloway is a busy man. Are you finished looking around?"

"By all means. I've been ready." Gabby gestured at the door. If anyone should be pissed, it should be her. She was early and still had to wait over twenty minutes after her appointed time.

The woman knocked on the door. A loud booming voice from inside yelled, "Come in."

The woman pulled the door open and stepped inside. "Mr. Holloway, Ms. Stileano to see you."

"Send her in."

The old lady smirked at Gabby as she walked by. She wanted to slap her silly for saying her last name wrong again. She knew she did it on purpose this time. Instead, she kept the smile on her face and thought of Mia. This was all for Mia.

"Ms. Stileano, have a seat," Mr. Holloway said from behind a huge oak desk, waving a hand at the chair in front of it. He didn't even look up from the stack of papers lying on his desk.

Gabby tried to keep the awe out of her eyes, and her jaw from hanging open. The view behind him was spectacular. New York City was a city worth sighing over any day. But sometimes, a view as magnificent as this needed extra time to take in and breathe in deeply. They weren't even on the top floor, but she could see the Statue of Liberty in all its glory, the sparkling water shining with elegance all around it. What a view. She would do anything to have a view like this to appreciate every day.

"Have a seat. I don't have all day, Ms. Stileano."

She shook her head clear of that misguided detour of beauty just to land on his face. Mia was dating *this* guy. She was glad she chose a pantsuit over a skirt. She imagined her legs would've blushed from all the heat gushing straight between her legs. Did legs even blush? Was that possible? Because it sure felt possible right at this moment.

She knew Mia had a knack for picking out handsome guys, but damn! This man was perfection at its finest, from his stylish hair to his angular jaw that looked meant for kissing to his suit that fit him like a glove. Even though he was sitting comfortably in his chair, she could tell the suit fit him to perfection.

Not that she cared how well the suit fit him.

She took a few more steps before sinking into the chair. Another plush, comfortable chair that made her want to groan with satisfaction. And maybe a little from the piercing depths of his dark brown eyes that seemed to stare straight through her. Right down to her very soul.

"It's Still-ano. Not Style-ano. And I apologize. The view from your office is amazing." She pointed at the window as she tried to make up for her complete lack of decorum.

She needed him to turn toward the window. She needed some time to regain her composure. He was sex wrapped up into a nice delectable package with a beautiful red bow to tie it closed. Merry Christmas to her. Or not. He was Mia's boyfriend.

That didn't mean she couldn't appreciate the gorgeousness before her. It was totally okay to look. But no touching. He had brown hair, about as deep as his sharp brown eyes, combed to the right with a slight wave. It was short but long enough to tame with a comb. She was curious if she ran her hands through it if it would stick straight up or fall flat, resting into the same pattern he combed it into.

Mia. Think of Mia. This was her boyfriend. You are not touching the man's hair.

They stared at one another for the longest time. At least, it felt like that. He needed to turn around.

"The view. Gorgeous, right? You must—"

"Moving along, Ms. Stileano. It says here on your application that the last time you had any sort of secretarial job was at nineteen. A few cooking jobs, a bakery, and a flower shop since then. What makes you qualified? I prefer not to waste anyone's time here. Especially mine."

"First off, Mr. Holloway, thank you for getting my last name right this time. I do appreciate that." For the moment, she'd ignore the fact he interrupted her. *Think of Mia.* Because, how rude. "Secondly, I'm a fast typer. Writing reports is my forte at my—" Gabby stopped, almost spilling beans about her real job. "At my last job at the flower shop. You have no idea how many inventory reports I had to write. I take meticulous notes because I hate missing anything. There are so many things you can miss if you don't write that shit down."

She cleared her throat. "I didn't mean to swear. I have a potty mouth sometimes. There's a quarter jar at work. I contribute to it...a lot. The main contributor, actually. My former work, that is. I don't work at the flower shop anymore."

That wasn't a lie. There had been a quarter jar at the flower shop because she made one, just like she created the one at her current job. And the one she had in her apartment. Not to mention one at Mia's. Not that the dumb swear jars ever stopped her from cursing. She had the worst potty mouth. The words came naturally out of her mouth, no matter how hard she tried to stop herself. But it was nice to have—especially at work—because it filled up quickly with everyone contributing to it. They always used the money to buy donuts, cupcakes, and anything else yummy to snack on.

She inhaled a patient breath and folded her legs. She never lost her cool like this. He was simply too easy to look at. His eyes, brown as the chocolate she ate this morning, seared into her as she spoke. It was unnerving. Thinking about that chocolate made her want to eat him up as well. She imagined he'd be just as delicious.

Stop it! Mia, don't forget about Mia.

"The qualifications said you needed someone who could write memos, take notes, file files." She laughed. Not that there was anything funny about this situation. His tepid expression said he wasn't amused at all. "I am very organized, some would even say anal—way anal. I've had that said to me way too many times. But hey, if it's in its place, you can't lose it. Am I right?"

She watched as his lips moved, barely. She couldn't tell if that was a smile wanting to be freed or an unconscious gesture. She had to say, though, she enjoyed looking at his lips. They looked like very kissable lips. She could already imagine them making their way to hers. Taking a light nibble, then making a slow trail down her neck to her breast where he would clamp onto her—

Mia! You are here for Mia. Stop letting your mind wander.

"Why did you leave the flower business? Any problems that I should know? Besides your potty mouth," he said, his gaze still unwavering and void of any expression but coolness.

But that twitch. She saw it again. Definite twitch of the lips. He wanted to smile. She could tell. Oh, how she wanted him to smile. She imagined it would personify his handsome features. The added five o'clock shadow on his cheeks added a hint of danger. Like he was tempting her to close the distance and kiss him. Brush her cheek against his scruffy one.

Stop this nonsense.

"I needed a change. So, here I am. What's to lose? I would love to work for your company. You design and build things. I love watching things come alive. I rock at Legos with my five-year-old nephew. Not that that has anything to do with this." She could feel a blush coming on. *Seriously, Gabs.* She never mumbled and sounded like an idiot. "The most you can do is say no. I didn't lose anything. But if you say yes and give me a chance, I win. I gain a job. And you win. What's not to like about that scenario? You'll see within an hour what kind of wonderful secretary I would be if you gave me a chance."

And you better because Mia will cry. I hate it when Mia cries. Then she pasted on the best smile she owned.

"You're not like any of the other applicants I've interviewed. I like your honesty, Ms. Stileano. I'm a busy man—"

"So you said several times. Don't you take time for yourself at all? Have a little fun and let loose? You can't always be busy."

"Don't interrupt me. Ever."

She nodded in agreement. "You're right. That was rude of me. But you shouldn't interrupt me if you don't like it. You did earlier if you're confused about what I'm talking about. Just sayin'...Mr. Holloway."

A lone brow rose as if he were amazed at her audacity. She liked the look on him. It made him look sexier somehow, his cheekbones rising a little, the ridges on his face contorting into a slight shock that made her want to kiss each spot.

No kissing! Mia. Mia. Mia. If she needed to repeat her friend's name a billion times in her head, she would.

Why was she having these illicit thoughts about a man who was—in all reality—cheating on her friend?

Because it had been a long while since she had sex. She needed to rectify that problem, especially if she had to work with him for the next week. Hopefully. Not too hopeful, though, because she couldn't act on her impulses—like vault across his desk and devour him from head to toe. Nope. Just hopeful for Mia's sake.

"I must be losing my mind," he muttered, then ran a hand through his hair. Oh, wow. The gesture turned her on further, making her wish she could do the same thing.

No! She did not want to run her hands through his hair.

"I have work to do, and this is wasting my time. You want your hour? Here's your chance. I need this memo typed up, twenty minutes ago. I need this phone call returned that I can't make the meeting on Thursday. Reschedule it for Friday at a nice restaurant. I need to impress the client. After twelve but before four o'clock. And not Decello's. Don't ask why. I need emails to these people on the change of construction on the new building in Brooklyn. To the contractors, finance department, and investors. I don't have the time to hold your hand or explain further about what I said. Do it in an hour, or you can leave. That's my answer." He held out a stack of papers and sticky notes, his expression indicating he wasn't messing around.

"A kind 'please' and 'thank you' would go a long way. Just sayin'." She grabbed the papers from him and stood up. "Thank you for the opportunity. See how easy that was?"

His face was still void of any emotion, not even a flicker of what he was thinking. "Get to work, Ms. Stileano." His lip twitched again as if he wanted to smile. "Before I change my mind."

Duly noted. He was the biggest Scrooge in the office. She walked out of his office, happy to be free and clear of his handsome face. This was going to be the longest week of her life. She hoped he hit on her. And no, not that she could revel in the fact he found her attractive as well and how he wanted to throw her across his desk and have his dirty way with her. Definitely not for that reason, as tempting as it may be. But because she would know he was a lying, cheating, dirty scumbag. She could rid Mia of him and get the hell out of this building away from his enticing, sexy face.

DANE RUBBED a tired hand over his face after his new secretary walked away and closed his office door. What was he getting himself into hiring her? He had to be out of his mind. She swore, she stated her opinion without thinking, and her last job was working at a flower shop five months ago. A flower shop! Here he was hiring her to work as his secretary, where she would be making more money than she ever saw in her life.

Not that he thought about the money he made. He didn't have time to think about things like that. He worked too much.

But he worked to get that kind of money in his bank account. He liked his job.

No. He loved his job, and he wasn't in it for the money. He didn't need to rise to the top like *some* people without working hard to earn his way there.

Of course, he didn't want his thoughts to derail there because then he wouldn't get anything done. He was already behind schedule on his latest project. He needed Ms. Stileano to pull through for him. If she did her job well, she deserved each penny given to her. Because he would work her to the bone. He had with every other secretary.

Not that they stayed long enough for his liking. They always quit within a few weeks, or he fired them. He couldn't stand incompetence or slacking. He needed his work done, and he needed it done right away.

How long would she last?

He couldn't quite put his finger on it, but there was something about the woman that had him taking a chance for once. He never took chances. He always investigated, analyzed, and scrutinized every tiny detail before making a decision. He didn't get to where he was without being precise. He always had to work hard to make his way—even in his own father's company. Yet, here he was, hiring her on the spot.

But her honesty. That had him hooked right away. Honesty was hard to come by. He didn't see it very often, especially in his own family. Unlike some people, he always tried to be honest. Whether people saw that as a weakness, he didn't care. Honesty was important—critical in any relationship. He knew where he stood with Ms. Stileano, and that wasn't something he could ignore. She wouldn't hold back her opinion. He liked that about her—a lot.

Dane ran another hand through his hair. Damn. Was he making a mistake hiring her? He couldn't afford to get behind any further in this latest project.

Would she get everything done? Would she screw anything up?

She looked the part, like she knew how to run an office with efficiency and organization. She was dressed very conservatively, very dull that wouldn't attract too much attention. But she had an elegance that wasn't hard to miss: long, wavy hair, half pinned to the side, giving a nice view of her cheekbone. For a moment, he had lost his train of thought, wondering what it would be like to kiss her along her jawline to her mouth.

Damn it.

Not something he could afford—a distraction. He had too much work to get done.

Double damn. Perhaps hiring her had been a mistake. She would be a huge distraction. She had since the moment she sat down in front of his desk. Her blouse had pulled tight across her chest, revealing a nice set of breasts that made a man want to touch. He was thankful it only lasted a second before she settled into the chair, making her blouse loose again. He couldn't believe he even noticed in the first place. He never noticed things like that.

He had to admit, his favorite part had been when she walked out. The way her ass swayed from side to side, her pants fitting snug. He never considered himself an ass man, but he had been tempted to stand up and follow her. To grab her from behind and squeeze. Thank heavens he stayed seated and hid the hard erection that formed from watching her walk away.

An erection, for God's sake. At work.

He needed to keep his thoughts away from the bedroom. He didn't have time for a woman. And he didn't need to screw things up by sleeping with his secretary. Never had he stooped so low in his life. Things like that were despicable in his eyes. He wasn't about to start now. Maybe none of that would matter. Could she last an hour with his high expectations?

To his surprise, she did more than he expected. She completed his long list he threw out to her in their initial meeting, not once needing to clarify anything. She returned a few phone calls that needed to be taken care of via the sticky notes posted on the computer screen on her desk. She also tackled the phone calls as they came in, learning quickly he didn't want to be bothered by just anybody.

He knew he was abrupt—to most people if he was honest with himself. If he expected honesty with others, he had to be honest with himself as well. He didn't have time for nonsense. Most of the calls he received were nonsense. He needed a secretary who would weed out the nonsense right away and take care of the problem. He had given her a small reprieve by explaining what calls he wanted to take and what calls should be directed to the office manager down the hallway. He had bigger things to deal with than what color he wanted the walls painted in the new building in Brooklyn. Paint them white, for all he cared. It was the structure, the magnificence of the building itself that made his heart soar.

An hour and a half into her probation period, he decided he liked her efficiency. He canceled the other three interviews he had lined up that afternoon. He was sick and tired of looking for a secretary—three long days of interviewing, coming up empty in each one. None of them spoke to him like Ms. Stileano had. By noon, he left for a lunch meeting and told her he'd be back by two. He told her to grab lunch and finish completing the memos he placed on her desk.

He knew it was a large stack he set forth for her to complete. But he was three days behind schedule. Three days without a secretary that too much work had piled up. He hated being behind, and he hated rushing even more. He liked everything to run smoothly. So far, she had proved to make things run very smoothly for him indeed.

Until he went to the filing cabinet in his office and couldn't find the file he needed. Nothing was in its spot.

"Ms. Stileano, my office! Now!" He shuffled through the files, his irritation rising by the second. He glanced over to the door to see it closed. Where was she?

"Ms. Stileano!" Slowing down as his fingers ventured forward through each folder, he made sure to take his time so he wouldn't miss the file he was looking for.

What was taking her? This was ridiculous.

"Ms. Stileano, I need you. Now!"

His fingers paused between the files. It couldn't be. He blew out a deep breath, wondering how much nerve the woman actually had.

A kind please and thank you would go a long way. Just sayin'.

"Ms. Stileano, come here...please."

No more than three seconds passed before the door opened and she walked in.

"Yes, Mr. Holloway. You needed me?"

"Were you standing outside the door waiting for me to say please?"

"Was it so difficult to use the word? I am a person with feelings. I may be your secretary, but I am not a doormat or a dog. I don't jump at commands."

He steeled his mind not to lash out. She was right. He could be more polite at times. But he needed this file, and he needed it now.

"Did you mess with my files?"

"Do you mean to ask if I organized them? Then, yes, I did mess with them. I completed everything you asked of me. I took a phone call from Mr. Shelburg, who needed some information on the Duncan building. I came in here to look for it, and let me tell you, your filing sense is atrocious. I almost didn't find the damn thing. I had to apologize to Mr. Shelburg—multiple times—for keeping him on hold for so long. You weren't back yet from your meeting, so I organized your filing cabinet for you."

"But I can't find anything now."

"Could you seriously find anything before?"

He paused, not wanting to answer the question. Then, because he couldn't stop himself, he said, "You swore again. Do we need a swear jar, Ms. Stileano?"

A tiny smirk appeared on her gorgeous face. "Maybe."

He forced himself not to return a smile, smirk, or even a tiny grin, but damn, he wanted to.

"I need the Marcelli file. Where is it?"

"It's simple. I promise. It's under M."

She smiled brightly, making him want to shake her silly and remove that damn smile. Then it hit him. He knew the perfect way to remove it. What would she do if he suddenly kissed her? That'd wipe her smile off with ease. That sounded like a much better plan than shaking her.

Damn it. He couldn't kiss his secretary, no matter how enticing it sounded. But, oh, it sounded very enticing.

He pressed his lips together to hold back another smile that wanted to let loose. "Do you enjoy being a smartass?"

She tilted her head, tapping a finger on her temple. "On occasion. But I didn't mean it sarcastically. I meant it literally. It's really simple. I organized it by sorting everything alphabetically. It'll be much easier for you." Then another beautiful smile appeared. "Perhaps I should make a swear jar. You can't seem to control your impulses to swear either."

He averted his attention back to the cabinet. She was right on one account. He couldn't control his impulse to swear, and he was almost having a hard time controlling the impulse to cross the distance and kiss her senseless.

Ignoring what he knew would be a terrible idea, he pulled open another drawer where he found the Ms. He saw the file he needed immediately, grabbed it, shoving the drawer closed.

"Ms. Stileano, I need a cup of coffee." He walked back over to his desk.

"You can get your own coffee."

"Excuse me?" And he thought she had already managed to surprise him enough for the day. Apparently, he was wrong.

"I'm your secretary. Nowhere in the job description did it mention fetching you a cup of coffee. I'm not your personal servant. Although, you've felt the need to almost act like I've been just that all day. I have a lot of things to do, thanks to you. I don't have time to get your coffee. If you want one, you'll have to get it yourself."

"Do you like testing me?"

"No. It's simple manners. You didn't even add 'please.'"

"Do you want to be fired already?"

"Are you firing me?"

2

GABBY PULLED her feet onto the couch, rubbing her toes with a rough hand. She needed a good massage. A deep massage. She hadn't worn heels in a long time. Not some cheap heels with little height. But no, tall, make-me-break-my-neck heels. Only because Mia suggested she wear the damn hazardous shoes. While one would think a secretary sat at a desk all day, she didn't. That damn aggravating man had her running back and forth between her desk, his office, and the file room down the long, long hallway.

Way too long of a hallway.

She glanced at her hallway when she heard her apartment door swing open, and the sound of tiny clicks come her way. She reached for her wine glass, raising it to Mia as she plopped down next to her.

"Cheers."

Mia leaned closer. "So? What are we cheering? Is he cheating on me? You found out already. The scumbag!"

Gabby smiled behind the rim of her glass. "No. I didn't find out much other than the fact he works too damn much. And don't you dare tell me to add anything to the swear jar.

I'll add five bucks later. My feet hurt. Rub them?" Gabby tried to lay her leg over Mia's lap, but she pushed her away.

"I'm not touching your feet. I told you that you needed to wear heels more often. This is what happens when you don't." Mia cocked a brow. "Five bucks? You're anticipating swearing a lot tonight."

"You do realize I can't wear heels at my real job. I hate wearing the damn things. That right there incites me to swear heavily because they made my feet hurt."

Mia grabbed the glass out of her hands, taking a huge gulp. "Hmm, this is the stuff from that wine festival we went to last year. I love this stuff. So, dish? How'd the day go?"

"It went. He worked me dry. He was still at the office when I left. I don't even know how he has time for you. He doesn't even have time to appreciate the gorgeous view from his office. He needs a serious wake-up call." She scrunched up her nose in distaste.

"So, that's why he bailed on me tonight. He said he had to work late. He wasn't lying." Mia smiled, taking another sip of wine.

Gabby grabbed her glass back, almost spilling the contents. "Get your own glass, girl. This one is mine. I'm tired. He wasn't lying. He was working when I left. It didn't look like he was going anywhere anytime soon."

"This is good news. Maybe I'm creating it all in my head. Something always goes wrong, I guess I'm making nothing into something." Mia blew out a sigh of relief. "Wanna watch a movie? I don't have a hot date anymore tonight."

"Sure."

Gabby kept the happiness plastered on her face and in her tone of voice, even though she wanted to crumble into a tiny ball and cry her eyes out. Hot date. Yeah, Mia's boyfriend was hot, alright. That's all she had been thinking about since she came home—that, and how aggravating the man was. He could use a manners 101 course. Despite how he worked her to the bone with barely offering a please or thank you, she felt bad for him when she knocked on his door.

He had looked up from his desk, his face full of shadows and tired lines. He nodded once and waved a hand for her to close the door. She didn't think he even processed who was at the door, he had been so engrossed in the paperwork on his desk. He needed to let loose once in a while. Smell the fresh air.

She almost let those sad eyes of his suggest she stay and help him with whatever he needed. Which was crazy—she didn't even like the man. He was abrupt, arrogant, and most of the time, rude. Ha! Try all the time. And he was Mia's boyfriend, and potentially cheating on her.

Although she got the vibe he wasn't that type of man. He was focused on his work, his mind only on the project in his hand. She imagined he would be the same when it came to a woman. He would focus his attention on that one woman. Her gut told her he wasn't a cheater or a liar. She liked to follow her gut.

She was lucky he didn't fire her for her loose lips. She always had a hard time keeping her mouth shut. That saying, "think before you speak," applied to her. She never mastered that once in her life. It put her in some tight jams, mostly at work, but her fast-thinking always managed to get her right back out of the trouble. She also knew that's why she had a hard time keeping a man around. Most men she dated didn't like a strong-minded woman. Well, good for them. She wasn't about to change for anyone. A person either liked her or they didn't.

She should, at least for now, be a little less abrasive with him. He could've fired her today.

"Are you firing me?"

A muscle ticked in his jaw. "No." Then he said, surprising her, "If I ask nicely, will you get me a cup of coffee?"

"Is that you asking nicely?" she asked with a grin, enjoying the way his eyes leveled into tiny slits like he was thinking about changing his mind to fire her. Which she totally shouldn't enjoy.

"You don't give up, do you? You want it straight forward and concise."

"Well, it's easier to understand a person if you're straight forward and concise. Why beat around the bush with things? You asked a question, but not the direct question you want answered."

He sighed, leaning against the front of his desk and crossed his legs. "I think you like testing me."

"What am I testing you for? Midterms?" Shit! She closed her eyes, then opened them with a distressed expression. "I didn't mean to say that. Well, I did because it came out. But I sometimes forget who I'm talking to. I'm not trying to get fired here. I can be sarcastic at times, joking around. I'm not testing you. Unless you want me to. You could use some lightening up. Life shouldn't be so serious."

He eyed her for a while with an expression she couldn't decipher. His gaze unnerved her. It looked like he barely moved his gaze, yet she felt like he was roaming her body from top to bottom. Or maybe that was her imagination wanting him to. To check her out from head to toe. To grab her around the waist and fling the things on his desk to the floor with one fell swoop of his arm. Then ravish her to the point of bliss on that very desk.

Neither spoke for the longest time. Maybe they were both having naughty fantasies in their minds. She could only hope.

Then Mia's name popped into her brain. She shouldn't even be having a tiny fantasy about her friend's boyfriend.

"Ms. Stileano?" he finally said in a soft voice. Or she imagined it coming out of his mouth softly. She didn't think he knew how to talk softly. Abruptness was more his style.

"Yes, Mr. Holloway."

"Will you please get me a cup of coffee? I would appreciate it."

"I can do that. I'll be right back." She had to give in. He asked very nicely. The first time anything came out of his mouth so nicely. How could she resist that? Simple. She couldn't.

"Ms. Stileano?" he called to her before she stepped through the double doors.

She turned around. "Yes?"

"Thank you."

As she walked out, she swore she saw a slight tilt of his lip. A smile. Maybe he did know how to smile.

"Yo, earth to Gabs. Did you want a refill?" Mia asked, waving a hand in front of her face.

Gabby shook her mind clear of the memories and handed her glass to Mia. "Refill sounds awesome. Action flick tonight?"

Gabby got up from the couch to dig through her movies. She hoped Mia agreed. She didn't want to watch a romance. That would only make her mind drift to a man she shouldn't even think about. Since when did one person dominate her thoughts? She never had a man take over her mind and make her act like an idiot.

"Yeah, works for me."

Thank goodness for small favors. She rifled through all her movies until she found the movie that had the most action possible.

DANE PINCHED the bridge of his nose as the words sitting in front of him started to blur into one big spiral of nonsense. He was tired. He stayed way too late last night. This latest project had to go smoothly because the last one didn't go as well as he had hoped. He could only blame himself. He refused to blame anyone else. These projects were his responsibility—at least, in his eyes. When he put his fingers to work to create something, he expected it to come out with perfection. If it didn't, it must've meant he did something wrong.

He needed caffeine. Lots and lots of caffeine. He opened his mouth to yell for Ms. Stileano, except he found himself closing it. Almost like a fish gulping for air. She didn't like it when he yelled for her. Something she told him several times this morning.

She had even produced a mason jar and set it on the edge of his desk. In her straightforward, honest way, she smiled and said, "It helps remind me to keep my potty mouth in check."

Which he doubted, considering she had already added five quarters to the jar. It made him chuckle—not in her presence, of course—how adorable she was when she swore, then looked aggravated at herself for swearing in the first place. Her forehead crinkling, her lips puckered in annoyance. Then a silly smile would twist her lips as a quarter clinked to the bottom of the jar.

He almost smiled, thinking back to those times.

What? Why would that make him smile? He didn't appreciate her wasting his time by derailing his train of thought. Which she often did. The smile punctured his expression anyway. He couldn't help it. No one else ever stood up to him, put him in his place with simple words and a sweet smile. She may say things she shouldn't, but she always said it with the sweetest smile.

She made him realize how much of a jerk he could be at times. He didn't mean to act that way. He just had so much to do. Work. Work. Work. That's all he ever did. Even his mother commented on how much he worked. Although, he'd never tell his mother he liked to work so much because it was the best excuse to stay away from them. Not her. But his father and brother. He'd never admit that to her. He loved his family. He did. But he could only handle them in small doses. Especially his brother. He couldn't be happier his brother worked several floors above him. He wouldn't be able to handle seeing him every day.

He stood up, taking his time. What the hell was he doing? He must be more tired than he realized. Or he wanted to see her sweet smile. It was so wrong of him to even think such things. It didn't stop him from grabbing his jacket, opening the door, and stopping in front of her desk.

"Ms. Stileano, I need a cup of coffee. And—"

"You forgot 'please.'" She looked up from the computer with a straitlaced face, not amused by his behavior. Where was the smile he enjoyed every time she talked back to him?

He almost smiled despite himself but held his face neutral. He wouldn't let her see what her attitude did to him. He liked her honesty way too much for his liking. If she ever found out he liked her—more than as a simple secretary—she would quit, and he couldn't have that.

Oh, shit.

He liked her.

Not only as a secretary. That wasn't good. Maybe he should start looking for a new secretary.

But he'd miss her. Miss her bossing him around and

sending sweet smiles his way when he did something she didn't approve of.

"Tsk, tsk, Ms. Stileano. What happened to not interrupting each other? You didn't let me finish."

She cleared her throat, a small blush appearing on her cheeks. "You're right. Forgive me. Please finish speaking."

He liked the way her cheeks bloomed a rosy color. It made it that much more enticing to brush a hand across her face to see if her skin felt as soft as it looked. He jammed his hands into his pockets before the impulse took over.

Then he copied her by clearing his throat. Now he felt awkward with what he wanted to ask her. Nothing scared him, though. He came out here for a reason, and he'd ask her, regardless of how much tension floated between them at the moment.

Oh, the tension. Not the angry, you-upset-me kind of tension.

Oh, no. That would be too simple.

More like the I-want-to-jump-your-bones kind of tension. Or maybe he was the only one feeling that sort of awkward tension.

Right. He had to be the only one feeling that kind of tension because her facial expression didn't say she was wanting to jump his bones right now. And if she did, he wouldn't stop her.

And he was derailing from his original goal. He needed to focus.

"I need a cup of coffee. I was going to ask if you wanted one as well. I need some fresh air. I was going to go across the street to the coffee shop. Would you like to join me?"

He couldn't believe he said that. He meant to ask her if she wanted something. Not if she wanted to join him. He could tell she was also surprised. Her mouth hanging open couldn't be a good sign. Why did he ask her to come with again?

She stood up, a mask of indifference on her face. "I guess I could use a small break." She reached down to the bottom drawer of her desk and grabbed her purse.

"Well, then, after you." He put his hand out in front of him for her to take the lead.

She nodded, doing as he suggested. Which after he thought about it as he followed her, it was a horrible idea. He enjoyed looking at her ass. Like, really enjoyed it. He always turned away from his work to watch her walk out of his office. Here he was, following behind her with the perfect view of the very thing he loved to look at. And within reaching distance. He shoved his hands in his pocket, squeezing them into tight fists to stop himself from doing the one thing that could ruin everything. He couldn't lose her as his secretary. She was perfect for him.

Shit.

He walked a little faster to match her pace so he could walk next to her instead of behind. Hitting the elevator button, they waited in awkward silence while the elevator took its wonderful time to get to their floor. He still couldn't figure out what possessed him to ask her to join him for a cup of coffee, or that he even wanted to leave the building for one. He never did things like this.

He thought he should say something, anything to erase the silence, but nothing came to his mind. He didn't lack female attention when he felt inclined to have it. Lately, he hadn't had much female attention, but only because he had too much work to get done.

This was unusual behavior for him to feel nervous with a woman. Nervous. He couldn't believe it. He was nervous to talk to a woman. Geesh. She was nothing more than his secretary. There was nothing to be nervous about.

He moved his mouth to say something when the elevator doors dinged open. Instinctively, his hand ventured to her back and urged her forward. Electrifying desire pulsed through his veins. Damn it. This was worse than when he took his fill of her. He immediately dropped his hand from her back and hit the button for the first floor. She moved more to the right, closer to the wall than to him. She didn't like that he touched her. Good to know. Although he couldn't say the same thing. He had liked it. The short zap of desire that hit him. When had a small touch from a woman ever affected him like that?

Well, it wouldn't happen again if she didn't like it. He didn't even mean to do it in the first place. Nothing good would happen to upset her other than her leaving him. Unacceptable. He couldn't lose her. She ran his office better than any secretary he ever had.

"My mother's birthday is coming up next month. I thought a nice arrangement of flowers would be nice. What is the best flower this time of year?" They were the only two in the elevator. They had way too many floors to go in complete silence. He couldn't stand the silence anymore.

"Why would I know?"

"You used to work at a flower shop." His brows puckered. He couldn't be mistaken. A lot had been on his mind during her interview, but he swore that had been one of her previous employments.

She laughed. "Oh, yeah, I did."

This time he lifted a brow in amusement. He couldn't help but grin as well. "And? What would you suggest?"

She brushed a hand across her forehead to wipe away a strand of hair. "Right. Um...white lilies are beautiful. Throw in a few more flowers, maybe a few roses for a splash color. Or all lilies would be fine as well." She brushed another hand across her forehead before placing a hand on her hip, then turned to him. "Is this a test?"

"Are we still testing each other? I hadn't realized. It was an honest question."

"Okay."

"Okay," he repeated, wondering why he, of all things, had to ask her about flowers. She didn't think he was sincere. Why in the world were they so defensive toward each other? Since the moment they met? Well, he could think of several reasons, except he didn't want to admit to any of them.

The rest of the ride went in silence. When the doors to the elevator opened, he almost placed another hand on her back to guide her but stopped himself at the last second. He had no claim to her. Placing a hand on her in such a manner spoke volumes. As much as he ached to touch even one part of her, he couldn't. Plus, he couldn't take her retreating again. A small pang to his heart already hurt from her first rejection.

They walked outside, where she stopped in the middle of the sidewalk. She put her head in the air and inhaled deeply. She turned toward him and smiled. He would never tire of her smiles. He couldn't be happier that she was smiling once again.

"Go ahead. Try it."

He looked at her, confused. "Try what?"

"Smell the fresh air. You said you needed some."

He glanced around, watching as people walked by them, not paying them much attention. But still. They were standing in the middle of the sidewalk.

"I can smell the air."

She shook her head with annoyance. "You can smell it, yes, but you're not appreciating it. You work too much, Mr. Holloway. Live a little."

"I am. I'm grabbing a cup of coffee across the street instead of down the hallway from my office."

She chuckled, her eyes lighting up with pleasure. "Baby steps. You're right. That is progress for you. Come on, Mr. Holloway. You have a meeting in thirty minutes. I imagine you're rarely late for anything."

"No. I've never been late in my life."

She stopped before stepping off the curb to cross the street. "You were late to interview me."

Well, that was something he'd never let happen again. For her, he'd always be on time. No matter what.

GABBY SHUT DOWN HER COMPUTER, organized the papers on her desk, and grabbed her purse from the bottom drawer. Then she slammed the drawer shut, ready to get the hell out of here. Her feet were killing her. Again. They killed her more today than they did yesterday. She didn't know how Mia did it all the time, wearing killer high heels that made her feet ache to the point of pain.

While they had a nice reprieve, managing to be cordial for the short coffee break they shared, Mr. Holloway had worked her to death the rest of the day. She couldn't remember how many times she ran to the file room down the long hallway to grab another file he needed. That room was as disorganized as the filing cabinets in his office.

As much as she hated this job—knew she wouldn't be here next week—she couldn't help herself. She tried to organize what she could in the little time she found for herself.

She couldn't stand the disorganization. She hadn't lied to him when she said others called her anal at her other job. She was always organizing the files at that place as well. She knew some of those jokers she worked with purposely put things away wrong to see if she would put it back correctly. She did. It was a compulsion she couldn't control.

Throwing her purse strap on her shoulder, her eye caught the empty coffee cup in her trash can. She still had a bit of a shock that he asked her to join him. The ride down the elevator had been awkward, to say the least. But once outside, they had meshed into an easy conversation.

She wasn't sure how it happened, but one minute they were talking about the fresh air, then the next, they were talking about baseball. She loved baseball, and she loved her home team. Surprisingly, so did he. Not that she was surprised a New Yorker loved their home team, but that he enjoyed baseball. He worked so much, she didn't think he made the time to enjoy anything.

That fact alone made her like him just a little bit. Which was a very bad thing. She didn't need to develop feelings for her friend's boyfriend. He had tiny moments when he could spark the desire in her. She hated the feeling every single time. Only two days with the man and she found herself daydreaming about what it would be like if he was her boyfriend.

But that's where problems started. Nothing could happen between them. Absolutely nothing. Her friendship with Mia was worth more than just a guy. She would never ruin what she had with Mia for anything. Not only would he be considered a cheater and liar, so would she.

Yet, sometimes it was hard to get his face out of her mind and the soft way he touched her. She almost froze in place when his hand hit her back. His touch scorched right through her shirt straight to her skin. She had wished for her shirt to magically disappear and for his hand to glide up her back and to her front. Of course, she had been glad when he let her go. His touch had made her lose her focus, the ability to function like a simple step forward. It was a very good thing he urged her forward; otherwise, she didn't think she would have made one step.

She walked to the double set of doors and knocked. She opened the doors when a loud voice told her she could enter.

"I'm leaving for the night. You should walk down with me." She didn't want to see the tired lines on his face tonight. She didn't want to leave him alone with his work for his only company. Even with his abruptness and rudeness at times, she didn't want to see him working so hard by himself.

"I still have things I need to get done. I'll see you tomorrow, Ms. Stileano. Thank you for another great day. I do believe you're the best secretary I've ever had."

He smiled at her. A full-blown smile that suddenly made her feel guilty.

She was lying to him. She would be quitting by Friday, thereby leaving him secretary free again. He would have to interview more people for the position. She could already imagine the torture he would go through in doing so. He was a very particular man. Very set in his ways. She wasn't sure how she managed to mesh with him so well in such a short amount of time. But she did. They made an excellent team. She would be destroying all of that soon.

Sure, his regular secretary would be back in a few months after her maternity leave was over, but he needed someone else in the meantime. She hated how she'd be letting him down.

"Don't work too late tonight. You need downtime sometimes."

His face fell into a frown, rubbing his whiskered chin delicately. "What can I say? When you have nothing to go home to, work seems to be the only solace."

"What about your girlfriend?"

What about Mia? Was he saying Mia was nothing? How dare he! Mia was an amazing person, full of life, full of fun and laughter. Which made her realize, these two were complete opposites. Sort of like he and she would be complete opposites.

"Good night, Ms. Stileano. Close the door...please."

Too shocked by his words and his refusal to answer her question, she did as he asked. She closed the door and walked out.

She changed her opinion, just like that.

He was cheating on Mia. Cheating on her with his work. Maybe she wouldn't have to come back tomorrow. Maybe that would satisfy Mia. She deserved better.

3

To Gabby's great annoyance, Mia found nothing wrong with him ignoring the question or his words that he had nothing to go home to. She said they weren't living together, so he had nothing to go home to unless he knew she would be there. She had a late show that night and couldn't make any plans with him.

Mia worked backstage doing costume and makeup for a small theater. She hoped one day to move up to the big leagues on the big Broadway plays. But for now, she was happy working where she was. She worked with some talented people who made her job worth walking into every day. And Mia loved dressing up. She didn't care she wasn't dressing herself up. As long as she had someone to beautify, she was a happy camper.

Instead of finishing her vacation putzing around her apartment or taking in the sights, it was a beautiful city not to enjoy now and again, she returned to her job, to the man who started penetrating her nightly dreams.

She tried her hardest to keep her focus on the notepad

in front of her instead of his handsome face when he needed her to dictate a few things. But it was a hard thing to do. His eyes lit up with excitement as he talked, his hands making motions in every direction. It's as if he needed to talk with his hands, impossible to keep them by his sides.

Every day, he inquired whether she wanted to join him for a cup of coffee. It took her by surprise as it had the first time. But unlike the first time, the elevator ride wasn't awkward or stilted. She found herself laughing with him. Laughing. She had no idea he had such a boisterous laugh, he barely smiled.

They didn't talk about anything personal. They talked about baseball, the crazy things going on in the news, a book she recently read—which in turn made him mention a book he also read. She didn't know when he had time to read. She knew he always stayed late at the office. Sometimes she wondered if he stayed until the next morning. But she knew that wasn't possible as he always had a new suit and tie on the next day.

A suit and tie that fit every delicious inch of him.

Talking about reading had her thinking about Mia's dislike for reading before sex. Which had her thinking about sex. Which had her thinking about sex with him. She couldn't dispel how many times she pictured him taking her across his desk and having his wild way with her. There were a few times she had to back up from his desk to stop the urge to fling herself across the desk.

She couldn't be any more excited that it was officially Friday. Her last day of work. Even with all the times they shared talking, although never getting too personal, she still had no concrete evidence that he was cheating on Mia. Her gut, though she didn't like what he said a few days ago, still didn't think he was a cheater. And that's exactly what she would tell Mia. She would also tell her that she should move on from him. For two reasons.

Reason one—he worked way too much. She had no solid proof because she always left before him. But she had a strong feeling he stayed at the office way late into the night. Mia shouldn't date a man who had no time for her. She deserved better than that.

Reason two—a very selfish reason. A reason she would never utter to Mia even under duress. She liked him too much herself. She wasn't sure how she would be able to stand it if they progressed into a serious relationship, like marriage. Plus, she was dying to know how Mia would explain her working for him when, or if, they met. That would be one awkward conversation she didn't want to be a part of.

Sort of like the conversation she needed to have with him about quitting. She had a real job to return to on Monday. A job she loved. She would miss his handsome face, but she wouldn't miss the secretarial work.

She figured she owed him the whole day, though. Instead of heading to his office to tell him the bad news, she took the long, long walk down the hallway to the filing room. To organize.

"What are you doing?" a soft voice asked behind her.

She had been in here for almost twenty minutes. She should have known she couldn't be gone that long without him needing her for something. And she knew for a fact that she didn't imagine anything this time. He definitely spoke in a soft voice.

With the drawer left open, she turned around to face him. "Organizing. I wanted this place to look better before I

—" She stopped speaking when she realized she didn't want to tell him yet.

He crinkled his face with confusion, yet a slight tilt of his lip emerged. "Before you what?"

"Before I went for lunch. It's almost lunchtime, isn't it?" she asked with a beaming smile.

God, she would go to hell for lying to him. She despised the fact she'd have to confess later she was quitting. She knew it would hurt him so much.

He glanced at his watch, wrapped perfectly on his wrist. "I suppose so. I couldn't find you. For some strange reason, I thought I would find you here. Why do you like organizing so much?"

"Do you dislike that I organize as I do? Do I not make your life easier?"

She leaned against the drawer, the corner of it digging into her back when he stepped closer to her.

"You do make my life easier. I'm not sure how I functioned before you."

"Oh, I'm sure you functioned fine and will continue to do so when I'm not here anymore."

He looked confused again. "You're not leaving me, are you? I can't have that." He took another step closer.

She felt the drawer move a little as she moved back. He was so close she could reach out and claim his lips if she wanted to. She couldn't do that to Mia. She *wouldn't* do that to Mia. "You needed me? What can I do for you, Mr. Holloway?"

At the sound of his name on her lips, said in a very professional manner, he backed up a step. He cleared his throat nervously. Very nervously. She couldn't recall a time he ever acted like that. He had been on a few heated calls, too, where she would've been nervous the client would bow out of the deal. Not him. He didn't break a sweat or display an ounce of nerves.

"I need you to deliver these papers to my brother, two floors up." He held out his hand with a thick file.

"Your brother? You have a brother...who works here?" Well, wow. What a surprise. She didn't know why that surprised her. Maybe because Mia never mentioned a brother.

"Yes. And I prefer not to deal with him that much when it comes to work."

"But you work at the same company. It seems a little impossible to avoid the man."

"Perhaps. But not impossible. That's why I have a secretary. And if I ask her nicely, she'll take these papers upstairs for me."

The smile that caressed his face made her weak in the knees. She could never resist him when he smiled. Except she didn't remember him asking.

"I'm waiting."

He leaned forward, his mouth getting dangerously close again. "For what?"

She laughed, the nerves beaming forth with ferocity. Great. Now they were both nervous. For the same reason? She didn't know how much longer she could resist the temptation standing in front of her. "For you to ask me nicely."

"Oh, of course. Will you please take these to my brother? Two floors up, like I said. His office is at the end of the hallway."

"Of course, it's at the end of a hallway." She sighed, wiggling her feet in her heels that had yet to make her feet feel comfortable.

"Is there a problem with the hallways?" he asked, amused.

"Only when my feet hurt to walk. I'll take them up, then take my lunch break." She tilted her head, glancing at his watch. "You have that phone meeting in a few minutes. You better get back to your desk."

"Yes, Ms. Stileano. Thank you for reminding me." He turned to leave, then glanced back at her with a morose expression. "You should wear different shoes, so your feet don't hurt. I didn't realize it. I've made you come back here a lot this week. I apologize."

"I'll survive. I've survived a lot worse. Trust me."

She watched as his face flushed with a variety of emotions. She thought for a minute he was going to say more. But he didn't. He gave a slight nod of his head and started to walk away.

"Mr. Holloway?"

He turned around, advancing at her with quick footsteps. She thought she saw excitement on his face. "Yes, Ms. Stileano."

She glanced at his hands, where he gripped the thick file. "I need the file."

He glanced at his hand, lifting the file. "Right. Here you go. Thank you." He handed her the file and walked out of the room.

She leaned against the drawer, almost falling in the process when the drawer slammed closed, making her lose her balance.

Well, he asked nicely. In fact, in the last few days, he had been more polite than when he first hired her. It hadn't taken him long to get with the program. She didn't bend over backward for assholes.

Boy, she'd miss him.

Best not to think about it.

She walked to the elevators, eager to get this task over with. She needed her lunch break. Now! She needed to form the perfect words in her head for when she would tell him she was quitting. They had to be perfect. She could already see the devastation that would mark his face.

She slammed the file to her chest, wrapping her arms around it. She couldn't believe she wanted to kiss him back in the file room. What was wrong with her? Maybe she was lacking some serious sex. It had been a few good months since she had a nice lovely romp between the sheets. Greg. He had been nice. A little duller than she liked, but overall, nice.

She should call him again and see if she missed the spark that was there. She just hadn't been paying attention. There had to have been a spark. Because she was definitely not feeling a spark with Mr. Holloway. No way. No sir-ee she wasn't.

She stepped off the elevator, almost tripping on her feet again.

Nothing like her own clumsiness to tell her the truth. Of course, she felt a spark with him. Every time his eyes glossed her way, a rare smile touched his face, or even the super rare moments when he laid a hand on her. Those tiny, electrifying sparks shot throughout her body like the Fourth of July.

She needed sex, all right. And she needed it with Mr. Holloway. Which meant she needed to quit as soon as possible. No sex would be had.

She walked the few small steps from the elevator to the big counter several feet away.

"I need to bring these files to Mr. Holloway. They're from...Mr. Holloway, two floors down," she said awkwardly to the receptionist. That sounded silly coming out of her mouth.

"He's in his office. Give them to his secretary. His office is through the set of doors at the end."

Gabby thanked the young woman and made her way down yet another long hallway. She was throwing away these heels when she got home tonight. Hell, she might even grab a metal trash can and burn them in a flaming ceremony in the alley behind her apartment building.

She pulled open the big double doors and stepped into a room that looked like her desk area, but much bigger. Much, much bigger.

Not that she was jealous. She liked her workspace.

A desk sat near another set of double doors, several plush couches and end tables next to each couch with various magazines covering them. The walls also had more great works of art. But unlike finding meaning in the ones that hung in her domain, she found these a bit more plain in comparison. A picture of a bird, not even that pretty. A picture of the moon. That's it—just the moon. But there was no depth to it. Boring. Like the pictures surrounding her that had wonderful images of buildings, this room held nothing of the sort. She thought it should, especially since that's what they did here. They were architects. Strange.

Besides that, the room was empty. No secretary. She saw his door, slightly ajar, and low murmurs of voices coming through. She walked to the door and pushed it open without listening to what was being said. She should have. She really, really should have.

"Oh, Champ. Yes, Champ, right there," a blonde woman moaned as she lay half-naked on his desk, his round ass glaring in Gabby's face.

"Champ? You're Champ? So, you are cheating on Mia, you dirty, rotten bastard," Gabby said with disgust.

His head whipped around. "Who the hell are you?"

"Your worst nightmare, pal." She sneered at him with the best one she could manage without running full speed in his direction to pummel his face into the ground.

Oh, she wanted to eviscerate him until he was nothing but a pile of ash. Instead, she turned around and slammed the door on her way out.

———

DANE PACED his office after he walked away from the file room. He almost kissed his secretary. His beautiful, demanding, spunky secretary. He never had sexual relations with another employee, an employee who worked with him day in and day out. He never had the want, the need, the burning desire to have sex with his secretary. Until *she* walked in.

"Stupid. Stupid, Dane. Keep your hands to yourself."

For a brief moment, he thought she wanted him to kiss her. Of course, not when she retreated, a small cringe tingeing her face as she backed into the file drawer. But when she said, "I'm waiting." He swore she meant she was waiting for him to make his move. What an idiotic thought because that wasn't what she meant.

He had needed to flee the room with a passion, to get his bearings back down. Then she called his name. He rushed to her like a lovesick puppy. And all she wanted was the file dangling from his hand. Not him. Not the man in front of her. And why would she? He was her boss. Her demanding, arrogant boss. That was all.

He needed to remember that. He couldn't lose focus on

what was important. His work was important. Not some woman who made his heart feel things that he hadn't ever felt in his life.

He dated women. Lots of different types of women. Not as often in the last few years as work consumed his time more than anything. But he wasn't a stranger to the opposite sex. He was a man. He had needs. But when he thought of all those other women, they failed in comparison to her. He knew that even only knowing her less than a week.

He had a serious problem. He couldn't fire her. He had no solid reason, other than the raging hard-on he experienced most of the workday. That wasn't good enough. And he couldn't fire her because he'd miss seeing her face, even if it were for the day. He ached to see her out of the work element, out in the real world. Out on a date. What would that be like?

Spectacular.

She could only be described in one word. The best word. She would make the date spectacular.

Shit. He couldn't fire her. He couldn't ask her out on a date while she was his secretary. That put him in a very serious predicament. And burning a hole in his floor as he paced back and forth wasn't helping him come up with any brilliant ideas. Damn it. He should be working, not contemplating ways to get into his secretary's pants.

He would simply have to suffer. He didn't want to risk losing her by firing her. Because there were no guarantees, she would accept a date from him if he let her go. And he couldn't date her while she was employed by him. He was screwed either way.

He sat down behind his desk, resting his hands on his head as he thought about his future misery. He knew he should mentally prepare himself for the meeting he was about to conduct, but he couldn't. She wouldn't leave his thoughts—a natural occurrence since the day he hired her.

He somehow managed to divert his thoughts for the moment when the phone rang, and he started his meeting. He almost dropped the phone when his door busted open, and the woman of his day—and nightly—dreams stormed inside his office.

Whoa.

With a level of anger he had never witnessed before.

He did something he had never done in his life. He ended the call without one word goodbye.

He stood up. "Ms. Stileano, what's the matter?"

"What's the matter? What's the matter, you ask? What is your damn name?" she yelled, her face coloring into a deep red.

"My name? It's Holloway."

"Don't jerk me around. Your first name."

Okay. He had to tread carefully here. He wasn't quite sure why she was so upset, but she wasn't about to tell him until she had her questions answered.

"Dane. My name is Dane Holloway. Your full name is Gabriella Stileano. Are we good now? Can you tell me what has you so upset?"

"Dane. Your first name is Dane. There are two Mr. Holloways here. You have a brother. I solved my mystery within seconds of meeting Mr. Holloway number two. An entire week..." She pierced her lips as her voice trailed off, and she shook her head.

Dane walked around his desk as if he were approaching a frightened animal. "You've lost me. What's going on? I just hung up on Mr. Gordon. You know how important that meeting was. I deserve an explanation here."

She met his eyes square-on. "Your brother is disgusting. Despicable. A downright sleazy scumbag."

"While I would agree with that, I'm not sure why you think so."

"His secretary wasn't at her desk. The door was ajar. I pushed it the rest of the way open without knocking. My bad. Very, very bad. I may need to wash my eyes out with chemicals to remove the nasty scene I witnessed. He was screwing his secretary on his desk. Some blonde chick. Definitely wasn't Mia."

She turned around, still distressed. He wanted to be surprised by his brother's behavior. But he wasn't. That was Champ to the T. He thought life was a joke. That everything came easy and handed to him with ease. Which wasn't completely off when he thought about it.

"I'm sorry you witnessed that. I...I don't know what to say. Who's Mia?" He swore he heard her mutter that name under her breath.

She turned back toward him, taking a few steps closer, almost within his reach. The thought disgusted her of his brother banging his secretary on his desk. Yet, Dane had the insane urge to reach for her arm, spin her around, and push deep inside her on his desk. Make her forget everything she saw. Make her see how wonderful they could be together. Make her smile. He hated the anger plastered on her face. He wanted to see her smile instead.

How disgusted would she be if he actually did that? How disgusting was he to even contemplate it at a time like this?

"I forgot to leave this behind. Don't even ask me to go back up there. It's not happening. Even with a please and thank you." She held out the file.

"Of course. I would never ask you to do that." He reached for the file, brushing her fingers as he did. The tingles that jolted from his fingers and up his arm almost had him giving in to his earlier urge. Damn, he wanted to pull her closer. Wipe the anger from her face with a light kiss. Erase her memory and fill it with something better—something that would put a smile on her face. He loved her smiles.

"I'll talk to my brother. That never should've happened. Ever."

She pressed her lips together, a sad shadow filling the worried lines dotting her face. "You do whatever you want. I'm sorry, Mr. Holloway. I really am. After you get under that thick skin of yours, there's a very nice man, perhaps even sweet. Try to lighten up once and a while. It'll help."

"What are you talking about?" His chest started to pound with a fear he didn't like feeling.

"I quit. But you are much better organized now."

His mouth dropped open as she turned around and headed for the doors. "You can't quit. Don't do this...please. It was my brother who made the idiotic mistake. Not me. I didn't bend you over my desk and have my wicked way with you."

He pressed his eyes closed and cringed. Holy. Shit. He did not just say that.

He opened his eyes as she turned back around toward him.

"I truly am sorry."

"Gabriella, don't quit." He took a step forward as she continued toward the door.

"You're better off without me."

"That's not true. I'm better when I'm with you. You make me a better man. I didn't realize how aloof I could be with people. How abrupt and rude I can be. You make me better. Don't you see that? I'll never ask you to take anything to my brother's office again. I promise." He knew his voice was getting closer to the sound of desperation.

"Like I said, it doesn't matter."

"Gabriella. Don't leave. Please." He took another step toward her. "I need you."

"Maybe...as a secretary. I never liked being a secretary. I'm sorry for lying. I hope you can forgive me someday."

With that, she walked out of his office, closing the door behind her.

Walked right out of his life.

4

GABBY CURLED her arm around Mia as the tears trailed down her face. "Stop crying over that shithead. You cried earlier over him when I first told you, and you were better when you left. Why are you back at my apartment crying over him again? He's not worth it."

"I can't...help...it," Mia said between sobs.

Gabby rubbed Mia's arm, wishing she would've given more of her wrath toward Champ. He deserved the biggest ass beating on the planet. He made Mia cry, and that always made Gabby want to murder someone. "All right, this might call for some drastic measures. Do I need to get the tequila out?"

Between the frenzied cries, Gabby heard a laugh escape. Before long, Mia's crying subsided to minimal. Enough for her to have a conversation without sounding like a blubbering idiot.

"I went over to his house. I wanted to see him admit it to my face." Mia sniffed, wiping her nose with her shirt sleeve.

"Eww, Mia, don't do that. Let me get you some tissues." Gabby walked to the kitchen and grabbed the box of tissues she kept on the edge of the counter. "Here, blow your nose."

Mia tried to compose herself, using several tissues before she sounded better.

Gabby took the tissue box from her and set it on the coffee table in front of them. She hated to do it, but it was time for some tough love. "Now, tell me why you went over there. I'm pretty sure there's nothing left to say to that asshat. I don't want to describe what went on in that office, but if I have to, I will."

"No tough love right now, Gabby. Please." Mia grabbed for her purse on the floor and found a hair tie. She roughly grabbed her hair, pulling it into a messy bun. "I wanted to see what he would say. If he would deny it. He tried calling me several times before you called me. I was busy working. His messages were weird until I talked to you."

"What did he say when you saw him?"

"That it wasn't what it looked like. That the crazy bitch misinterpreted what she saw."

Gabby looked indignant. "He called me that. I should've punched him in the face like I wanted to. I know what I saw, Mia."

"I know. I told him that. Then I told him I wasn't surprised and that I thought something was going on."

"Oh, no, Mia. Please, you didn't. Please tell me you didn't tell him why I was there."

"It just came out. I told him I wanted to know the truth and that you would find out the truth. And you did."

"Yeah, well, I almost didn't. I was working for the wrong brother. You said your boyfriend was the one who needed a new secretary for a while. How in the hell did I get an interview with his brother Dane?" Gabby stood up from the couch, more annoyed by the fact every time she thought about it. And oh, boy, she'd been thinking about it nonstop since she left Dane looking lost and confused. She'd never forget the hurt on his face—the pain in his eyes. It hurt her, knowing how much she hurt him.

"He laughed when I told him why you applied for the job. He thought it was funny that you got the wrong guy. He said that his secretary was on maternity leave. He didn't want to be bothered to get a new secretary. He said his brother Dane goes through secretaries more than anyone else in the building because he's a hardass and doesn't like any of them. So, he took his brother's secretary without asking him. Champ told him that he'd end up firing her anyway. I didn't know he did that. I didn't realize it was his brother looking for a new secretary. I would've never asked you to do that otherwise. I'm sorry, Gabs."

"It's not your fault. Champ sure sounds like a winner," Gabby drawled, the sarcasm clear in her tone. "What an asshole! To his own brother."

"I agree. But, I mean, he did make it sound like his brother is a real jerk. Maybe he deserved it if he was going to fire the woman anyway."

Gabby turned toward Mia, her face twisted with rage. Dane was far from a jerk. Sure, he had a hard exterior, a little arrogant at times, but once a person got underneath his protective shell, he was a—well, a good boss. Thinking any other term, like sweetheart, was not a path she should venture down.

"He's not a jerk! He didn't deserve his brother taking his secretary without asking. Listen to you. That same woman is the one he was screwing on his desk. Don't make him a victim. Dane is not a jerk."

"But you said he worked you to the bone." Mia stood up. "Remember, your first day, I came over here to see how it went. You didn't sound like you liked him very much."

"That's true. He was a little abrupt and rude. But after you get under the surface, he's very nice."

"Oh, my God. You like him, don't you? How long have you liked him?" Mia walked around the coffee table to stand in front of her. She leaned in close, almost as if she was inspecting for any tiny reaction. "You like Champ's brother."

"Don't be ridiculous." Gabby turned around, fleeing to the kitchen. There was no way she could admit she liked Dane because that would be admitting she had liked Mia's boyfriend. Because when she first met him, that's who she thought he was. How shameful. There was no way in hell she could admit that. Not to her best friend.

"Then why are you walking away from me? You never walk away. Admit it."

Gabby grabbed a glass from the cupboard. "There's nothing to admit. He was a jerk at first, but as I said, you have to get to know him to like him. He's nice."

"We've been friends for twenty years. We've been through so many things together. Tough and rough stuff. I know when you're lying."

Gabby clutched the glass tighter. Damn. Mia knew right where to hit her. "What do you want me to say? You want to hear that I was attracted to your boyfriend? That I felt guilty as hell all week because I liked him?"

"He's not my boyfriend." Mia smiled wide, a giddiness in her step as she came closer.

"Yeah, well, for an entire week, I thought he was. It wasn't my proudest moment, having dirty thoughts about a man I thought was your boyfriend."

"No worries. I know you wouldn't go behind my back. And even better, he's not my boyfriend. Never was."

"What is so better about that? Shit." Gabby sighed, setting the glass on the counter.

"Um, you can make your move. Fulfill your dirty thoughts. Which, by the way, you should share with me." Mia wiggled her eyebrows in playful anticipation. "And I'll even pretend I haven't been counting how many times you've sworn tonight. That's what besties are for."

Gabby rolled her eyes, glancing at her swear jar. She'd pay up later regardless of Mia's reprieve. "I'm not sharing any of those thoughts with you. I never should've said anything. It doesn't matter, Mia. I lied to him. For an entire week. Do you know why he hired me? Because of my honesty." Gabby laughed in disbelief. "What a joke. I was dishonest the entire time. He'll never forgive me. I was his secretary. I'm sure he didn't see me as anything other than that."

"You don't know if you don't try."

"Not gonna happen. I'm not stepping foot in that building again. And you're not stepping foot in Champ's place again either. Move on. You don't need any lame excuse from him. Don't shed any more tears over that jerk. Okay?"

Mia nodded her head. "Okay. I know we only dated two months, but those two months, he was a dream. He was attentive to my needs, and he was dynamite in bed. I just wanted to be wrong. I hate that I was right, and he was cheating on me."

Mia grabbed the glass sitting next to Gabby and put it back in the cupboard. "You're feeling down as well. You like his brother, and it's my fault you can't have a chance with him. I'm the reason you had to lie." She walked over to the stove and reached high above to the top cupboard. She pulled down two shot glasses. "I do think we need the tequila. Let's drown our sorrows for the night."

"We shouldn't."

"Maybe. But we're going to." Mia grinned, waggling the glasses in her hand.

"Oh, alright. Start pouring." She missed Dane's handsome face. His sweet smile that he shared sparingly.

I need you.

That's all she heard in her mind since she walked out of his office. The devastation in his tone. The plea. The sharp ache of how much he needed her to stay. He didn't need her. He needed a secretary. Her wishful thinking wanted it to mean more than the simplicity of it. But she knew it was ridiculous. He never saw her more than a secretary. After his brother told him the complete truth, he'd wish he never laid eyes on her.

DANE LOOKED up from his paperwork sprawled across his desk as his office door opened without a knock or word beforehand. Damn. He should've locked his door. He wasn't in the mood for company.

"You know I hate it when you don't knock or announce yourself before you step inside my office."

"Which is why I don't do it," Champ said with a devilish smile. "We need to talk."

"Yeah, what would you like to talk about? The fact you stole my secretary, then decided to screw her on your desk with the door wide open? Or the fact you're the reason my new secretary, the best secretary I've ever had, quit because you decided to screw your secretary on your desk with the door wide open."

"First off, the door wasn't wide open. Maybe I didn't close it firmly, but it wasn't hanging wide open."

Dane stood up, clutching the desk hard, his fingers started to turn white. "That's all you have to say? You want to talk about semantics? I lost my best secretary because of you. I'm sick and tired of you coming in here and ruining my peace. Get the hell out, Champ! I have nothing to say to you."

"You are right about one thing. You lost your secretary because of me. But," he grinned like a Cheshire cat, "you also would've never had her because of me."

"Get out."

"She lied to you," Champ said as his sly smirk grew bigger. His damn brother was trying to bait him, knowing how he hated liars and dishonesty.

"She's the most honest person I've ever met. She has more honesty and integrity than you. And you're my brother. That's pretty sad."

"What's sad is that you can't get over the fact Dad gave me reins to the company and not you. Grow up."

Dane rounded his desk. "Grow up? You're telling me to grow up? I'm not the one banging his secretary with the door. Wide. Open." Dane made sure to enunciate the last two words just to piss him off.

"It wasn't wide open." Champ grounded his teeth together. "Do you even want to know what your precious secretary lied about?"

"Nothing. She's not a despicable human being like you."

"And why am I despicable? Because Dad chose me over you, or because I live life to the fullest? You don't even know what the word fun means."

Dane shoved his hands in his pockets to hide the fists he wanted to shove in Champ's face. He never had the urge to punch his brother as he had right now. Sure, the impulse came over him now and again, but not this intense fury to let loose all the pent-up emotions he always held inside when it came to Champ. Good ol' Champ. The boy who could do no wrong.

"Excuse me for wanting to work hard and make my way into the business the correct way. So Dad gave you control of the company when he retired. I like doing the hard work. I don't like being handed shit for no reason. That's exactly what Dad did for you. You do nothing the hard way. You've always been handed everything. You've always been the favorite son."

"I'm the favorite son?" Champ exclaimed. "You're the oldest. Mom loves you more than me."

"Well, Dad seems to favor you more than me. I guess we're even. I'm done, Champ. I don't care to keep reminiscing over family dynamics anymore. I have work to do."

"It's past nine o'clock. You know, I didn't even try your place. I came straight here, knowing you'd still be at work. You should move into the building. Why'd your secretary quit?"

Dane wanted to wipe the smirk off his face. Two little words would do it with ease. "Why do you think?"

"Well, I know it's not why *you* think."

Dane decided to sit back down. The temptation to charge at his brother and have a roll 'em on the floor fistfight was too much. "You've been dying to tell me something since you walked in. I'm sure it's nothing but nonsense since that's all your life is. A bunch of nonsense. Go away, Champ."

"My girlfriend, Mia, broke up with me tonight. She was told I was cheating on her."

"What, you're kidding me?" He pretended to sound shocked. Then he snapped his fingers. "Oh, wait, you were cheating on her. Forgive me if I don't feel bad for you." Dane picked up his pencil and the mock drawing he was working on.

Mia? The name sounded familiar.

"Your secretary, Ms. Stileano, is the one who told her. They're best friends. She lied to you, Dane. She's a liar." Champ stepped closer to the desk when Dane raised his head slowly.

It couldn't be. Not Gabriella. She was the most honest person he knew.

"Are you saying you weren't screwing your secretary on your desk? She lied about that." Of all the things Dane expected, he didn't expect that. He knew she didn't fake the kind of reaction she had in his office. He knew his brother did what she said exactly happened.

Mia! That's why the name sounded familiar. She had blurted the name in her tirade before walking out of his office—and his life—forever.

"She lied about why she applied for the job. She thought you were me. Mia told her I needed a new temp secretary. Mia thought I was cheating. She convinced her friend to apply for the job and do some undercover work." Champ laughed. "She got the wrong brother. She thought you were dating her friend Mia."

No.

No way.

Yet, he saw the truth written on his brother's face. Champ wasn't lying, and he could tell when Champ was lying. He did it so often. He watched as Champ continued to laugh as he walked out of the office.

An entire week.

She had lied to him for an entire week. What he had thought so real had all been a big sham. God, he was such an idiot. She played him. She thought he was a womanizing cheater and liar while he had been having lustrous thoughts about her.

His pencil snapped in half as the anger swirled inside. He didn't like being made a fool of. How dare she.

I'm sorry for lying. I hope you can forgive me someday—her last words to him.

She tried to tell him in her own way what she had done.

Forgive her? Not likely. He couldn't stand liars. His brother was a compulsive liar, and he could barely stand him. He only did because he was family, and his mother would disown him if he cut Champ out of his life.

She was nothing. He had no problem forgetting about her.

That's exactly what he did as he grabbed a new pencil.

5

GABBY GROANED, grabbing her head as the pain skyrocketed from her temple down to her toes. She pulled a pillow over her head to drown out the insistent pounding going on. When it wouldn't disappear, she threw the pillow to the floor. Her visitor wasn't going away.

She got out of bed and swiped her robe that sat in a tangled mess on the floor. Untying the kinks as she walked to the front door, she had just shoved her arms through the sleeves when she approached the door. She grabbed for the ties to knot it together as her hands fumbled with the door locks. Her expression told her visitor she wasn't impressed or happy about the wakeup call when she finally opened the door.

"You look like shit, Gabs," her longtime friend and partner, Jaxson Brandt, said as he stepped inside and closed the door. She sneered at him as she continued to tie her robe closed.

"Gee, Jaxson, is that what you tell all the ladies? You owe me a quarter, too." She needed coffee—lots of coffee.

Without waiting for his response, she turned toward the kitchen.

"You know I never go anywhere without a handful of quarters," he said with a low chuckle. "Late night last night? What happened? Did you have a hot date, and it got a little rowdy?"

"When's the last time I had a hot date? Junior high?"

Jaxson leaned against the counter as he watched her get the coffee ready, chuckling. "Oh, someone's cranky. You always get ridiculous with your sarcasm when you're cranky."

"Well, someone did wake me up way too early."

"Hey, Gabs, look at the clock on the wall. It's noon. Not that early."

Gabby watched as his finger pointed to the clock on the wall that read it was indeed twelve o'clock.

Well, shit. It was late.

Then she looked at her swear jar. "Pay up, mister. Don't think because I have a helluva headache, I'll forget."

Jaxson chuckled but dropped a quarter in the jar.

"Dish. I need details."

Gabby rolled her eyes. His words reminded her of Mia's from last night. She had asked her several times to dish out the details about Dane before she finally caved. "I was with Mia, who must've left already. She normally has to be at the theater by now."

"So you had a late night with Mia. That explains things a little better, sort of. Care to explain a little bit more?"

Gabby turned around from the coffee pot, weighing her decision. It didn't take too long. She rarely kept anything from Jaxson. Twenty minutes later, after explaining the past week—every sordid detail—Jaxson refilled her coffee cup and handed her two painkillers.

"Bottom's up, Gabby. Your headache isn't disappearing like you wanted it to with only coffee. Take the pills."

"Thanks, Dad. What would I do without you?" she asked with her usual attitude when she didn't feel well.

Would she ever feel better after the way she treated Dane?

"You'd never survive, that's for sure. Are you okay? I mean, truly okay. You and Mia never grab the tequila unless it's desperately needed."

Gabby swallowed the pills, taking a quick sip of the coffee. "Mia's boyfriend was cheating on her. That screamed tequila loud and clear."

"Yeah, but you know that wasn't what I was talking about. You, Gabs. Are you okay? We've been friends for nine years; I know what's hidden underneath the words you don't say. This Dane guy, you liked him."

"Stop being a detective for once."

"Not possible. Like it's not possible for you."

She gave him a strangled laugh. "I wasn't much of a detective this past week."

"Not your fault. You got bad intel." He sighed, nudging her shoulder lightly, so she didn't spill the coffee. "Are you okay? That's all I want to know."

"Yeah, life goes on. It always does." She smiled, hoping to ease his worries. She didn't want to continue this conversation. "What are you doing here? I still have two more days of vacation before I should see your ugly face."

"And I can't bug you on your vacation? You know you find me charming and handsome. Don't lie." He grinned at her with the most dazzling grin he had. "I can't believe you used vacation time for something like this. Only for Mia. The things you do for her."

"And always will." She took another sip of coffee, nudging him this time. "What are you doing here?"

He pulled his phone out, scrolling to his texts. "A little drunk texting went on last night. I have to say that you made me laugh a few times. I figured you wouldn't be feeling well this morning. I wanted to make sure you were all right. You usually don't drink like this. I now see why you were."

She cringed at some of the horrible texts she sent him as he continued to scroll through them all, laughing as he went.

"Alright, buddy, I've seen enough. So Mia and I had fun, big deal." She laughed when he raised his eyebrows teasingly. "Thanks for coming over. Want to take the ferry to see the Statue of Liberty today?"

"Seriously?" He shook his head, his adorable grin making her feel better. "Never mind, of course, you're serious. Yeah, why not? It's been a while since I've seen it up close and personal. I'm game. Grab a shower first. You stink."

"Gosh, Jaxson, you sure know how to win a woman's heart." Gabby stood up, placing a hand over her heart as she flicked him a mocking look.

"I never stop trying when it comes to you." He winked at her as she walked down the hallway to the bathroom.

Several hours later, after taking a trip to the Statue of Liberty, they were back in Gabby's apartment. They had an amazing time, not that they actually went up to the top. You needed tickets in advance, but Gabby hadn't minded. She enjoyed the ferry ride to the island and walking around the magnificent statue. Seeing the view from Dane's office had given her the idea. She had wanted to visit it since that day.

Although, she had envisioned going with him. Relishing

in the way his face would light up with excitement and look relaxed for once.

Dreams.

Only in her dreams would that happen.

She had a wonderful time with Jaxson. She wouldn't let the thoughts of Dane distract her from the nice time she had.

"Game starts in an hour. Up for some baseball?" Jaxson asked, plopping down on her couch.

"That's a dumb question. You know I'll always watch baseball. Damn, we should've gone to the stadium." She should've thought of that sooner. That would've rounded out the evening perfectly.

"Wow. You want to take in all the sights. What's up with that?"

"Going to a baseball game isn't taking the sights in. It's fun. And I'm on vacation, remember?"

"Ah, yeah, almost forgot. You know, normal people go on a cruise, or an exotic island, or some shit like that," Jaxson said with a laugh, grabbing the remote control from the coffee table.

Then they both pointed at each other and laughed, "Quarter!"

"Mia asked. You know I always do anything for her. Even if it is ridiculous." Gabby started to walk toward the hallway to the bathroom.

"If she asked you to jump off the Brooklyn Bridge, would you?" Jaxson asked, his facial expression devoid of all teasing.

"She's my best friend. She's more fragile than people realize. I need to protect her, sometimes even from herself."

Jaxson rubbed his chin, grimacing. "I know, Gabs. Forget I said anything."

She nodded, knowing that Jaxson did understand.

While she looked out for Mia all the time, he liked to look out for her. As she walked to the bathroom, she wondered, who looked out for him? She did, for the most part, but not like she did for Mia.

She changed clothes and took her time using the bathroom, trying not to think about a man she should forget about. Nothing good would come from her daydreaming about him. But damn it. It was so easy to picture Dane's handsome face. She couldn't help but daydream. Picture the rare smiles he had bestowed upon her. He would hate her when he found out the truth. She knew it. For once in her life, she wished she would've said no to Mia.

But if she'd said no, she never would've met Dane. She couldn't be sorry about meeting him. She was sorry for how it all happened.

"You're not stinking the joint up, are you? I have to use the bathroom too, you know," Jaxson hollered from the living room.

She laughed, shaking her head. She should've stunk up the bathroom to irritate Jaxson. She wiped her hands dry and walked back to the living room.

"Bathroom is as fresh as the day I cleaned it. Settle down."

Jaxson stood up, heading toward the bathroom himself. "You were in there forever. What were you doing, if not stinking it up?" He frowned. She must not have shielded her sadness well enough. "Ah, shit, Gabby. I'm sorry. Why don't you try talking to him? It would make you feel better. Obviously, I'm not helping like I hoped."

"I don't think that would help. I don't want to hear the nasty words he'd say to my face. And you always help me,

Jaxson. You're the best guy friend a girl could have and the best partner."

"Ah, shucks, don't make me blush." He grinned sheepishly, as if embarrassed, then a bright sincere smile emerged. "You're the best partner and friend a guy could ever ask for. Mia's pretty lucky that you're such an awesome friend."

They didn't have heart-to-heart talks like this very often. She didn't know how much more she could take. It meant a lot to her that Jaxson cared as much as he did. "Go take a piss already. Did you find the channel for the game?"

"Yeah. Be right back. Don't take my spot."

She smiled with a wicked twinkle in her eyes, watching as he shook his head while walking away, knowing that she was going to sit in his spot. Which she did. She sat down, wiggling her butt to get as comfy as possible when a knock sounded on her door.

She wasn't in the mood to be bothered by anyone. Probably one of her neighbors looking to borrow something. Mrs. Stenson, two doors down, loved to bake and was always knocking on her door to borrow sugar or flour or whatever other ingredients she ran out of. Gabby didn't think she ran out of supplies as often as she claimed. She figured Mrs. Stenson liked the company since her husband had passed away not more than a year ago. Of course, if it happened to be her, Gabby wouldn't turn her away.

She knew it wasn't Mia. She always walked in without knocking. Jaxson did as well if the door wasn't locked.

She glanced through the peephole, her lips twisting with surprise as she jumped back.

It couldn't be.

Leaning closer, peering through the hole again, she

almost thought about rubbing her eyes. They had to be deceiving her.

Dane stood on the other side.

What did he want? And why did she have to be so honest and write her real address on the application?

He knocked again, making her jump back for the second time. She finger-combed her long hair, knowing it didn't look the best, especially after the day on the ferry. The wind had a heyday blowing it around like crazy.

Well, she had never backed down from a fight. She wasn't about to start now. She took a deep breath, then pulled open the door.

"Mr. Holloway, what can I do for you?" She made sure to keep her tone positive and in control. Not like she was on the verge of tears. Because damn it, she suddenly felt like crying.

He didn't look happy. In fact, he looked downright pissed. Perhaps she shouldn't have opened the door. "We're past the formalities, aren't we, Gabriella? I would like to talk to you for a moment. May I come in?"

She wasn't sure if she should let him in, especially with the way his face still contorted with rage.

Again, not afraid of a fight. She deserved whatever he had to say. And she didn't think he'd physically harm her.

She stepped aside for him to enter and shut the door.

Plus, Jaxson was here. He couldn't hurt her with any bodily harm with Jaxson here. Not that she thought he would. She really didn't. He looked angry but angry enough to hurt her? She didn't think so. He wasn't that type of man. Or was he? She didn't know him that well.

Of course, she could hold her own. She wasn't scared— of anything.

"What did you want to talk about?" She turned around, realizing he hadn't made a move. He stood a breath away from her. So close, he could wrap his arms around her with ease.

Oh, how she ached so much for him to do that. Forgive her and see where this—whatever this was between them—could go.

Ha! That was her wishful thinking that he saw her as anything more than a secretary.

"You know what I want to talk about. You lied to me."

"You might not like my explanation, but it's a good one."

"Explain away. I'm dying to hear it." His expression didn't indicate he was happy to hear anything.

She started to open her mouth, yet was unsure of what to say.

"Yo, Gabs, grab me a beer."

Oh, shit.

Not good.

Jaxson just had to open his loud mouth.

Dane looked at her, confusion morphing with his anger. Or was that pain? She couldn't be sure. Damn it. She hated the unknown.

There was a moment of silence because she still didn't know what to say.

"Please, Gabs. I forgot the 'please.' Pretty please."

Okay. Enough was enough. She had to take control of the situation before it completely spiraled out of control.

"Yeah, hold on." She met Dane's irate gaze. "Do you want one?"

"Who is that?"

"Jaxson...my partner. I'll take your avoidance of the question as a yes. I think we could all use a drink." She tried to walk toward the kitchen without touching him, but it was impossible. She almost fell into his arms when her arm grazed his chest. The small touch was electrifying. She wanted more.

She heard his shallow steps follow her. She grabbed three beers from the fridge and held one out to him, even though he never officially answered her. He made no move to take it.

"You don't want one?"

"You know what I want."

She wanted to ask, "Me?" Because that was what she wanted. She wanted him to want her—desperately.

Of course, she couldn't blurt that out.

She walked around the counter toward the dining room that connected with the living room. She took a few steps near Jaxson, tossing him the beer.

He caught it with ease. His mouth started to open as if he wanted to ask why she was throwing it at him when he noticed Dane standing behind her.

"I didn't hear the knock on the door. Who's your friend?" Jaxson asked, casually, although he eyed Dane like a suspect in a lineup.

"I was wondering the same thing. What does 'partner' mean, exactly?" Dane's eyebrows burrowed further into a frown.

Gabby shifted so she could see them both. "Partners. You know, as in work partners."

"Work? What do you really do, besides take a job under false pretenses?" Dane asked with a strained breath. His jaw clenched, then unclenched.

She wanted so badly to walk up to him and smooth her hand across his scruffy jaw, relax the tension in his features. Erase the pain she put in his eyes.

Jaxson stood up. "Oh, shit, is this him?"

"If by him, you mean, Dane Holloway, then yes," Gabby replied, her heart breaking. She honestly had no idea what to say or do anymore. The situation was becoming more awkward as each minute passed.

And, for the first time, she didn't do awkward so well. Where was her usual spouting out whatever came to the tip of her tongue? Her loose lips. Her sarcasm. Her finesse with words in any situation.

"Interesting," Jaxson said with a sleek smile.

She responded with a glare.

Jaxson could rankle her nerves without even speaking. His sly smile inched up a notch as he looked at Dane. "We work for the NYPD, in the homicide division. We're partners."

"You're a detective?" The shock coated Dane's features from his eyes to the aching frown to the subtle way he jerked back.

"Clearly not a very good one." She couldn't hold in the ridiculous laughter. Nothing was funny, but it slipped out.

She raised one of the beer bottles to her head to cool herself down and the raging headache she could feel coming on.

"Hey, Gabs, why don't I step outside on the balcony. You two can talk." Jaxson walked around the couch to the sliding glass doors, then turned toward Dane. "Let her speak before you judge. You can be pissed, that's your right. But Gabs doesn't do anything unless it's important to her."

Gabby waited until Jaxson stepped outside, then walked around Dane with a wide birth, careful not to touch him, and stepped back into the kitchen. Because if she touched him, she might crumble to pieces, and that was the last thing she wanted. She refused to let him see her in a moment of weakness.

She put the two beers back in the fridge and turned around, wondering if Dane followed her.

Of course, he had. She wasn't sure why she thought he might leave. His expression still wasn't inviting. He looked like he wanted to punch something.

"Maybe I wanted a beer."

She scoffed. "Then you should have grabbed it when I offered." Her face morphed into sadness. "I'm sorry, okay? You have every right to be mad at me. What did your brother say? That's why you're here, right? He told you."

He leaned against the counter, folding his arms and legs like he used to do in his office when they had their little spats.

God, it felt like a lifetime ago. Had they only known each other for a short week?

"My brother is a known liar. He lies more than he tells the truth. I wanted to hear it from your lips. I told myself it didn't matter. That you didn't matter. But it does matter."

She folded her arms as well but didn't lean against the fridge where she stood. "My best friend, Mia, was dating your brother. She came to me last week, saying she thought he was cheating. I told her to dump his ass if that was the case. No man who does that is worth the time. She wanted proof. She begged me to apply for his temp secretary position and find out the truth. She wanted solid proof before she accused him of anything. I've never been able to say no to her."

"Why? Why can't you say no to her?"

DANE WAITED for her to answer. He could see it was a difficult one to answer.

Interesting.

The array of emotions that flashed through her eyes told him it was a very complicated answer.

So strange. Why was it so complicated?

And why did he want to pull her into his arms and smooth her erratic emotions away?

"I just can't. She didn't realize your brother stole your secretary and that you were the one needing a new secretary. She didn't even tell me that Champ had a brother. She didn't know that. She simply said his name was Champ Holloway. I never heard anyone call you anything other than Mr. Holloway. I just assumed you were him. Doesn't show very good detective skills on my part, does it?"

Her version wasn't much different from Champ's. He couldn't figure out why he had come here. He told himself he would forget her with ease.

Except he hadn't.

He dreamt about her all night. The entire day crawled at a pace with nothing but her on his mind. Suddenly, he found himself at her doorstep.

The minute she opened the door, he wanted to yell his rage at her for lying.

The other part of him wanted to grab her into his arms and kiss the daylights out of her, like now.

"So, what did you tell her? You worked an entire week with me. I imagine you came home every night and gave her updates. What did you tell her?"

Why was he torturing himself? What did he expect her to say? That she thought of him in sexual ways she shouldn't —like he stupidly had all week.

"I told her that you work too much. That I didn't think you were cheating on her. That if you were cheating on her, it was with your work, not a woman." She took a step toward him. "You do work too much, you know. We saw the Statue of Liberty today. I thought of you. You don't even appreciate the view from your office. You need to get out more, Dane. You look tired."

"I would never cheat on a woman. I'm not my brother."

He didn't want to focus on the "we" part of that conversation. She had to have been talking about her partner Jaxson. Jealousy, an emotion he had never felt before regrading a woman, flooded his system. Hit him straight in the heart like an arrow hit a bullseye. She shouldn't be doing anything other than working with that man.

"That's what I told her. But it doesn't matter because I was working for the wrong brother. I'm sorry for deceiving you. I couldn't care less about Champ's feelings, but you, I never meant to hurt you. I'm sorry, Dane."

Before Dane could respond, not even sure how he should—because damn it, he still wanted to kiss her breathless despite the fact she lied—the front door opened. Small clicking sounds reverberated through the hallway. A beautiful redhead stuck her head into the kitchen, faltering in her steps when she saw him leaning against the counter.

"Hey, Gabby. I didn't know you had company."

"Yeah, lots of company right now. My life's never this busy, and suddenly, it is." Gabby blew out a breath, pointing at Dane. "This is Dane. Cha—"

"Champ's brother," the woman finished for her. "It's all my fault. I made her do it. Don't hate her."

So, this was Mia. His brother was a complete idiot for cheating on such a gorgeous woman. Beautiful red hair that cascaded around her shoulders in simple, yet perfect waves. Her deep brown eyes shined with glory as the makeup surrounding her eyes grabbed your attention. She wore bright red lipstick that screamed to a man, "kiss me!" She had on a tight black dress that showcased her every curve, giving her an elegant yet trendy feeling. Her high heels reminded him of Gabby and how they'd probably hurt Gabby's feet if she were wearing them.

His eyes glided to Gabby for a brief second.

Long brown hair with a tint of red. It looked a bit messy. Windblown, most likely. She said she had taken a ferry ride. Yet, on her, it looked sexy instead of making her look like she had a rat's nest. No makeup, except for a light shade of pink lipstick. Loose lounging pants and a ratty old t-shirt that looked like she wore all the time, indicating it was a favorite.

Gabby looked ready to relax for the night and veg out in front of the TV.

Her friend Mia looked ready for a night out on the town.

Dane wanted Gabby more and more with every breath he took, with every short glance her way.

But she lied to him.

"I'm sorry what my brother did to you," Dane said. He wasn't even sure why he apologized. He hadn't done anything wrong. He never apologized for his brother, either. That was a first.

"Uh, thank you." Mia shifted on her feet and didn't meet Gabby's eyes as she asked, "Is someone else here? What did 'lots of company' mean?"

"Jaxson's on the balcony." Gabby glanced at the clock. "Why aren't you still at work? You look a little too dolled up right now."

Dane looked over at Mia, taking in her outfit once again. She was a beautiful woman. She wasn't Gabriella, though. He knew everyone kept calling her Gabby or Gabs, but he could only see her as Gabriella. He would continue to call her only that.

"I needed...you know, some time off. I wanted to pop in and say hi. You were out cold this morning when I left, I wanted to make sure you were okay."

"I'm fine. But you're hiding something from me. Let me see your phone," Gabby demanded, holding out her hand.

Mia circled the island counter, moving farther away from Gabby and more toward him. "There's nothing on there of importance."

"Mia! Did Champ call you? Are you seriously thinking about seeing him again? I worked a whole week with the wrong man just to find out if that man was cheating on you. Newsflash—he was!"

"I know. I hear you. I need to get a few of my belongings from his apartment. He asked me to come get them and talk a little. That's all," Mia said in a small voice.

"You are not dressed for a little trip to get your belongings. But if that's the case, I'll go with you."

"Can we not do this in front of his brother? I'll be fine on my own. I—"

"You're not going there alone," Jaxson interrupted, popping in as if out of thin air. He took a place close to Dane, glancing between Gabby and Mia. "You're not going there either, Gabby."

"Oh, you're going to stop me?" Gabby shoved a hand on her hip, raising her brow in defiance.

Dane wanted to chuckle at her cute stance. So fierce and demanding. It reminded him of the times she reprimanded him in the office.

"Unless I miss my guess, you haven't finished talking it out with Dane. And you should. Not to mention, you have a hot head sometimes." Jaxson shook his head, rolling his eyes. "All the time. You wanted to punch the man in his office when he was screwing the woman on his desk. I'm not sure you can control your impulses this time."

Jaxson looked at Mia. "Did you hear the part where I said he was screwing another woman on his desk? You're a beautiful woman, Mia. You're amazing. You have the best friend in the world who took a vacation from her real job to help you out in some crazy scheme. If she would've told me about it, I would've talked her out of it and helped you handle this guy. You deserve better. You shouldn't even be contemplating going back to this asshole."

Jaxson glanced at Dane. "No offense to you. I know he's your brother."

Dane shrugged, suddenly not so worried. The jealousy vanished—almost, but not quite—as Jaxson's concern for Mia was clear. "He is an asshole."

Jaxson nodded with a smile. "See, even his own brother thinks so. I'll go with you to get your stuff. You can go exactly like that, even though it's a little too beautiful, in my opinion. But hey, we can use that. We can shove it in his face. I'm your new date for the night. That'll grate on his nerves. Trust me."

Mia bit her lip, the indecision clear.

Dane stood up from the counter. "My brother is a liar. He's not worth your time. Go with Jaxson and get your things, then leave without another word. It'll irk my brother to see you arrive with another man. I almost wish I could see it."

"Wow, you really don't like him, do you?" Jaxson asked with a small laugh.

Dane turned toward him. "Only when I have to."

Dane waited with the other two for Mia's decision. He wanted to push her and Jaxson right out of the apartment.

He had made up his mind. He was done being mad at Gabriella.

And he wanted her all to himself now.

"We could be here all night with your indecisions. Gabby makes executive decisions all the time for you. I'm making one right now. I won't see you dating that guy again." Jaxson rounded the counter, placing his hands on her shoulders. He pushed her forward.

"Okay, Jaxson," Mia said quietly, as she obediently let him push her out of the kitchen.

Dane saw Jaxson wink at Gabby and throw her a sweet smile. He wasn't worried about that anymore. That was nothing.

"What the hell just happened?" Gabby asked after she heard the front door close.

"You have no idea, do you? You *should* brush up on your detective skills."

She glared at him. "Excuse me?"

"Your partner, Jaxson. He likes your friend, Mia. I have to say I was jealous of the man for a moment. Not anymore."

"Jealous?" she whispered.

He took a few steps toward her. "Jealous. I would've pushed them both out myself if he didn't take the initiative. Before you quit, I was debating whether or not to fire you."

"Fire me? I was a damn awesome secretary. You had no reason to fire me." She advanced at him, poking him in the chest.

He grabbed her hand, letting the fireworks explode throughout his body at her electrifying touch. His gaze caught a large jar filled halfway with quarters.

"I have no idea why you even have a swear jar when it doesn't seem to stop you." He stepped closer. Her eyes flashed with fire. "I couldn't justify dating my secretary. I also didn't want to lose seeing your face every day. I had such a dilemma. And now, I don't."

He tenderly brushed her lips with his. The soft moan that left her mouth had him dropping her hand and embracing her within his arms as his tongue dove in. He never wanted to let this woman go, or lose the intense emotions rushing throughout his body.

6

———

GABBY TORE HER LIPS AWAY, pushed her hands against his chest, and backed up a few steps, almost running into the fridge. "What's going on?"

He looked confused. "I'm pretty sure we were kissing and enjoying it."

"You're mad at me. Your Scrooge-like face said so."

"Do I look like a mean, unsmiling slimeball right now?" He lifted his lips into a grin, washing away the previous angry vibes.

She could never resist his smiles. Especially since he rarely smiled.

A very unladylike chuckle slipped out. "Calling Scrooge a slimeball is a bit harsh."

"He almost destroyed Christmas. Everyone should love a holiday that tries to milk every dime out you for the sake of presents people don't need." The twinkle in his eye and the smile still brightly displayed had her heart racing. Something was about to happen, and she wasn't sure what—or if it should.

And he was joking with her. At least, he better be joking with her because she loved Christmas and not his version he so eloquently pointed out.

Her lip tilted up. "You better tell me you like Christmas."

He closed the distance, placing a gentle hand on her cheek. "I like Christmas, especially if you like it because that means I get to see one of your beautiful smiles. I shouldn't confess it, but I love your smiles."

Wow. How they both thought alike, loving each other's smiles.

He sighed, yet he still displayed a gentle grin. "You're right; I was furious up until you opened the door. It melted away when I saw your beautiful face again. I missed seeing it today."

Oh, she wanted to keep teasing about Christmas. He had made her heart pound even faster at his sweet words, but she couldn't dispel the odd feeling he was still upset. "You're not mad anymore? Just like that. I only have to flash a sweet smile and boom! All better."

His smile dimmed but didn't completely disappear. "What you did...I don't forgive people who lie to me."

She clutched his wrist, where his hand still held her cheek. "Then why are you kissing me? Is this some sort of revenge? Because I could kick your ass ten ways to Sunday."

He kissed her as low masculine laughter echoed between them. "I almost want to see that happen. You'd probably do it very well, as well as you organized my office. You're different. You've been so different from the moment I met you. I can't stand dishonesty." He ran a hand down his face as a low moan escaped. "I guess I understand why you did it." Then his sweet, delicious grin reappeared. "I don't want an ass-whooping from you. I forgive you. Let's move on."

"Moving on sounds nice," she said softly.

It sounded so nice. It felt surreal. Like her dreams—and she had quite a few of them over the past week—were coming true. Was she in a dream right now?

"You don't look so sure. If you want me to leave..." Although he said the words, he made no move to step away.

Apparently, with him, she couldn't hide her emotions. Because when she was working, she never displayed what she was thinking.

Her hand clamped around his wrist tightened, then softened. She needed to keep her cool and go with the flow. Not let her emotions get the best of her. Keeping her cool was always something she struggled with. At work. With relationships. In life.

"I've had these...thoughts in my head since I met you. I don't want you to leave."

He twisted his hand, where she was forced to let go of her grip. But instead of stepping back, he linked hands with her. "What sort of thoughts?"

She smiled wickedly, yet sadness filled a part of her soul. "The sort of thoughts I shouldn't have had because I thought you were Mia's boyfriend. Very naughty thoughts."

He squeezed her hand, leaning in close, almost a breath away. "I'm not her boyfriend. I've never been her boyfriend and never will be. You can have all the very naughty thoughts about me that you want. I've had plenty of you. It was a very, very long week of work."

"You have no idea." Her words were like a kiss upon his lips, said so soft and low.

He decided to make it a real kiss, picking up where they were before the intense conversation. He kissed her deeply, locking his lips to hers, even a crowbar couldn't tear them apart. It's as if they both wanted to be as close as possible.

She let go of his hand and wrapped her arms around his neck, digging into his hair. His hand circled her waist, pulling her closer.

She never wanted this to end. To think he was holding her in his arms like he never wanted to let her go. It seemed unreal. If it was a dream, it was better than any other one she had.

She pulled away again. "What are we doing?"

He crinkled his eyebrows in confusion as his hands strengthened their grip on her waist as if telling her with his touch what was going on. He was claiming her. Letting her know he would not let her get away. "I thought we established that. Scrooge, Christmas, dirty, sexy thoughts." His frown deepened. "What's the matter, Gabriella? If you want me to leave, I will. I would never force you to do something you didn't want to."

She grabbed the front of his shirt, clutching the material as if he would vanish into thin air. "I went from regretting everything I did because I knew I lost my chance with you, to this. To you holding me in your arms, kissing me with a passion I never thought possible. I feel...this is unfamiliar territory. I don't know how else to explain it. It doesn't feel real."

He let go of her waist and covered her hands. "I'm real. I'm going to show you how real I am." He peeled her hands from his shirt and swung her into his arms.

She gasped, then giggled and wrapped her arms around his neck. "What are you doing?"

"I'm going to walk around this apartment until I find your bedroom. Unless you tell me where to go."

She had to force herself to keep a straight face. "What... no please and thank you?"

His lips curled into a delicious smile. One that said sweet, sweet pleasure was soon to be had—as long as she quit messing around. Oh, she never ever wanted him to stop smiling. She couldn't believe all the smiles he had been bestowing upon her.

"Sweetheart, I'm going to have you begging me for some pleases and thank yous. But not if you don't tell me where the bedroom is."

She chuckled, pressing her face into his chest. She had never begged a man in her life, but for Dane, she was already on the verge of begging him to do every naughty thought in his head. Because the gleam in his eyes said he had some very dirty thoughts going on.

She inhaled a hint of cinnamon, something she had never smelled on him before. Not that she had gotten this close to even get a sense of what kind of cologne he might be wearing. Although she didn't think it was cologne. Did men wear cinnamon smelling cologne? That just sounded odd. Now, she was officially losing her mind. Or perhaps her nerves were kicking in. Ha! Kicking in? They'd been full-blown since the moment she spied him through the peephole.

This was nothing. They were about to get it on in the most blissful way. Something she had ached to do since the moment she walked into his office—what a hussy.

She wondered if he even realized he called her sweetheart. She never was one of those women who needed pet names. Anytime Mia talked about her latest beau calling her something silly like baby, doll-cakes, or darling, she always laughed at how ridiculous it sounded. She wasn't laughing now. She loved how the word rolled off his tongue like a sweet caress. How could she get him to say it again?

"Are you debating whether to tell me? Because you're making me nervous now. That's not something I freely admit either," he whispered near her ear.

She lifted her head, a ridiculously happy smile on her face. "I lost my train of thought. You smell delicious. Like a tasty cinnamon roll. And I'm ready to eat you up."

The throaty chuckle that escaped his lips made her insides melt even more. God, she could listen to him laugh all day, every day. "I swear. You surprise me one minute, then manage to knock me off my feet the next."

He had no idea how his tender, thoughtful words he slipped out now and again were sweeping her off her feet with finesse.

She tossed her head toward the hallway that led to the front door. "Lock the door first. Then take a left. My bedroom is at the end of the hallway. It's not that big of an apartment."

"Are you security-minded all the time?" he asked with a smirk as he made his way to the front door with her in his arms.

How silly was it that she didn't want him to let her down? She liked the feeling of him holding her so close, his strength flowing through his veins and straight into hers. Each step he took gave her more courage, let her nervousness die away.

What was there to be nervous about? It's not like she'd never had sex before. She didn't need a manual to tell her what part went where. And she'd been dying to get her hands on this man for a week. She had nothing to be nervous about.

She flipped the locks herself as she cocked an eyebrow. "Unless you want Jaxson or Mia to walk right in, then I better lock the door. Those two never knock."

"And it's a possibility they'll come back?"

She swore she heard a hint of disappointment. She couldn't begrudge him for that because it would disappoint her as well because she didn't want anything to interrupt what they were about to do. "They could. I'm not even sure why Mia stopped by before heading to your brother's. Most likely, she knew I would talk her out of it and needed me to do that."

"You still haven't explained why you would do anything for her."

She rested her head against his chest, not wanting to think about that. Definitely not a conversation she wanted to have right now. "I thought you wanted to know where the bedroom was."

He made no sound in response except to turn around and make his way to their destination. He closed her bedroom door with a swing of his foot and gently laid her on the bed.

"I don't like distractions. I have too much work to get done. You've been nothing but a distraction since you walked into my office."

His body hovered above hers. Not one inch of him touched her, and it was driving her insane. As if he was teasing her, already wanting her to beg for more. For the slightest touch from him.

The words teetered on the edge of her lips to beg. She needed his touch.

"Live a little, Dane." She grabbed his shirt, yanking him down to her mouth. But she was never one to beg. She was one to take charge and get shit done.

He didn't resist, and honestly, if he would've, she would've had no choice but to show him her version of an ass-whooping. Oh, yeah, she'd love to smack his ass. Hard.

Their lips tangoed fiercely as if all their pent-up emotions from the past week were finally coming to a head. He pressed firmly into her, his hard cock telling her how much he wanted her. Damn it, she wanted more. She wrapped her legs around his waist to get as close as she could, refusing to release his mouth for even a tiny breath. Her delectable moan mingled with his low groan as his fingers brushed through her hair with a tantalizing caress. It was a mixture of fierceness and tenderness.

"There's too much between us," he said with a raspy breath as he unhooked her legs from around him and stood up. He removed his jacket, letting it drop to the floor.

"You're right." She started removing her clothes, tossing them to the floor as quickly as he did.

She could feel the frenzy swimming in her veins, just as she could see it in his eyes. They wasted no time getting naked. She tried to wrap her lean body around his again when he climbed on to the bed, but he shook his head. How dare he not let her have her way. She whimpered and frowned. "Not nice, Mr. Holloway."

A sly grin formed. "You've been a naughty girl, Ms. Stileano."

If not for his grin, she would've sworn he was about to exact the revenge he declared he wouldn't do.

Then he ran a hand down the length of her, eliciting an electrifying shiver. "And I want to touch every inch of you with my lips first."

Oh, dear, he was exacting revenge, alright, and sweet, sweet torture.

"I can't wait for that. I want more now."

He pressed a few kisses along her collarbone. "It's too bad you didn't say 'please.' Manners, Ms. Stileano, you can't forget your manners."

She sighed in pleasure as his mouth continued a path to her breasts, taking his time as he went. Yep. He was out to torture her with his soft lips. They didn't miss a spot on her skin. His mouth clamped down on her tight nipple, swirling his tongue with lavish delight. Another moan escaped as she ran her hands through his hair. A grin appeared when a low growl echoed from his lips at her touch. It was good to know her touch made him as mad as his touch did to her.

And his touch was maddening. He didn't simply take his time, he slowed down as if time stopped. The seconds ticking by as if long minutes. He took turns going from one breast to the other, several times before continuing his trail down her stomach. She dug her fingers deeper into his hair when his hot breath hit her aching desire. His tongue dove in without restraint, making her lift off the bed like a shooting rocket.

"Dane, I want you," she whispered breathlessly.

He continued to ignore her as he licked, swirled, and devoured her with abandoned pleasure. She wanted to lift his head, move his mouth up to hers, and have him plunge deep inside. Yet, she couldn't seem to make her hands move. Her body moved restlessly beneath him as he refused to stop his torturous assault.

"Did you hear me? Dane..." she murmured in between her tiny moans of pleasure.

She could feel the pinpricks of bliss wanting to escape. She was so close, yet not quite there. His tongue continued to move, making her yearn for more. Much, much more. Then, like a firecracker shooting straight to the sky, ecstasy burst through, making her cry out with satisfaction.

She waited for her body to come down from the high, the feeling of relaxation covering every corner of her body. Her eyes closed with joy. That had been better than she ever had. Not that she had dated many guys who wanted to go down on her. But damn, if Dane wanted to ignore her pleas to do that again, who was she to argue?

She felt tiny kisses on her thighs, hovering near the spot he just claimed.

"Dane, what are you doing?"

Of course, she wouldn't mind his sweet, tortuous kisses again, but not so soon. She wanted him deep inside her. That's what she wanted.

He still ignored her, his kisses raining all of her body. He made it very difficult to concentrate. Every time his soft lips touched her skin, her body begged for another one. And another one. And another one.

Until it hit her.

He was giving her payback for all the times she made him wait until she heard the magic words.

"Dane, please. Inside me. Now."

She couldn't resist being a little demanding while at the same time giving him what he desired.

She watched as his head lifted with a mischievous smile. "It took you long enough. Although I could kiss you all night."

"Who knew the word please was so magical?"

"I never did." He moved over her body, resting his forearm next to her head as he swiped a lock of hair back. "I don't have any condoms on me. I'm hoping you have some. I want you so badly, the scenarios in my head are scaring me. The last thing I expected when I came here was this."

"Scenarios?" she asked with a giggle.

He returned a wondrous laugh of his own. "Oh, they range from knocking on every door on this floor to bribing the doorman to run to the store. Trust me, those are the tamer ones."

As much as she'd love to see Dane ask Mrs. Stenson if she had any condoms—since she always knocked on her door for things, not that sugar compared to condoms—she decided she'd put Dane out of his misery. And her own. She wanted him just as badly.

"Bathroom. Underneath the sink." She didn't move from her spot as he hopped off the bed and opened the bedroom door. "Hurry up."

In the brief seconds he was gone, her mind went from one thought to another.

What was she doing?

How long did it take to grab condoms from underneath her sink? They weren't hiding in the back. Or were they? No, they were right next to her tampons in the front. She kept things very organized in her bathroom. Like she did everywhere else.

Should she be doing this? She barely knew him.

What was taking him so long? She couldn't wait to get him deep inside her, sending more delicious tingles down her spine.

Round and round her mind spiraled in the seconds he was gone. She couldn't help herself. Part of her thought she should wait and get to know him more. Why didn't he seem to like his brother? Why was he willing to forgive her when he said he never forgave liars? Was he now lying to her? Exacting revenge in the worst kind of way? Would he be that cruel? She never meant to hurt him.

Part of her thought, who cares. She'd been dying to get her hands on him since the first penetrating look in his eyes. She'd deal with the consequences after the fact.

He walked back into the bedroom, swinging the door closed again. The look of anticipation and excitement in his eyes had her worries disappearing for the moment.

He tossed one condom package on her nightstand as he rolled one onto his thick, hard cock. A seductive, slow smile emerged as he crawled back onto the bed. That wasn't the look of someone trying to get revenge.

"We're going to need to make a pharmacy run. Or bribe the doorman. Or knock on a few neighbors' doors. That's all the condoms you have," he said, positioning himself over her.

She giggled, enjoying the picture of him knocking on anyone's door asking for a condom. Then she glanced at her nightstand, where the other condom package sat waiting to be used. "Oh, we're using two condoms tonight...and more. So ambitious of you."

He pressed forward, slowly entering her. "When it comes to you, Gabriella, I imagine one time will never be enough. You know how ambitious I am. There's no stopping me."

She gasped. A mixture from his words and feeling her body stretch to his hard length. She never felt such yearning for a man. He barely entered her, and she never wanted him to leave. She wrapped her legs around his waist as he fully penetrated her. He couldn't leave her now.

"Hold on, sweetheart. I've been wanting this all week. I'm going to take you fast and hard," he whispered into her ear as he started to thrust into her.

Yes. Oh, yes. Hard and fast was what she wanted, too.

She squeezed her legs tighter, loving the way the endearment left his mouth. She absolutely loved it when he called her that, and the way her name rolled off his tongue. She would embrace his sweetness for as long as he was willing to give it. Because she imagined he didn't give it often.

She clung to him as he thrust deeply, letting loose. He didn't hold back. He meant it when he said fast and hard.

His muscles were strained, pumping, exerting himself as he was, yet he looked relaxed for once. As if he was letting down barriers he kept tightly around him. And why? Why did he push himself so hard at work? Why did he never let himself have a break?

She tried to keep up with his pace, wanting him to let loose as much as he could. He needed this. She imagined he never let himself go in such a manner. How could he when he worked so damn much?

A moment of panic entered her mind. How much would she have to contend with when it came to his job? Would she have to fight his job to get any affection from him? She thought it was a high possibility. But as he continued to pound into her over and over again, a wicked smile stretched across his face, she knew he would be worth the fight. She would make him take a break. She would make him smell the fresh air.

She could feel another beautiful orgasm making its way through her body. She didn't want to ruin the moment by coming first, but she had no way to stop it. With the way he moved so freely inside of her, she couldn't hold back. She gave way to the joy, moaning his name, the neighbors down the hallway had to have heard.

"Oh, Gabriella," he whispered roughly as he thrust a few more times and followed her into glorious bliss.

She didn't relax her legs around his waist even after she felt his heavy weight pressed on her. His hot breath tickled her neck, waiting for his breathing to slow down. She didn't want him to leave her side. It was suddenly such an irrational fear. She never felt such pleasure, so close to another man. She didn't want to lose this. The minute he pulled away, she would never get it back again. She had no idea why she feared it, but she did.

He lifted his head, kissing her lips. "Did I tell you how beautiful you are? I thought so since the first time I met you."

She loved hearing that, but she was never good with compliments. They always made her uncomfortable, unsure of how to respond. Instead of responding with words, she brushed her hands through his hair, enjoying the softness. He enjoyed it if his low groan was any indication.

"I should get rid of this condom." He tried to extract himself, but she refused to move her legs.

Maybe she should've said something to his sweet comment. It's not like a guy never said she was beautiful before.

But it was the first time she believed it. How did one respond to that? A simple thank you didn't seem enough. Not to mention awkward. Did she say he was handsome back? He was, but that also felt awkward.

"Gabriella, can I get up?"

"You don't like where you are?" she asked with a teasing grin. But the panic was setting in. He wanted to pull away from her already. She should've responded to his comment.

He kissed her again. "I want to toss this condom away, grab us some beers, and have round two—slower this time. I want to love your body as slowly as I possibly can, savor every single minute. Because I like exactly where I am."

Oh.

Wow.

This, at times, arrogant, thoughtless man, who could work her until her feet wanted to fall off, could also be the sweetest, kindest man she had ever met. Every time he said such wonderful words, it broke a part of the impenetrable wall she had built a long time ago to keep from getting hurt.

Because keeping people outside of the wall was always easier than letting them in.

This wonderful man was creeping his way inside her walls.

She bit her lip as a smile appeared. "I like exactly where you are, too."

7

DANE SWIRLED his fork around the noodles as he peered at Gabriella out of the corner of his eye. She looked cute and delectable in only a tight white tank top and black lacy panties. He still couldn't believe how the night was going. Not that he had expected any of this to happen. When he left his office after pacing from one end to the other until he thought he'd explode from more questions than answers, he knew he needed to see Gabriella. He hadn't known what he'd say to her, but this... This hadn't been on his agenda when he left his office in a huff.

Of course, he wasn't complaining.

They had used both condoms, then left to get food and a refill of condoms. They stopped at a small Chinese restaurant not far from her apartment that had him concerned. The place had looked like a dive. Would the food even taste good? But she had smiled at him and said, "Trust me."

And he did. When she smiled like that, it was hard not to listen and follow her instructions. But should he trust her? She had lied to him.

When he looked at her beautiful face and sweet smile—oh, that smile did something to his heart—he trusted her.

The more everything rolled around his mind. The heartache on her friend Mia's face. His asshole brother. He understood why she had done what she had. He did.

But he felt like he was missing a piece to the puzzle. Like, why would she do anything for her friend Mia? Every time he tried to ask, she clammed up and refused to tell him. It only made his curiosity worse.

Which made him think she could still be lying to him.

"So? It's good, isn't it? Really, really good, huh?" she said with a devious smile, nudging him in the shoulder.

"I already told you it was. No need to rub it in anymore. Even cold, it tastes delicious." He took another bite, winking at her.

"Well, mister, it wouldn't have been cold if you didn't distract us first."

"You distract me so easily." She distracted him more than he cared to admit. "I couldn't help myself." He thought back to the new box of condoms they bought. He didn't waste any time opening it up and putting them to good use. He couldn't seem to keep his hands off her.

He didn't know yet if that was a good or bad thing.

"I like distracting you. I have this strange feeling you work Saturdays. Don't you?"

He paused, twirling the noodles around the fork and frowned. "There's a lot that needs to be done. There aren't enough hours in the day."

A warm hand caressed his cheek. He couldn't resist leaning into it. "How many times do I have to tell you that you work too much? Life shouldn't be so serious."

He turned toward her and kissed her. "You're starting to convince me."

Which he also couldn't determine if that was a good or bad thing. Work was very important to him. It was his livelihood—his sole focus.

"We'll never get this food eaten if you keep distracting us."

He nibbled on her bottom lip. "You're the distracting one."

He was about to set his food down on the nightstand and start another round between the sheets when her phone went off. A low groan slipped out before he could stop himself. Her eyes twinkled with a bit of mischief and confusion as she set her food on the nightstand and grabbed her phone.

Yeah, he should've kept his groan to himself. His emotions were all jumbled and confused. He wanted her, yet he wasn't sure if he should leave and keep his distance. And any interruptions weren't going to help the tangled emotions raging a war deep inside him.

"It's Jaxson. I'm going to grab this quick and make sure Mia's okay."

She answered the phone and walked out of the room. His mind started to wander. Why did she have to leave the room to take the call? Had he misinterpreted Jaxson's feelings toward Mia? Should he be jealous?

He frowned, hating the confusion swirling inside his veins. He liked to be in control and in charge. Right now, he was nowhere near either of those things. Well, he liked to be in control and in charge of things that were right in front of him. He knew he'd never have control of his father's company. No matter how much he fought and demanded control—not that he even tried—he'd never be better than Champ. Not in his father's eyes.

He took a few more bites of food but lost the taste for

anything. This was why he didn't put in the effort to date anymore. Too complicated. Too much time worrying about why she did this or why she did that. He had too much to worry about at work and in his family to waste his time worrying about a woman as well.

He set the food down on the nightstand. His eyes caught a glimpse of her black lacy bra adorning the floor. The erotic image of extracting the lacy garment from Gabriella's gorgeous body flooded his mind after they returned to the apartment. He knew right then why he wanted to make a small effort to date a woman again.

She was worth it.

Or was she?

Was she still lying to him?

Did she like her partner as more than just a friend?

His mind fought a brutal battle back and forth.

She had so many endearing qualities that he had never seen in a woman. She had a sense of humor. He had been having fun tonight teasing her. And it always elicited one of her sweet smiles he adored. She spoke her mind without effort. He knew he would never wonder where he stood with her. That was refreshing. That should ease his mind some. Yet, it didn't. She still held back part of herself.

Especially the part about her friend Mia. Why couldn't she open up to him? He asked, and she dodged. Perhaps she thought they needed to know each other a little better.

Glancing around the bed, he thought they knew each other pretty well now. Physically, anyway.

And maybe that's all it would ever be. The thought saddened him. He wanted to know more about her. He wanted to know her inside and out. He wanted to know her fears, her dreams. What made her happy, and what made her sad. He wanted to know her favorite movie and how she liked to spend her spare time.

Or did he?

Maybe it wouldn't be smart. She had lied to him in the beginning.

He shivered from the directions his thoughts were taking him. He always kept it light with women. He should continue to do so.

He sat up straighter, thinking it was time to leave. There was a lot of work waiting for him in the office.

The door shut, erasing his decision to leave. He grinned as Gabriella rounded the bed with her own sweet smile.

"Whew. She's fine. I trust Jaxson, but I still worried." She hopped back in bed, taking a sip of her beer.

Wow. What did that mean?

"My brother's an asshole, but what did you expect to happen? He wouldn't physically hurt her."

Dane may not like his brother much, but he knew Champ would never physically harm a woman. Destroy her heart and leave the pieces without a backward glance? Yes. Throw a punch or push her or slap her or any number of physical traits? No. He was offended she thought so.

She shrank back from him, knitting her brows in confusion. "I never thought that. Mia may not look fragile, but she is. I didn't want her to break down in tears again. Jaxson said they were in and out of his apartment without an issue. He said Champ glared at him the entire time and that he barely said a word to Mia. When Jaxson dropped her off at home, she seemed fine. That's all I meant."

"Why is she so fragile? Why would you do anything for her?"

She still hovered away from him, irking him further

each second she stayed that way. Why was she pulling away like that?

"She's my best friend. Do you need another beer?"

"What I need is for you to talk to me. You keep avoiding the question. Why?"

She set her beer down, scooting farther away from him. Damn it. The more she kept pulling away in such a manner, the more the decision cemented in his brain that leaving was the best option. She clearly only wanted something physical between them and nothing else.

Her lips were in a tight line, matching his stern features.

"Why do you hate your brother?"

"I don't hate him."

And why in the hell was she turning the questions around on him? Why couldn't she answer a simple question about her friend Mia?

She laughed, almost sounding like a hoity-toity woman he dated once. And damn, once was enough after hearing the woman's obnoxious laughter for two hours straight. "Yeah, right, and I'm a fairytale princess. Cue the singing animals."

"He's my brother. I don't hate him. I don't always like him, but I would never hate him. My mother would disown me if I did."

"There's more to it than that. You don't want to talk about it, then don't expect me to talk about my friendship with Mia." She stood up and stalked to her dresser where she pulled out a pair of drawstring pants.

"I asked my question first. Answer my question, and I'll tell you anything you want to know about the issues between my brother and me." He stood up from the bed, wondering whether he should shove his clothes back on as she was rushing to do.

Hadn't he wanted to flee a few minutes ago? She was giving off the vibe they were done.

Yet, it proved to have the opposite effect on him. Instead of wanting to leave, he wanted to forget this conversation and make sweet, slow love to her.

"It doesn't matter."

What doesn't matter?

He didn't matter? The issues between his brother and him? Her friend? He hated that she refused to open up. He hated that he wanted to forget this happened and pull her into his arms and hold her tight. Because it felt like she was slipping away, and he didn't want that. Sure, he had been confused before. Hell, he was still confused by his swirling emotions. But his heart was telling him that leaving was the wrong move. The rapid beating, the erratic pace—he knew walking away would gut him.

"Why are you getting dressed? A few questions you don't want to hear, and you run. What is this?" He whipped his hand to the bed. "We sleep together, but we can't dig deeper than that?"

"What do you want from this? I'm still trying to figure out why you forgave me so easily. Is this what you wanted? A romp in the sheets and 'see you later, babe?'" she fired back.

"Did those words come out of my mouth? Because I, as sure as shit, don't remember them." He growled with frustration as he dragged a hand through his hair. "You didn't believe anything I said earlier. Maybe I was wrong about you." He grabbed his pants from the floor and whipped them on.

A man could only take so much. *He* could only take so much. The anger fueled inside him. It didn't take long for him to get the rest of his clothes on.

"So, you're just going to leave?"

He looked up from the words that left her mouth tonelessly. "You started to dress first. And it doesn't feel like we have anything left to say to each other. You don't seem to trust me, and I'm beginning to think that I shouldn't have trusted you in the first place. You lied to me from the moment I met you."

"See, you're still mad. You never did forgive me."

He stared at her for the longest time.

Trying to gauge what she was thinking. Trying to figure out how this situation spiraled out of control. Trying to understand how he could want to walk away without another word, yet also want to grab her and never let go.

No matter how long he stared at her, and she stared back, he couldn't determine what she was thinking. No expression marred her face. Most women would either be yelling at the top of their lungs or crying in hysterics. She was doing neither—just a blank expression.

"Why did you sleep with me?" Her whispered words broke his heart. That she even asked such a question ripped his soul to shreds.

He clenched his jaw. So many things wanted to spew out. Angry words. An apology. A bit of begging. He couldn't believe what he was hearing from her. Why would she ask him that? Didn't his touch tell her why he slept with her?

Yet, she was reducing what transpired between them to nothing but sex. Nothing special. Nothing momentous. Nothing where he thought she might be the woman of his dreams.

He grabbed the box of condoms behind him and tossed them in the trashcan near the door. "I don't think we'll be needing those anymore."

There was work to be done. He had enough of this bullshit.

Heading for the doorway, he stopped before stepping into the hallway. "I've never been dishonest with you. Never. And I never would be. That's not who I am."

———————

THE MOMENT she heard her front door slam, the tears rained down. She glanced at the bed, the rumpled sheets laughing at her. She wanted to rewind the last few minutes and go back to the lighthearted teasing and fun-loving Dane. She didn't like the side of him she witnessed.

Although he had never raised his voice, he hadn't needed to. Every time he spoke, it came out with venom laced in each word.

She dropped down on the bed and curled into the side he had occupied. Her tears fell as the silence threatened to choke her.

What happened? How did they go from the sweet bliss of lovemaking to fighting with each other?

She believed him. She should've never said that she didn't believe he forgave her. Of course, he wouldn't lie to her.

He was an honorable man. She knew this. Only working one week with him told her that. He worked hard. Sure, he treated other employees abruptly. Yet, with underlying respect. She didn't think he was being rude on purpose; he was simply too focused on his work that his words came out clipped.

And the clients. If they asked a difficult question that would not help in his favor, he still answered with honesty. He would never lie to a client to make his way in the business. The few phone calls she had been a part of—dictating every word said—she could hear the awe and respect in the client's voice at his honesty.

Her eyes started to hurt, her nose stuffy and snotty. She couldn't stop the tears. A sharp ache in her head formed. Why had she screwed everything up?

Always screwing things up, especially with men. This was why she never managed to maintain a healthy relationship. She either dated losers or screwed it up in some way that could have been prevented. She had no one to blame but herself.

She could've just told him about Mia. She should've.

But she had her reasons. One being it was too painful to talk about. Another being it wasn't her story to tell. And those reasons for the first time had proved to be disastrous.

The people who knew always looked at Mia differently, even her at times. They judged. They condemned. It was a natural reaction for most people. Or they felt pity. The pity was the worst for Mia. She hated it.

A loud hiccup echoed in the quiet room. She should call Jaxson. He would be over in an instant. He would comfort her and tell her she didn't need that jerk. That it was none of his business.

But if she expected things from Dane, he would expect things back. That made it his business when he asked.

How would he react if she told the whole story? Her reasons why she always—always—did anything for Mia.

She feared his reaction. She feared it so much, she let him walk out without fighting for him.

Jaxson was the only person she knew, besides her parents, who hadn't reacted with anything but support. He didn't judge. He didn't show pity. He barely said a word, which had helped when she explained everything. But he had shown her in one simple look that none of it mattered.

She jumped when a hand touched her shoulder.

Oh, that touch.

She never thought she'd feel his soft touch again. Relaxing, a low sigh escaped as she relished in Dane's solid hand doing nothing but holding her softly. She turned toward him, tears still silently streaming down her face.

"Why are you crying?" Dane asked in a whisper as he moved his hand from her shoulder to wipe the tears from cheeks.

"I thought you left. I heard the door slam."

She tried not to let another needy sigh escape as he caressed her cheek again. "Why do you always dodge my questions?" He dropped his hand to his lap, a deep frown tarnishing his handsome face. "I realized I forgot my phone."

He grabbed his phone from the nightstand and stood up. He shoved the phone in his pocket as he started walking toward the door.

What was she doing?

Here was her chance. She couldn't ruin another chance when it was in her reach to fix things.

"Don't leave. Please." She sat up, wiping at her cheeks, trying to clear all the ugly tears away. Oh, she had to look ugly. Red, bloodshot eyes. Snotty nose. Rosy cheeks from the tearstains. Her head still pounded from all the ache she had shed. She grabbed a tissue from her nightstand to erase part of her embarrassment.

"I was crying because of how bad I screwed up. I know you would never lie to me. It's not easy answering the question you want the answer to." She watched the rigidness in his body start to relax as he turned around in the doorway. "I say things sometimes that slip out. You should know this by now. Call it a nervous tic. I know you didn't lie. I know you forgave me. Please, Dane. I'm sorry. Please, forgive me... again."

That sounded lame when she processed everything she said. How pathetic she needed him to forgive her once again.

He walked back to the bed and sat on the edge—close enough where she could reach out if she wanted to wrap her arms around him and beg him to stay. By the fierce frown on his face, she was afraid he was seconds away from leaving.

Then his expression loosened, yet the pain still lingered in his eyes. "Stop crying, Gabriella." He wiped another tear from her cheek that she hadn't realized escaped.

"I can't help it. I've never met a man who made me want to cry like this. In fact, I don't cry. It's...it's for the birds."

A low masculine chuckle trickled from his lips. "That's not a saying I've heard before."

She shrugged. What could she say? Nonsense came out of her mouth, especially when she was agitated, upset, or nervous. "I don't want you to leave. I want this," she waved her hand at the bed, "to be more than just a romp between the sheets."

His eyes followed her hand gesture. "I..." He hesitated.

No. She needed him to finish his sentence, but she was afraid to interrupt as the emotions flitting across his face looked intense.

He looked from the bed, then to her. "I want that, too. But not if we can't trust each other. I would've never slept with you if I hadn't forgiven you."

"I know. I know that."

She hiccupped, hating that she couldn't stop the water leaking from her eyes.

"Stop crying. Are you waiting for me to say please? I hate

seeing this." He brushed a few more tears away, the anguish clear in every feature. "Please stop crying, sweetheart."

Before she could tell him that she didn't need to hear the word please, he kissed her. So sweet. So soft. So full of tenderness, it melted her heart. All the tension slipped away.

Sure, a bit of tension still swirled around them, but the tension hampering her heart diminished. Her tears slowed down and died away. She wrapped her arms around his neck, putting everything into that simple kiss. She needed him to feel how sorry she was. To know how much she cared for him. Not just for a warm body in her bed.

She opened her mouth, savoring the taste and texture that she would always attribute to Dane. He didn't hold back, something she feared he would do. He tangled his tongue with hers, keeping the steady pace she craved.

She never wanted to end this kiss. If it ended, she was afraid of what would happen next. Would he still walk out? Was he still mad? He didn't give her much reassurance that he forgave her. Or maybe he did. She was on the verge of creating a new fiasco when it wasn't necessary. Why did she always do this to herself?

She felt him pull away, making her tug on his bottom lip before he extracted himself from her lips.

"You know what happens when I kiss you. If I don't stop now, I'll never leave this bed." He leaned his head farther back but didn't move his body away from hers.

"I don't understand."

He sighed heavily and gestured toward the door. "I threw the condoms away. I was about two seconds away from whipping all our clothes off and diving deep inside you without a condom. That's what you do to me. You distract me. You have since the moment I met you. Here I am again, not mad anymore. Just one tear had my anger crumbling to pieces. I would've never walked out if I would've seen one tear. You didn't even yell at me. What kind of way is that to fight? You should either yell or cry. Don't do this blank expression business. I don't like it."

She couldn't help it. A tiny laugh escaped. She laughed a little bit more when she saw the corner of his mouth tip up into a devilish grin. "Maybe you should dig in that trash can."

"Do I look like the diving dumpster type?" he asked with a mock grimace.

She playfully slapped his shoulder. "Does it look like a dumpster?"

He stood up, grabbed the condoms from the trash, and set them on the nightstand next to her. He resumed his seat and grabbed her hand. "Gabriella..."

Oh boy. No sentence ever turned out well when someone said her name with such anguish without saying anything else.

Since she was afraid of what he would say, she didn't say anything. What could she say? If he wanted to leave, she couldn't stop him. And as much as she wanted to beg, she had never begged a man in her life for anything, and she wasn't about to start now.

Although she was tempted. Dane seemed worth a little begging.

"I still think the air needs to be cleared. I thought we cleared it well enough before we even hit this bed the first time. But...we didn't."

She cringed inside. Oh, here it comes. The same damn question. She wasn't sure if she could answer it. She wanted to. It burned deep inside to let him know. But how would he react?

"Champ's younger than me by two years. He's always been the golden boy. He thinks our mom favors me while I know our dad favors him. I always tell him that evens everything out. He floats through life like it's one big joke. He's never had to work for anything in his life. College... Yeah, I'm pretty sure he paid other people to do his work. Sports... Always handed the best position even when he didn't work hard enough for it. Job... Our dad retires and hands over the reins when he barely lifted a finger in the company beforehand. I work my ass off at that company, and that's the respect I get. I'm the oldest."

He wove his fingers through her hand, clasping tightly. "I'm not jealous, even if I made it sound like I am. I like working hard. I don't want anything handed to me. It doesn't feel right. He can have it. His behavior will come back to bite him in the ass someday. I'll be there to laugh and say, 'I told you so.' I don't hate Champ, but I barely respect him. I'm not even sure how the distance between us happened. I think it was always there from the beginning. I remember when I was about five. Champ was three and was throwing a ball back and forth with our dad. He was catching them with ease and throwing back as if he was born to do it. I remember my dad saying, 'That's my champ. That's how's it done, son.' Then he looked at me and said, 'Why can't you be like your brother?' That's not the only time my father has said those words to me. I'm not very athletic."

"Champ's not his real name, is it?" she asked softly, almost afraid to interrupt him. She wasn't sure why he was suddenly sharing all of this information, but she wanted to hear it. Soak it up like a sponge.

"It's David. My dad called him champ one day, and it stuck. My mom supports me and loves me and encourages me to do whatever I want. My dad...I don't know. I think he wishes Champ was the oldest son. He seems to have more pride in him than in me. But that's okay. I'm happy. I love my work. That's what matters." He shrugged. "So, that's the issue between my brother and me. Nothing spectacular. I'm sure other people have it worse. It's rare, but we have moments where we get along."

"I know you love your work. What I don't understand is why you stay there. You could build your own company and create your own success. You'd never have to nicely ask your secretary to bring your brother files."

She smiled, hoping a little light teasing would elicit a small smile from him. She was rewarded for her efforts.

"You're the only one I ever asked. I made everyone else do it without arguing with me."

"Of course, you did, you hardass," she said with a laugh.

"I don't know why I've never branched out on my own. Maybe I'm still hoping one day my dad will say how proud he is of me." He looked away, releasing a lame laugh. "How's that for sharing my feelings? I've never said anything like this to any woman before. You make me want to share, to make this relationship work."

His words lingered in the room like the aftereffects from a loud bang of thunder in the distance.

Her heart started to pound. Giddy, yet frightened.

He met her gaze, his lips tilted up in a sweet, adorable grin. "That's what I want. A relationship."

She grabbed his face, his scratchy stubble melting her insides. So rough on the outside, yet so tender on the inside. She wanted to rub her cheek against his. Feel him everywhere. Soak up every part of him, inside and out.

"Me, too. I want that so much." She inhaled and let out her breath gradually. "Thank you for sharing. And I meant what I said. You should start your own company. You'd do wonderfully at it. I know it."

He leaned forward, kissing her. She dropped her hands from his chin to wind around his neck. Before she could dive in and truly claim his mouth, he pulled away. "Imagine how much more I would be working if I started my own company. I'd never see you. My mind is always focused on work that I'm trying to figure out how to even see you now."

She gave him a stern look. "Mister, you better make time for me. I will not compete with your job. I know you would never cheat on me...with a woman. That doesn't mean you wouldn't with your job."

"Give me a smile." He cracked his own silly grin. "I hate the look you're giving me right now. I won't cheat on you with my job. I will make time for you. I promise, Gabriella. I want this to work. I'm sorry for the things I said earlier. I don't want to leave tonight."

Her expression changed from serious to sultry because she didn't want him leaving anytime soon, either. "I'm sorry, too. Makeup sex sounds fun."

"Is it fast and dirty?" His eyes glittered with mischief as he let her hand go and stood up.

"For you, I'll be as dirty as you want me to be." She bit her lip coyly as she ran a finger down her stomach and stopped at the edge of her pants.

His eyes flashed with desire, and a delicious grin etched across his face as he took his clothes off again—everything except his boxers. He nodded his head to the other side of the bed. "Scoot over, sweetheart. You're sitting on my side. Don't make me spank your ass."

Her eyebrows lifted, considering her options. Spanking might be fun. But then she decided to move when his eyes said he wasn't joking. She had upset him—twice. He might spank her hard, and she wasn't sure if she was into that kind of dirtiness.

She moved over, the happiness in her heart starting to drop back to normal. Ten minutes ago, she thought she lost him forever. Now, here he was climbing back into her bed, almost gloriously naked.

She removed her pants and dove under the covers. Two could play this game. He hadn't taken off his boxers, she could tease him by hiding part of herself. She shifted closer when he joined her under the blankets. His arms reached around her, pulling her close.

"This is much better. I don't like fighting with you."

She leaned her head on his chest, inhaling his wonderful scent. "I don't either."

She felt his intake of breath, then a heavy sigh escape. She was almost afraid to ask what that meant. Turned out, she didn't need to ask.

"So, whenever you're ready to tell me the answer to the question that started everything earlier, I'll be ready to listen. No pressure. I want you to know there's nothing that you can say that will make me leave this room again. I'm right where I want to be."

She had her doubts about that. Maybe she would let him spank her.

It'd be better than confessing.

8

DANE WANTED to hold his breath as he waited for her to say something. But he knew that would be foolish. He'd die of suffocation, waiting for her to answer that burning question.

He opened himself up to her. He said things he had never told another soul. It felt good to release all that pent-up emotion. To unload about his brother. Because he bottled up way too much about his brother. He could never stand Champ's antics.

Sure, his other reason for sharing would be so she felt comfortable sharing with him.

But he also wanted to tell her.

If it came to the point where he introduced her to his parents, he needed her to know why it might be awkward. His father didn't keep his opinions about Dane to himself. He had no problem praising Champ and excluding Dane as if he didn't exist. His mother always tried to bridge the gap, but it never worked.

On second thought, maybe it wouldn't be the wisest decision for her to meet his parents. He was embarrassed, simply thinking about it.

He kissed the top of her head. The silence was starting to become deafening, but he wasn't sure what to say. He wanted her to say something first. Anything. Even something like, "Let's get this party started under the sheets," and he'd be happy.

Of course, he would drop the subject if that's what she wanted. For now, anyway. He wasn't sure he could drop it altogether. He wasn't made like that. When something bothered him, it festered like an infected wound. Nothing would solve a problem by letting it continue to fester.

Was it selfish of him? Probably. When he wanted something, he did everything in his power to obtain it.

They held each other for the longest time. The minutes ticked by as silence reigned. It wasn't an uncomfortable silence. He could've lain there all night holding her. He liked her in his arms. It was a very unfamiliar feeling. Foreign, yet wanted. He couldn't remember the last time he relaxed and enjoyed the silence—enjoyed the presence of another person. A woman. A very beautiful, enticing woman. It had been a long time since he had the urge to do something more than just work. Work was the furthest thing in his mind. He wanted to hold Gabriella, let this strange feeling—contentment, perhaps—soak into his veins and settle into his heart. He could get used to this.

But should he?

He shivered when her lips caressed his chest.

Soft, tender touches like that told him, yes, he could get used to this. He wanted more. So much more. By her simple gesture, she was telling him she wanted more as well. At least, at the moment.

He stopped brushing his fingers on her back, bringing them down her arms and to her waist, where he grabbed the hem of her tank top. He didn't need any further signal about what she wanted.

She didn't want to talk. That was fine with him. They had all the time in the world to talk later.

He pulled the tank top over her head, immediately clamping his mouth over a hard nipple. She moaned in delight, her body instinctively reaching for his cock. That small contact lit his body on fire. He pushed her to lay on her back and slid down her body as he removed her panties.

"I want you, Dane. Nothing else right now, please. Just you inside me," she whispered, grabbing at his hair when his mouth started to glide to her hot center.

He glanced up at her with a scorching grin. "Later, then. I want to taste you again later."

And he would. He had to. His need for her was all-consuming. A strange, yet intense feeling he couldn't get rid of. That he couldn't control. Look at him, not even working. That should tell him how much control she had over him.

He threw off his boxers, grabbed a condom, and ripped the package open with quick precision. Sheathing himself, he entered her in one smooth move. For one glorious moment, he let himself enjoy the feeling of her. Wet. Hot. And ready for anything he was about to dish. Fast and hard? Or slow and sweet? He wasn't sure how he wanted this joining to go, even though they had teased it would be fast and rough.

She stared back at him, smiling with one of her gorgeous smiles he loved. She grabbed his ass and gave him the cue to start moving. He could've held that position for a bit longer, enjoying the sweetness that surrounded him, but he also understood her urgency. The desire coursed through his body as well. He needed her like he needed his next breath.

They moved in a rhythmic pattern—thrust after thrust of delightful joy, perfectly in sync with each other.

Slow and sweet it was.

Neither made a move to do anything but connect their bodies as one—no kissing, no moving of their hands, just a simple embrace as they moved together. That spoke louder than any other action could have done.

The joining should have frightened him. He felt more connected to another human being than he ever had before. This wasn't like the other times with her.

This was more.

This was intense.

This was...love?

He wasn't sure he wanted to think that yet, but it ventured through his thoughts as he held her eyes and moved deep inside her with aching patience.

This did more than relax him. It relaxed his soul. He needed this connection. He needed to feel love for once.

There it was again. The feeling of love. Could he love this energetic, smart-mouthed, strong woman already?

Her lips twisted with bliss, her eyes sparkling with what looked like the same thing he was feeling.

Impossible.

They barely knew each other. Only one week had passed. He shouldn't be feeling such emotion. Neither should she.

He had to be mistaken. This was only intense lust. That's what it had to be. Pure lust. He could handle lust. But love? He wasn't sure he could handle love at the moment. He knew a relationship with Gabriella would not be easy. She hadn't made anything easy for him since the moment he met her.

He wouldn't take her any other way either.

Their pace increased as if they both needed to ignore what was floating between them.

The heat increased. Hot and erotic. Each time he thrust into her, he swore he saw the same emotion he felt reflected in her eyes. That only made him increase the movements. They couldn't be feeling anything but good sex. Yet, the way she devoured him with her eyes made him even hungrier for her. He had to remind himself a few times that what he saw was lust, not love. It couldn't be love.

They suddenly both exploded into ecstasy together. His body stiffened as she clenched around him. He almost wished the condom would magically disappear so he could feel her skin to skin.

A slice of disappointment hit him. The moment was over. He didn't want it to end.

His mind trailed to the box of condoms sitting on her nightstand. Thank the heavens he bought the largest pack he could. He planned on using quite a few more before the night ended.

What an idiot he'd almost been. He almost left her place filled with anger, just as he had arrived.

Bending his head, he kissed her neck, his lips lingering. "So beautiful."

She shifted under him. "Me, or this moment?"

He met her eyes, the teasing light shining within in her depths. "Both. It's always beautiful with you. You've ruined me for any other woman."

The surprise in her eyes at his candid words mirrored his own. Did he admit he loved her?

Of course not.

He was speaking of lust.

"Let me get rid of this condom. Then some more food— being with you has increased my appetite." He smiled, trying to clear the sudden awkwardness that shifted between them.

Perhaps it only felt awkward to him. He couldn't tell if it was disappointment in her eyes or not. Regardless, he needed a moment to himself—some space.

He used the bathroom, taking his time. When enough time had passed, that would make her start to worry—which he didn't want—he walked back into the room. He climbed back into bed and grabbed his food.

Gabriella didn't say a word, but she smiled. He could never resist her smiles. It almost made him want to set his food back down and pull her into his arms. Make sweet, sweet love to her once more.

Although he couldn't quite decipher what her smile meant. Happy and content? Confused and worried and hiding it by smiling? He should've never said what he had. *You've ruined me for any other woman.* The magic they shared would not be dampened by what he said afterward. He refused to allow that to happen. Yet, she still hadn't said a word—only smiled.

He needed to decipher what that smile meant. He wasn't sure what to make of her silence.

She shifted closer to him. He twirled his fork around some noodles and offered her a bite. She shook her head, and her smile disappeared. He almost dropped his fork by the sudden change in her expressions.

"Mia killed her father...and I helped."

At that, he did drop his fork into the container.

He wasn't sure if he heard her correctly. His hand was frozen in the air as he tried to process what she said.

"That's the answer to your question."

His brows dipped low. "No. That just raises another slew of questions. I don't understand." He set his container to the nightstand. "Don't leave me hanging here, Gabriella. Please explain."

Her eyes moved straight ahead, glaring at her closet as if it were the entrance to a mountain of treasure. "He was abusive. Beat her mom up until the day she died. Mia was sixteen when her mom died from cancer. He never hit Mia when her mom was around. But she wasn't around anymore. So, he went to his next best target—Mia."

He watched as her face morphed into so many emotions; it was hard to keep track of what one she was experiencing at the moment. The urge was strong to pull her into his arms, but he knew she needed to finish.

This had to be a sick joke. He couldn't believe what he was hearing. Yet, by the stiffness in her posture and the fact she refused to look at him, told him this was no joke.

"I never knew anything. She was very good at hiding it. At masking her bruises with makeup, even her mother's when she was alive. It's no wonder she works at the theater costuming people and applying their makeup. She's perfected it from a young age. It's sad when you think about it."

He watched as she fiddled with the end of the blanket. It took all his strength and control to wait for her to continue. If he interrupted, he feared she wouldn't finish her story.

"We were coming home from a movie when I found out the first time what was happening. It started raining on us, and it washed part of her makeup off. You should've seen the nasty bruise on her face. It didn't take long for her to confess it was from her dad. I didn't give her much choice. I demanded she call the police. She wouldn't. But I wouldn't give up. I made her go."

She sighed—a huge intake of breath followed by an

equally large exhale; her entire body moved from the exertion.

"They didn't believe her."

"What?"

At his shocked tone, she finally turned in his direction. "Her dad was a cop. I made the mistake of taking her to the precinct where he worked. I guess he had a habit of saying how mentally unstable Mia was—hurting herself after her mother died. I guess he needed an excuse if she was ever brave enough to rat him out. It worked. They wouldn't believe her. Of course, that didn't stop me. I raised the roof, spouting out things a sixteen-year-old shouldn't say. I wrote letters to the captain about how horribly he ran his department, how filthy and despicable his officers were."

"I can picture that very well." He smiled. She was a force to be reckoned with; he could only imagine what she had been at age sixteen. She didn't magically turn out to be this strong, defiant woman in a day.

A small grin tinged her lips. "Mia started to hide herself better after that from me. She insisted he backed off since I made a stink with the cops. I didn't believe her. I knew she was lying. But there wasn't anything I could do. The dumb cops wouldn't believe her. Her dad even made her go to therapy as if she was the one who needed help."

She glanced back at the closet. "She called one night—crying, hysterical. I could hear yelling and banging in the background. She had locked herself in her room. He was in a drunken rage trying to get inside. All she kept saying to me was, 'I need you, Gabby. Please help me.' I can still hear those words sometimes when I close my eyes. I didn't hesitate. I made it to her place as fast as I could. It didn't even cross my mind to call the cops who probably wouldn't have believed me anyway. The front door was unlocked. I ran up the stairs and started screaming at him to leave her alone. I didn't know he had his gun, and neither did Mia. He turned to me and fired the weapon."

"What?" He grabbed her by the shoulders, turning her to look at him. "He shot you. Where?"

A soft hand landed on his cheek. "He was drunk. He had horrible aim and only grazed my arm." She pointed to a tiny scar on her right bicep. "I don't know what came over me, but I charged at him. This two-hundred-fifty-pound man and I charged him like I could honestly kick his ass. I did manage to knock him to the ground, but that was about it. He got the upper hand and started hitting me. Mia rushed out of her room and joined in the fray. Two seventeen-year-old girls fighting a drunk bastard with a mean temper. When he knocked Mia out of the way, he lost the gun in the process. He started wailing into my face."

Dane slid his hand down her arms in a soothing caress when she stopped speaking. He finally understood why she didn't want to answer what he thought was a simple question. Forcing her to continue was the last thing he wanted to do, but he could tell she needed to finish her story even though she had paused. The determination was in her eyes to keep going. She inhaled deeply. Then she slowly let it out.

"Mia did the only thing she could think of. She picked up the gun on the floor and fired. I swear my heart stopped for a moment when his dead weight fell on me. That was almost worse than when he was beating me."

He squeezed her hands when a shiver rippled throughout her body.

"The cops had no trouble believing us that time. My face was proof enough, as was the toxicology report that came back, indicating he was heavily under the influence. To my surprise, Mia kept very detailed documentation of every single time he hit her. The number of apologies we received was amazing." Her face turned hard as granite. "Do you know what I told them they could do with those apologies?"

He chuckled as he pictured his beautiful Gabriella giving those men a piece of her mind. "To go screw themselves. Because that's exactly what's going through my mind."

She laughed. "You do understand me."

"I'm beginning to understand so many things." He couldn't resist any longer. He kissed her softly. "I see why you don't like to talk about it. But thank you."

"You asked why I would help Mia no matter what. Because every time she asks for the simplest of things, I don't hear that simple request. I hear that terrified voice crying, whispering to me to come help her. It took a while for both of us to move on, but we managed together. Mia still has bad days. She's so fragile."

"This is why you became a cop." He was in awe of her. Her bravery. Her strength. Her ability to keep fighting when it's not always easy to fight.

She nodded. "I want to help people. I never want someone, like Mia and me, to ever feel like there isn't help out there. I make sure to remind the cops that still work there that we dealt with back then how despicable they are. Needless to say, I'm not popular at that precinct."

He kissed her again. Oh, the beauty in his arms. Would he ever get enough of her?

"You continue to amaze me. God, you're beautiful. Every single part of you."

She brushed her fingers down his chest. "I like it when you say such sweet things."

It wasn't something he normally did with women. Sure, he made them feel special and appreciated, but he didn't express his feelings and say half of what he said to Gabriella. Because she was the most special woman of all.

She was everything.

"So, I think we're both good with sharing our deep, dark secrets."

He could hear the strain in her voice even though she laughed as she said it. The confession took more out of her than she wanted to admit. Not that he'd make her admit it.

He pulled her into his arms, then shifted until they were lying down. Rolling slightly, he hovered above her body, tracing his fingers lightly across her face. Smoothing out the worry. Letting her know with a simple touch, he'd erase the ugliness.

"I'm okay with no more talking." He replaced his finger with light kisses. From one cheek to the other. On top of her nose. Across her chin. Down her neck. Then he stopped.

Sinking onto her soft body had him craving her to the point of madness. Kissing her delectable body wasn't helping either.

He needed her.

He needed to replace the darkness she shared with something full of light and happiness.

"I need you, Gabriella."

Her eyes dilated with distress, then settled with pleasure. He didn't realize what he said at first, but then it dawned on him those had been the same words Mia had said when she called Gabriella in a panic.

What an idiot.

Yet, it didn't erase the fact he did need her. Completely and wholeheartedly.

"I want you," he whispered, then kissed her on the lips.

Her soft moan in response was all he needed to continue his pleasurable assault on her body.

9

GABBY WANTED to shield her eyes from the blasted sun that poured through her bedroom window. Except she didn't want to move and wake the handsome, devilish man sleeping next to her. It was nice to be able to take a moment and watch Dane unguarded, looking so peaceful for once. So relaxed.

It didn't matter how hard he tried to hide the tension or the stress in his life, she saw it. He masked it well, just not from her. She was trained to notice the slightest thing to pinpoint the tiny detail, especially when dealing with a suspect.

Yet, she had failed in her latest undercover assignment. Failed so miserably not detecting Dane wasn't who she had been looking for.

As she watched his slow, even breathing, the way the sun enhanced his features, she knew why. He had distracted her. Just like he said, she distracted him. Well, he had distracted her with one simple look. She could still picture him sitting in his chair, the gorgeous view behind him, the determination and focus in his eyes. Despite the fact she found him attractive and wanted to jump his bones, she had wanted to get him to loosen up as well. He fought her tooth and nail. She swore it was a lost cause until he knocked on her door, looking for answers. She finally got him to have a bit of fun and focus on something other than work.

She got him to focus on her.

But for how long?

He confused her. Excited her—made her ache for things she didn't know she ached for. He also scared her.

She opened herself up like she had never done with anyone, excluding Jaxson. He didn't count.

Her mind drifted to last night when she spilled her guts. No pity. No judgment. Nothing but sweet kindness and understanding.

It had surprised her. She couldn't figure out why it shocked her.

Why wouldn't he understand? He had a kind heart— once she managed to get past his hard exterior. It shouldn't be so surprising.

Maybe it surprised her because people rarely understood. They always judged and pitied. It was disappointing every single time.

But he had seemed to understand her immediately. Saying the right things. Shifting her focus to something else. Telling her thank you for sharing, but let's move on.

That's what she had wanted. Needed.

She knew when he spoke about his brother, it hadn't been easy. The words flowed out as if he were dictating to her. But she had seen the struggle in his eyes. Nothing about what he said had been easy—not one word.

After the stunning joining between them, she knew she needed to share with him. It was only fair.

Oh, and it was stunning. She wasn't even sure that was

the right word to describe it. She couldn't even be sure what transpired between them. Love, maybe?

"It's always beautiful with you. You've ruined me for any other woman."

Her? Ruin him?

Impossible.

Yet, he said so.

What exactly had that meant? She had no idea, especially when he walked away right after. She knew then, she needed to open herself up if she wanted to keep ruining him. She never wanted him to look at another woman again —only her.

What did that say about her feelings? Jealous? Yep. Possessive? Oh, yeah. Loved him? Hmm...not quite sure.

Confusion. That's all she felt.

"What is that beautiful mind of yours thinking? You're looking at me, but not really seeing me," Dane whispered in a groggy voice.

Gabby blinked a few times, hoping to clear the turmoil going on in her head and smiled. "That I didn't get much sleep last night and wish the sun hadn't woken me up."

He lifted his head to rest on his elbow as a sexy smirk emerged. "You didn't get any sleep last night? That's strange. I slept like a baby."

She poked him in the chest. "You kept me up very, very late. But I slept pretty well after all the exertion we had. You make a very nice pillow."

"Yes, I do believe you drooled on me." He chuckled as shock lit up her features.

"I did no such thing. Snore, maybe. But drool? Never."

Another chuckle fell from his lips that had her heart skipping a beat. Aww, she could lay here all day listening to him laugh and displaying his sexy, sinful smiles. It seemed he kept easing out smile after smile, and she wanted to keep him delivering even more.

She waited for him to respond to her teasing. His only response was to lean closer and kiss her.

"Breakfast? Then what shall we do for the day?"

She didn't miss the flash of regret enter his eyes.

Damn it. She was already losing him. He wanted to work today. She could feel it in her bones. Why would he want to end this wonderful weekend? That was the farthest thing from her mind.

Or she was coming on too strong. This relationship—if that's what they were calling it—was new. She shouldn't expect him to spend the day with her.

"You want to spend the day together? We spent yesterday together."

His words confirmed her fear.

She *was* coming on too strong.

Came on too strong, not strong enough. She was clueless when it came to guys and how she should act.

"We spent the evening together, not the day. There's a difference." She smiled, hoping to show he hadn't disappointed her. The last thing she needed was pity. If he wanted to leave and go to work, she wouldn't stop him. She had no control over the man.

Except, she didn't want him to leave. "It's my last day of vacation, and I want to spend it with you. Are you going to deny me that?"

He shifted under the covers as he sat up, running a tired hand through his hair. She wanted to know what he was thinking. Lucky for her, it didn't take a genius to figure it out. It was written on his face. A deep pain expanded inside her chest.

"There are a few things I need to get done today. Things I should've done yesterday, and I didn't."

Was this how it would always be with him? Fighting for attention? Fighting with his work?

"It's Sunday. You shouldn't work on a Sunday."

"I always work on Sundays."

He said it as if it were written in gold and couldn't be changed.

More pain exploded. Why was he doing this to them? Would it kill him to take one weekend off?

"I want to spend the day with you, Dane, but I won't beg. I will never beg you to spend time with me if it's work you'd rather do."

"Damn it, Gabriella. I want to spend time with you. I do. I don't want to fight with you already this morning. We just woke up."

"I'm not fighting." Although her words hadn't hidden the anger she was feeling spreading like wildfire in her veins.

But she didn't lie. She wasn't fighting. If he wanted to work, then so be it. She had better things to do than fight with a man who would ultimately break her heart. They always did. Which was why it was easier to walk away first. No sense letting someone completely in just for them to destroy her.

It already felt like he had broken her heart.

She tossed the covers to the side and stretched as she stood up from the bed. The evil part of her wanted to make him drool a little, like his teasing comment he made. He didn't want to spend the day with her. Fine.

She stretched her arms high, moving her body in a sensual way. She bent down to the floor, bending slowly as she swayed her ass from side to side.

Feeling rejuvenated from that small exercise, she grabbed her robe lying across the chair near her bedroom window and slipped it on.

She glanced at Dane, who sat motionless on the bed, watching her. His eyes were dilated with passion. A passion so deep, she almost expected him to jump out of bed and grab her. Throw her back onto the bed and have his wicked way—again for the umpteenth time. She would let him.

"I'm hungry. I'm going to see what's in my cupboards. You're more than welcome to eat something before you leave." She didn't wait for a response, especially since she didn't want to hear him confirm he would be leaving.

Damn the man for making her believe they could have something real. But what kind of relationship could they have if he always wanted to work? She refused to beg for his attention. He either wanted to spend time with her, or he didn't.

Opening the fridge with a trembling hand, mad at herself for caring so quickly about the obstinate man, she had to blink a few times to focus on what she was seeing.

Eggs. Milk. Bacon.

Well, why not? He wanted to leave her already to work when that's all he ever did with his time. She'd make him a breakfast fit for a king and show him what he'd be missing.

She pulled the eggs and milk out, taking care not to slam the eggs on the counter. But damn it, she wanted to smash every egg in sight. Preferably at Dane himself. It had been crazy to think he would spend the day with her. She should've realized she wouldn't be able to keep him from work long. His work was his livelihood.

She grabbed the counter as a sharp pain hit her. She'd never be able to compete with his work. Not even after a glorious night together. It's like it never even happened with the way he barely blinked about leaving this morning.

How foolish she had been to think what they'd shared was even an ounce of love.

She sniffed, hoping to prevent a tear from escaping. She would not cry. Nope.

Would. Not. Cry.

This was ridiculous. Why should she cry over that irritating man?

Why was she so upset? This was new—whatever this was between them. She shouldn't expect him to stay. He spent the night, and she should be thankful for that.

Time away, some space, was normal in any new relationship.

As the pain weaved a treacherous path through her heart, it was hard to remember that.

She pulled an onion from the fridge and grabbed a cutting board and knife. Chopping with a delicacy and familiarity like she was born to do it, she diced the onion. Her hand shook, squeezing the knife tighter when a warm pair of hands wrapped around her waist.

"I didn't mean to upset you, Gabriella."

Sinking into his body, she sighed. "You didn't upset me."

Liar!

She promised not to lie again.

His hot breath fanned her neck. "I thought we said you wouldn't lie to me again."

Damn it. Even he knew she was lying.

Dropping the knife, she twisted around in his arms. "I told you I'd have to compete with your job, and I already am. I don't like it. But this thing between us is new. So, I understand. Go to work today. It's fine."

He framed her face and stared for a moment before

touching his lips gently to hers. "From sunrise to sunset, my mind is used to thinking about work. Even after the sun goes down, work is on my mind. That's my life. Suddenly, you walk into my office with this attitude and spunk and this gorgeous ass and legs, and now my mind is struggling to focus on work. What's between us scares me a little bit. You surprised me this morning, and I have no idea why. Because when I think about spending the day with you instead of work, it sounds much better."

He lifted her onto the counter, pushing the cutting board of onions away. Pulling her close against his body, he grabbed another kiss. Slowly. Tenderly. "Please give me time to rework my brain around work. You will have a place in my life. I promise. I might make a few mistakes along the way. It won't be easy to toss my work to the side."

She wrapped her legs tighter around his waist, whispering fiercely, "I'm not asking you to toss your work to the side. I didn't mean to make it sound like that. But it *is* Sunday. It's the weekend. You can take some time for yourself on occasion. And the weekend seems like the perfect time to do that. I give you permission to ravish me silly at any time today, too."

A devilish grin punctured his handsome face. His eyes glittered with desire. "You tempt me now to ravish you right here on this counter. You didn't let me finish. I'd love to spend the day with you." He kissed her lips, then began a soft trail down her neck.

She opened her neck to give him better access. "You said you had to get things done today."

"It can wait until Monday. It normally can. But I'm used to doing it right away. Don't worry, Gabriella. I'm right where I want to be."

Oh, God, she loved it when he said those words.

His kisses left a scorching touch as he made his way to her ear. "You smell delicious. You left the bed too soon. We didn't have morning sex yet."

"I only smell the onions. Are you telling me I smell like onions?"

He chuckled, nibbling on her ear. "I love onions. I'm curious to know what you're making, but not that curious."

She laughed, holding on tight as he lifted her from the counter and started walking. "Where are you taking me?"

"I told you. You left the bed too soon. I want what my mind was thinking about before you left."

"Oh."

"You'll be saying more than that in a few minutes."

Her eyes shined with laughter as he tossed her onto the bed, then joined her. It was the first time she noticed he was still gloriously naked. He had walked out of her bedroom and into her kitchen with every intention of bringing her back to the bedroom.

Perhaps she had worried for no reason at all.

Her spine tingled with anticipation as she saw the predatory gleam in his eyes. He was about to devour her. And she couldn't wait. Food definitely could, though.

"I wish I could say I'm sorry for not going to the stadium, but I like right where we are," Dane said, wrapping his arms around Gabriella a little more snuggly.

Was he being too clingy? He had a hard time keeping his hands to himself. If she was in his reach, he pulled her closer.

"You're right. It would've been nice to go to the stadium today, but I'm all for hanging out on the couch and watching the game on the TV. I'm glad you stayed." She wiggled until she was settled the way she wanted in his arms.

"You're hard to resist."

He meant that. It had taken extreme control to resist her when she worked for him. And he shouldn't let his mind wander to work for even the smallest of reasons because part of him was dying to get things done. This was a very new and unfamiliar territory for him. Just relaxing. He never just relaxed.

She smoothed a hand across his cheek. He needed to shave, yet he liked how she rubbed his cheek back and forth as if she loved the feel of his stubble.

"But you're itching to go to work, aren't you?"

How could she tell? So odd. No one could ever read him this well.

He kissed her lips, then laid a tender kiss on her forehead. "A little. My work is important to me. But now, so are you."

She leaned her head against his chest, sighing with contentment. At least, he hoped that was contentment he heard. Had he said the wrong thing admitting she was right? Should he've denied it?

"Well, I'm glad you stayed."

"Me too." He kissed the top of her head before he said something else that would ruin the moment. Because he swore a bit of tension swirled between them.

Suddenly, she sat up. "Want some popcorn?" Then she extracted herself from him before he could even answer.

The minute her warm body left him, he wanted to yank her back down. He enjoyed sitting on the couch, doing nothing but holding her. Even though his fingers tingled like he should be doing work.

"I guess I could use a snack." He looked confused when

she started toward the hallway that led to the bedroom. "That's the wrong way."

Although he'd follow her in a heartbeat if she was looking for a different kind of snack.

She glanced behind her shoulder with a sly smile. "I have to use the bathroom first, silly."

"Oh, my bad. I was thinking you wanted a snack of another variety," he said with a chuckle, ready to leap off the couch if she agreed.

"Perhaps I am. Let's see what kind of fun we can have with popcorn."

She disappeared down the hallway with those parting words. His cock immediately stood at attention, waiting for her to get back. Screw the popcorn. He would devour her body on the couch without any food. Although he did enjoy her spirit and sense of adventure.

He groaned at the TV when another run scored from the opposing team. Gabriella distracting him with her gorgeous body would not upset him at all. But he hated watching his team lose.

He jerked his head toward the front door when a knock sounded. Glancing toward the hallway, he listened for the bathroom door to whip open but heard nothing.

The knock sounded again. Not persistent, but also not like whoever was on the other side was planning to leave. He stood up and ambled his way to the door, peeking through the hole before unlocking the door.

Raising an eyebrow at the visitor, he unlocked the door and swung it open.

"Good afternoon, Jaxson." He made sure not to let any jealousy tinge his voice, although he wasn't fully cordial about it either.

Why was Jaxson here? How often did he pop by unannounced to her apartment? He wanted to know, but not enough to ask. It annoyed him, but it could also lead to an argument. The last thing he wanted to do was get into it with Gabriella's friend and have her upset at him for starting it.

But if the man wasn't going to announce his intentions to Mia, that didn't mean he needed to revert his attention to Gabriella. *His* Gabriella.

Okay, so he was still jealous of the guy.

"I didn't expect you to still be here." Jaxson wasn't as good about keeping his emotions out of his tone of voice. Dane heard the shock. Maybe even a bit of jealousy.

Why was he jealous? He was supposed to like Mia.

"Well, I am."

"So you are."

They stood staring at each other, not saying another word. Mere words weren't needed. It's as if they told each other with their heavy stares what they wanted to say. Dane arched his brow, letting Jaxson know that Gabriella was his. Jaxson smiled back with a smirk that couldn't be disguised, but it had a slight reassurance he had no intention to swoop in.

"Well, this isn't awkward." Jaxson chuckled as he shifted on his feet. "Can I come in?"

He didn't want to let him in, but he knew he couldn't slam the door in his face without seeing Gabriella's wrath.

"Sure." Dane backed away from the door, figuring Jaxson could shut it himself. Otherwise, the temptation might be too great to slam it himself.

"How's Mia?" He turned around when Jaxson slammed the door harder than he expected.

"Why would I know?" Jaxson asked, confused.

"Why wouldn't you know?"

"Why should I know?"

"Shouldn't you?"

"Why should I?"

"You don't think you should?" Dane countered, wondering what Jaxson's problem was when it came to Mia.

He liked her. He should just tell her.

"This is turning into awkwardness again. I don't get it."

Dane shook his head. "I know you don't. That's the problem."

"What the hell does that mean?" Jaxson clenched his fists. "You have a problem with me, Dane?"

Dane stepped closer, getting toe-to-toe with him. "Only if you get between Gabriella and me. You seem very close to her. I didn't think I had anything to worry about last night when you left with Mia. I could see how you felt. Yet, here you are at Gabriella's, and you have no idea how Mia is."

"You feel threatened by me?" Jaxson asked with a laugh. "Wow. You must like Gabby a lot. I've never gotten that reaction, and yes, I've always been around the losers she's dated."

A muscle ticked in his cheek as he clenched his jaw tight.

Was this asshole insinuating something? That he was a loser? He'd hate to have to hit Jaxson and get Gabriella upset at him. But if Jaxson kept it up, he couldn't be sure he'd be able to control his temper.

"I can see why they never lasted. You hang around too much."

"Oh, is that the problem she has? It's me?" Jaxson stepped closer. "No, the problem is they're all losers. They can't handle the type of woman she is. Can you handle her? Why do you feel threatened by me?"

"Why haven't you checked on Mia?"

Jaxson backed up a step. "Why would I?"

Dane laughed. "Are we going through those series of questions again?"

"No, we're not. Excuse me," Jaxson said as he brushed by him.

Oh, the nerve.

Dane was tempted to push him but refused to fight with Gabriella again. And that would cause an argument. Not to mention, it was such a childish gesture. He wasn't in middle school, fighting for the attention of the most popular girl.

Why was he acting jealous anyway? He knew Jaxson liked Mia. He saw it plain as day last night, even now as Jaxson tried to avoid it.

Yet, he couldn't control the jealousy that coursed through his veins when he thought about how close Jaxson was with Gabriella.

Perhaps that was the problem. He wanted that closeness with her. And he didn't want to share it with anyone else.

Sharing had never been one of his strong suits. Especially having a brother who always wanted everything he had, taking it without a thought. Champ didn't know what sharing meant. He wanted something, he took it. Mostly taking what was his, which he refused to allow and would snatch it back. Then hearing his father say more times than not, "Share with your brother, Dane. You're older. You know better."

Damn it! He wasn't sharing now. This was his time with Gabriella, and he didn't want to share a moment of it with anyone else, least of all Jaxson. Not going to happen.

He walked back into the living room just to see Gabriella walk from the hallway and grab a quick hug from Jaxson. Seeing red was a saying he never understood until that moment. But, boy, he was seeing hazes and hazes of red.

Did Jaxson always hug her in greeting? Why the hell would he need to?

"How's your day going?" Gabriella asked Jaxson as if nothing was wrong at all for him to stop by.

She glanced at him and watched as the confusion slowly emerged. He realized his anger must have shown quite prominently. Jaw clenched. Fists tight. He was ready for an all-out brawl.

Which he could not do. Nope. He refused to fight once more with Gabriella. It was too painful, seeing the hurt in her eyes, knowing he put it there. Trying to remove the fierce emotion coursing through his veins took an amount of strength he didn't know he possessed. But for Gabriella's sake, he plastered on a fake smile.

"Fine. I wanted to see how you were doing." Jaxson glanced at Dane, then back to Gabriella. "How's Mia doing?"

Gabby grabbed a few strands of her hair and toyed with it. "You know, I'm not sure. I haven't talked to her today. I was planning on calling her later."

"Or," Dane said with a little too much enthusiasm, "you could always check on her, Jaxson. That would be a great way to show you care."

Dane leaned against the wall and crossed his arms with a real smile this time. He perversely enjoyed the way Jaxson squirmed and shifted on his feet.

"I'm sure Mia wouldn't want me to bother her like that," Jaxson replied. A little too quick. A little too defensive.

"Yet, you have no problem bothering Gabriella like that." His tone was clear, letting Jaxson know he didn't like it.

Gabby raised her eyebrows. "Am I missing something here?"

"Of course not, sweetheart." Dane stood up from the

wall and walked over to Gabriella, kissing her deeply. "I'll get the popcorn started. You want some popcorn, Jaxson?"

"Gosh, Dane, I'd love some popcorn," Jaxson said with a smooth smile.

Dane resisted the urge—again—to throw a punch in his face and walked out of the room. Damn, the man had nerves.

If he didn't want to avoid getting Gabriella upset, he would've knocked him on his ass.

10

GABBY PROPPED a hand on her hip and delivered a nasty glare that said Jaxson better start talking and fast. "Well?"

Jaxson leaned closer. "Your boyfriend is one jealous man, Gabs." He laughed. "Holy shit is he jealous. He does not like me coming to see you. He knows I do that a lot, doesn't he?"

Gabby smirked. "Well, I can't say we talked a whole lot, Jaxson. So, no, he doesn't know that yet, that we are very good friends. Friends. Only friends." She sighed. "He's not my boyfriend." Yet.

She hated to voice it because it implied they really didn't talk. Well, they did. But not about that.

Could she say he was her boyfriend? Had they moved to that stage? He was still here, so maybe she could say he was her boyfriend.

Jaxson rolled his eyes and stepped away, putting his fingers together like a cross. "TMI, Gabs. I don't need to know what you two were doing all night and today. I can figure that out on my own. He's a little intense. He had no problem getting in my face about you...or Mia."

"He can be abrupt, yes. But he means the best. I like him, Jax. I really like him. He's not like the other guys I've dated. He's different in a good way. You could check on Mia."

She saw the surprise flash across his features. "Are you kicking me out of your apartment? I'm wounded."

"No, you're not. I might not get as much time with him as I want, so I want to take advantage of it when I can." She raised her brow again, pursing her lips with devious intent. "And you ignored the part about Mia. Is there a problem for you to check on her? It was a very sound suggestion by Dane."

Jaxson shielded his eyes, swiping a hand through his shaggy black hair. "Mia and I are friends, sure, but not close like you and I are. I can't show up at her place like that."

"The only time you don't like to do something is when you're nervous. I never saw it before until Dane said it last night. You like her. Why have you never told me this before?"

"Don't be ridiculous, Gabs," Jaxson said with a laugh that sounded very forced. She propped her hands on her hips and added a tap with her foot. She gave him a look that said he couldn't escape, which made him cave. "It'd never work between us."

"And why not?"

Although she had never pictured Jaxson and Mia together, she thought they'd make a great couple. They'd be perfect for each other.

"You know everything about her, and she knows everything about you. You wouldn't have to go through all those awkward stages of getting to know each other. I'd say it would work quite well. You guys would be great together."

He took a tentative step toward her. "Does she see me other than a friend? Because I'll be honest, Gabs. I've liked her for a while. I hate seeing those losers she dates come in and out of her life. I never see her look at me like she looks at those jerks."

She shrugged. "I don't know, Jax. We've never talked about you like that, and I've never paid attention to whether she liked you more than a friend. But it can't hurt to try."

"And ruin a good thing we all have. Ruin a nice friendship. No, thanks, Gabs. I'll pass." He walked closer and placed a hand on her shoulder. "I know you like him. I can see that he's different from the other guys you've dated. Be careful. I don't want to see him break your heart. You're my best friend. When you hurt, I hurt."

She grabbed his hand that lay tenderly on her shoulder. "He makes me happy. He also makes me irritated, aggravated, and angry at times. But that also makes it interesting and enjoyable. Who wants a boring, plain relationship?"

"I hear you, but be careful. I'll leave. See you tomorrow at work."

He took a few steps before she said, "Are you going to check on Mia?"

Turning around with a pained expression she wasn't used to seeing on him, he replied, "I don't think so. Make sure to call her later tonight."

Gabby sighed and made her way to the kitchen where she saw Dane staring at the microwave, his face pulled down with sadness, as the seconds ticked down.

"You don't like Jaxson?" Her question came out quieter than she intended. Probably because she didn't want to ask at all. She didn't want her potential boyfriend and best friend not getting along.

He turned around. A muscle ticked in his jaw before he responded. "I'm not sure how I feel about him. I'm not sure I like sharing you with anyone. That sounds possessive and jealous, even to my ears. I don't want to feel like that. Yet, I wanted to shove him out of the apartment several times. Did I hear the door close?"

She stepped into his arms and rested her head against his chest. "He left because I told him I wanted you all to myself. He understood. He's my best friend, Dane. I also work with him every day, all day. We're very close. You can't ask me to shove him out of my life."

"Did I ask you to do that? I said I wanted to shove him out, but I controlled myself. I know this. I see it. One more thing for me to work through. Patience. Remember?"

"Lots of patience with you. Whatever will I do with you?"

He grabbed her around the waist, lifting her. She giggled, wrapping her legs around him as naturally as drawing her next breath. "I can think of several things you can do with me."

He started walking out of the kitchen. She glanced back at the microwave that had dinged loudly, announcing that their popcorn was finished. "What about our snack?"

"You're all the snack I need," he said as he sat down on the couch with her still wrapped around his waist. She started to try to get up, but his hands were stuck like glue on her waist. "I like it right here."

She pried his fingers off while smiling deviously at him. Standing up, she bent down to the coffee table where she had tossed a few condoms down. "Me too."

She took off her clothes, swaying her body in a way that she hoped he found sexy. Dancing provocatively for a man wasn't something she did. For Dane, she found she liked to do new and exciting things. And if him pausing as he removed his pants was any indication that he enjoyed it, she knew she would continue to do these sorts of things in the future.

Considering her small erotic dance had stalled him from removing his clothes, she took over the task for him. By the time he was gloriously naked for her, she had ripped open the condom package and sat down on his legs.

"You never give me the pleasure of putting this on. You keep your hands to yourself, mister," she said as she grabbed ahold of his hard cock that stood waiting for attention.

"I can make no promises, Gabriella," he said with a strangled voice.

"Then you won't get your treat. You sit still or pay the consequences," she said with a wicked smile as she slid off his knees to the floor.

"What...what are you doing?" he asked breathlessly, right before she clamped her mouth onto his rock-hard cock.

He had tasted, feasted, and devoured her body several times last night, giving her so much pleasure she could still feel the aftermath. Not once had he allowed her to do anything in return. No more. It was her turn for some fun. And she was having fun.

She sucked him harder when she heard a low groan leave his mouth. She swirled her tongue around, moving her hand in rhythm with her mouth. Up and down. No matter the words she said, he couldn't sit still, moving perfectly to her tune.

Relishing in the low growls that slipped from his mouth had her squeezing harder and sucking him like a yummy lollipop. Her other hand rested on his thigh and held the condom. But she yearned for more. He tasted delicious, the tiny lifts of his hips each time she moved her tongue in another direction had her wanting to move with him.

Slowly, like licking the side of an ice cream cone wanting to savor each bite, she slid her tongue to the top, detangling herself from the temptation in front of her.

"I want more."

He grabbed her arms, pulling her onto his lap. "Yes, more—now."

She rolled the condom on, slowly, even as her body flamed with desired to take him already. But the act of teasing him a little bit longer couldn't be contained. She enjoyed each time a throaty groan left his sweet lips. To know that he was enjoying himself, letting loose, made her feel special. She was making him feel like this. Nobody else. Just her. Like she had some sort of superpowers hidden inside. Because she imagined he never let himself act like this.

"Gabriella..."

Chuckling at his begging growl, she finally gave in to the torture. With delicious intent, she slid down his hard length and sighed. Bending low to his ear, nibbling, she whispered, "Is that better, Dane?"

"Much."

She stopped his hands from grabbing her hips, waggling her finger in his face. "Tsk, tsk, Mr. Holloway. Hands to your-self, remember?"

She laughed again at his defiant stare, knowing she was testing his control to the brink. He didn't like to surrender control, but she was making him. To think he was letting her. It was like sitting on the edge of a cliff, dangling her legs, knowing at any moment she could fall off with one tiny swing of her legs. She loved the exhilarating feeling. Perhaps seeing him lose control would be like free-falling off that cliff, the wind blowing in her hair, her arms wide open as if she could fly like a bird. But not yet. She was in control right now.

Slowly, because any other way would have defeated the delectable torture she was creating, she started to move. She bestowed a kiss on each of his eyelids when he closed his eyes to savor the way she moved. He was still letting her enjoy the freedom of having control. Simply amazing.

She took her time to love him on the couch, moving up and down, brushing her body against his, her nipples hard pebbles that had him shivering under her touch. No more words were spoken. Just their bodies as they started to move as one. He never moved his hands to her hips, or on her breasts like she cherished, or a smooth hand running through her hair. No. He sat there, moving his hips in tune to her movements, letting her take them for a ride. She couldn't have asked for anything better. Perfection.

Before long, her body needed more, craved more. She increased the speed. Dane kept up with the pleasure. She cried out when she hit the peak, her body tensing with burning tingles of ecstasy. All thoughts vanished from her mind. Even the fact he grabbed her hips to keep the momentum going, joining her a few seconds later in his own delirious climax.

Resting her body against his, snuggling her head into his neck, she inhaled his warm scent. "This has to rank as one of the best vacations I've ever had."

He chuckled into her ear, swiping a lock of hair away from her face. "Even the parts where I made you repeatedly walk to the file room in those treacherous high heels you hate?"

"Even those parts. I hate that I had to lie to you. I'm sorry." Lifting her head, she smoothed a hand across his stubbled cheek. A touch of roughness, like him sometimes. "I can't regret any part, though, because I never would've met you. I like what's happening here. I like you, Dane."

As those words fell from her lips, a part of her wished she had swapped "like" for "love."

But that was too soon.

Right?

Kissing her lightly, he lingered for a moment, brushing his hands up and down her body. "I like you, too, Gabriella."

She swore she heard a bit of hesitation of the word like from him as well.

Were they on the same wavelength? Was this love?

"And you were the best damn secretary I ever had. I have no idea what I'm going to do Monday morning."

11

DANE RUBBED a tired hand across his face, glancing at the clock for the twentieth time. The thought of moving the clock to another part of his office crossed his mind several times until he realized he'd have to throw his watch away as well. Because all he'd have to do is lift his wrist to see the time if he removed the clock from his office wall.

Concentration. He lost that weeks ago when he started dating Gabriella. Figuring out the meaning of that word couldn't even be put into words anymore. She was all he thought about every day. At work. At home. Hell, even when he was with her, his mind wandered to every wonderful thing he enjoyed about her.

Spectacular. That's what she was, just as he thought she would be when he first started daydreaming about her. She had lived up to that word, plus some.

A woman of many facets. Humor. Kindheartedness. Friendly. Lovable. Stern. Heated. Opinionated. Gorgeous.

He couldn't even describe her with all the words in the dictionary. She was too complicated of a woman to even try.

He treasured each day he had with her—something he

made time to do whether his work was completed or not. When five o'clock rolled around, he left the office.

It hadn't been easy at first. His work had been his solace for quite some time. To drop it all for something—a woman, no less—had been difficult.

He worked late that Monday after the glorious weekend they had. Like a jackass, he didn't even call her. She scared him. Messing with his emotions like she had, making him feel things that were foreign to him. He didn't know what to say to her, so not calling her at the time seemed like the best option.

He had been swamped with work. The energy to find a secretary never even touched his bones. He immersed himself back into his work like nothing had changed.

But his beautiful Gabriella wasn't one to let him get away with acting like that. And who was he kidding? When did she ever let him get away with something? Never. She always told him straight—another beautiful trait he liked about her.

She had stormed into his office the next day, wondering what they were doing that night. At first, only shock registered. Then complete numbness took over. Her beauty still had a way of distracting him with ease. He took one look at her and knew how idiotic he'd been by not calling her the day before. After the weekend they shared, he knew better than that. Something she told him, too. He had nodded in agreement, locked his office door, and proceeded to love her on his desk like he imagined since the day he hired her as his secretary. She hadn't argued once with him.

From then on, he had established a routine that fit them both. He worked a few nights while leaving at the normal time of five o'clock the other nights to spend with her. "A compromise," was what she had called it.

Except, as time went on, he found himself wanting to leave early and not work any late nights. He wanted to spend all his time with her.

What utter, complete foolishness.

He couldn't become an idiot over one woman.

But every time her face penetrated his thoughts, he knew why he was acting completely out of character. She was worth it.

Still, the rate at which their relationship was moving scared him at times. Keeping their compromise would be the best decision, no matter how hard it was to stay at work.

Dane glanced up at his office door with an annoyed glare when his brother stepped through. "I hate it when you don't knock or announce yourself. Why can't you ever do that?"

Champ shrugged. "Because you hate it so much."

Dane wanted to wipe off the ceremonious grin plastered on his face. "What do you want?"

"Do you have the specs for the Miller building? I've been waiting on them for a while now."

Dane tried not to roll his eyes as he pointed at the folder sitting on the corner of his desk. "There they are. I'm sorry I don't run to you like a little lap dog. I do have other things I need to get done. If you want it so bad, get it yourself."

Champ sighed and ran a hand over his jaw. "Are we ever going to have a peaceful conversation? A little respect."

Dane stood up, bracing his hands on his desk. "Geez, Champ, where's the respect when you walk into my office? You don't even respect my wishes about knocking on the door. If you want a little respect, show some yourself."

A small knock sounded on his door with a little blonde-haired woman peeking through.

"Yes, Ms. Wallace?" Dane gave her a small smile to try and ward off the tension swirling in the room.

It didn't work to dispel the tension, but he could see it made Ms. Wallace feel marginally better.

"Sorry to interrupt, Mr. Holloway. It's four-thirty. I need to leave. I wanted to let you know I was heading out the door." She didn't even glance at his brother Champ. Ms. Wallace was a very smart woman.

"Of course. Have a wonderful evening. I'll see you tomorrow."

Since Gabriella, he had worked very hard at being more respectful to his coworkers, and not being as harsh. He had his days where he failed, but usually not with Ms. Wallace. Besides Gabriella, she was the best damn secretary he'd ever had.

She nodded her head, then snapped her fingers. "I almost forgot. You were on the phone earlier, but Gabby called. She'd like you to call her back when you get a chance."

Dane had the intense urge to look at his cell, wondering why she hadn't called him on that but instead smiled with appreciation. "Thanks."

Of course, his brother zeroed in on that information as soon as his secretary walked away.

"Who's Gabby? That name sounds familiar. And since when do you let your secretary leave early?"

Dane refused to look at Champ as he pushed the button on his cell, lighting it up. A missed text from Gabriella. How had he missed that? Especially considering he'd been daydreaming about her, like usual.

"Ms. Wallace is a wonderful secretary. It's not going to kill me to let her leave early once in a while. Her son has a baseball game at five. She doesn't want to miss it."

Champ's mouth dropped open. "You're letting her leave for a dumb baseball game? What the hell happened to my brother?"

"Have you ever had a brother? Do we act like brothers? Grab your folder and leave. I still have work to do before I leave."

"You didn't answer my question."

Dane whipped the folder off the desk, shoving it into Champ's chest. "I don't need to answer any of your damn questions, especially when it comes to us being brothers."

Champ grabbed the folder before it tumbled to the ground when Dane let go without waiting for him. "I wasn't talking about that question. Who's Gabby? Was she talking about my Mia's friend, Gabby?"

Dane looked back at him, laughing. "*Your* Mia? She hasn't been anything to you for over a month. She deserves better than the likes of you."

"So, it is that Gabby? Why would she be calling you? In fact, why haven't you been working as much as you used to? I came here last week, late at night, and you weren't here. And you weren't at home. Shit, you were with this Gabby chick, weren't you?"

Dane advanced at Champ again, his fists clenched by his sides. "It's none of your damn business. But to get you to leave my office, we're dating. End of story."

"You're dating her? The woman who ruined it for me with Mia." Champ took a step closer to Dane.

"She ruined it? Are you kidding me? You ruined that, Champ. You screwed your secretary on your desk with the door wide open. That's your own fault."

"The door wasn't wide open," Champ ground out. "It was a mistake. One little mistake. Mia won't even give me the time of day to explain. I blame your girlfriend for that."

"That's not a little mistake. That's just plain stupid. And it's not Gabriella's fault. It's yours for what you did with the door wide open."

He couldn't resist needling his brother.

Champ clenched his teeth, the muscle in his cheek ticking like a time bomb. "It wasn't wide open. Lies. That's all your girlfriend knows how to do. She's still feeding you lies."

"Cracked open, a little bit open, wide open. What's the damn difference, Champ? You didn't have the brains to close the damn door. Hell, you didn't have the brains to respect the woman you were dating. Life isn't one big joke. You can't make a mistake and expect it to keep going your way. That's the real problem, isn't it? You can't get Mia back with a flick of your wrist. Not like you can with everything else in your life. As I said, she deserves better than you."

Champ softened his features, rubbing his chin with a sheepish grin. "You're right. I screwed up big time with her. I didn't realize how special she was until I lost her. I miss her, Dane. I truly miss her. You could tell her how sorry I am. I didn't mean to do it. It was a one-time mistake."

Dane stared at him, his brows pinched high. "You're serious right now? Do you really think by sounding sincere and using pretty little words that's going to persuade me to put in a good word for you with Mia? You're nuts. I would never do that for you."

Dane walked back toward his desk before he gave in to the urge to hit his brother. The audacity he had. "I've gotten to know Mia since I started dating Gabriella. She's a very nice, compassionate woman. She deserves respect. Not to be treated like garbage. I saw you look at my secretary, Ms. Wallace. You couldn't resist glancing at her chest, or her ass as she walked out. You can't keep it in your pants. And I doubt it was a one-time mistake. Leave Mia alone. And you better leave my secretary alone as well. She's not someone you can toy with. She's my secretary."

Champ lifted a brow as a sly smirk appeared. "Yeah, okay, she's your secretary. So, you wanna toy with her a little? Do you want to sleep with your secretary, Dane? What about Gabby...or what do you call her...Gabriella? You would never stoop so low, would you?"

"You have two seconds to get the hell out of my office before I do something we'll both regret. I would never do that to Gabriella. And Ms. Wallace deserves respect as well. Get the hell out!"

Dane pointed to his door, losing his patience with each breath he took. For once in his life, Champ didn't continue to argue. Shuffling his feet with a quick turn, he left the office without another word.

For added measure, he slammed the door.

Dane sank into his chair, resting his head back. The aching tremor to see Gabriella pulsed like he needed his next breath. He swiped his phone from the desk, almost dreading to read her entire text. Suddenly, he didn't feel like it would be a good thing.

"So, how did it go with the boss man? Did he take it as horribly as you thought he would?" Jaxson asked, glancing at her out of the corner of his eye, while still keeping a good look at the road.

"Eyes on the road, mister. Full concentration." Gabby snapped her fingers for him to focus. "Would it kill you once to call him by his name? You know, his real name. Dane. Try it out. It's a great name."

"You're in a snippy mood. Is it that bad you're stuck with me working a case late into the evening instead of hanging with *Dane*?"

Gabby turned her head, searing a glare his way. "The fact you used his name this time, but with a disgusting tone, does not make it better, Jaxson. What is your problem with him?"

He shrugged, flipping the turn signal to head left at the next intersection. "What's his problem with me? He doesn't like me. He hasn't since the moment he met me. You don't see it."

"What I see is my best friend and boyfriend, not trying to get along. You always have an attitude when you're around him."

He turned his head, his eyes bulging. "And he doesn't? You don't hear his attitude? What are you, blinded by love?"

Boy, what would Jaxson say if she responded with yes?

The word "love" flittered through her mind—and heart —constantly. It never left her mouth, though. Her relationship was going smoothly so far. She didn't want to do anything to upset the delicate balance it was on.

She pushed on his cheek to turn his head forward. "Eyes ahead. You know I hate it when you don't keep your eyes on the road. That's why I wanted to drive. Sure, I hear it in his voice, too, but I hear it from your voice first."

He slammed his hand on the steering wheel. "Damn it, Gabby, that's not fair. You're making me into the bad guy here. It's like he's a damn saint and can't do anything wrong. But, oh, no, one little wrong tone coming from my mouth, and you gotta lay into me."

He turned left, then rubbed his hand on his thigh from hitting the steering wheel so hard. "You're my best friend, and I feel like I'm losing you to him. You've never spent so much time with a guy before. I hate it. And I—"

"Please, Jaxson, don't say you hate him," she said with a firm voice.

"You hate when people interrupt you. You shouldn't do it to others."

"I'm sorry." She glanced out her window, afraid that he would see the swirling emotions embroidered on her face. "I don't think I can hear you say you hate him. He's become an important part of my life. I see the tension between you two and don't know how to fix it. I see the stress on his face from work, or perhaps me wanting him not to work. That's what he's used to, and I'm making him stay with me. Sometimes I think I'm demanding too much of his attention, but I don't know how to back off. I enjoy spending time with him. I'm not blinded by love."

Wow. When had she become such a liar?

He sighed. "Come on, Gabs. You're not acting like you normally do with a guy. Maybe you're afraid to say it—hell, even think it—but you're starting to feel the L-word."

When did she ever think she could get anything by Jaxson? He knew her too well. Still, she wasn't ready to admit it out loud.

"It's only been a month. We're still in the early stages of dating." She pulled her attention away from the window to look at him. "I know you two don't get along. And yes, I hear the attitude from Dane as well. But if you started trying harder, he would, too. You're an important part of my life. You always will be, Jax. He knows this, and it makes him feel threatened. But I think if you tried harder, then he would, too. Is that so much to ask of my best friend?"

He slowed down to a stop at a red light, turning his full attention to her. "A little bit, yes. I don't want to see him hurt you. I have a feeling he could do a lot of damage. I don't want that to happen."

"So, you won't be nicer to him? You won't try to be the bigger person in the situation?"

He rubbed a hand down his face, groaning in despair. "I hate being the bigger person."

"Pouting does not become you." She laughed to lighten the serious tension starting to fill the car. She hated the tension. When those two were together, it came in spades.

Jaxson thankfully laughed with her, reducing the tension some more. "For you, Gabs, I'll be nicer. I'll drop the attitude." He smiled sheepishly. "Or at least try."

She placed a tender hand on his shoulder, smiling in return. "Thank you, Jaxson. I know I can always count on you. You'll always be my best friend."

Gabby dropped her hand when he smiled wider and turned his attention back to the road. She didn't miss the frown that replaced his smile. Perhaps he didn't believe her that he would always be her best friend. Nobody could take him out of her life. Not even Dane. She also knew Dane would never ask her to do that. But his attitude could use some adjusting as well. Jaxson was right. Dane wasn't any better when it came to conversing with Jaxson. Put two raging dogs in a pit and sit back and watch them duke it out. That's what it was like when those two were in a room together. The testosterone filled the room, just waiting to be unleashed in a meltdown of great proportions.

Four hours later, after finding no new leads in the death of a real estate agent murdered while showing an apartment, Gabby unlocked her apartment door. The moment she stepped inside, a wonderful aroma wafted around her senses.

She flipped the lock on the door, then walked into the kitchen where Dane stood in front of her pantry.

"You cooked?"

Dane jumped, turning his attention her way. "You're home. I missed you." He shut the pantry doors and, with quick steps, had her in his arms, kissing her like he truly had missed her. "I hope it's okay I let myself in. I decided after you called to tell me you had to work late that I still wanted to see you. I thought you might be hungry when you got home."

She rested her head against his chest. She took in the small mess littering the counter. It was the first time Dane had cooked for her. What a wonderful sight to see. "It's more than okay. I'm so happy you're here. I missed you, too. And I gave you a key, it's okay you use it."

Funny how she was afraid to say the L-word yet she had given him a key to her apartment. Although he had also given her a key to his apartment, so it seemed right. Yet, they did find themselves at her apartment more often than his.

He kissed the top of her head. "Is everything all right? Was it a bad day?"

"A tiring day. Sometimes it's not easy doing this job. I had to tell a husband and a four-year-old little girl that her mommy wouldn't be coming home tonight. And the worst part for us, we have no leads yet. It breaks my heart sometimes."

He leaned back, cupping her cheeks with tender hands. "You have a heart of gold. I can imagine how difficult that job is for you. You want to help people so much. Sometimes more than you should."

He kissed her again, then walked over to the small wine rack hanging on the wall. "How about a nice glass of wine to unwind from the hectic day?"

She nodded and leaned against the counter, watching as he prepared their glasses. "What do you mean that I sometimes help more than I should?"

He stopped short of pulling the cork out. "That floral shop you worked at. The owner's son was murdered in a botched robbery. He was falling apart emotionally and neglecting his shop. You swooped in to help him back on his feet and regain a little life in him—while still working as a detective, I might add. Or the bakery shop you worked at. Again, helping out when the owners lost two of their best employees in a hit and run accident."

She watched as his face lit up with a magnificent glow. As if in awe of her. Yet, his eyes held concern she didn't understand.

"You worked all those jobs, not because you needed to for the money, but because you wanted to. You say I work too much, but I don't think I work as much as you do. Or for the same reasons. And my favorite of all? Recommending a wonderful, talented, hard-working, oriented individual for a secretary position even though she had no background as a secretary. Ms. Wallace has been great since the moment I hired her. I would have never given someone like her a chance if it hadn't been for your recommendation."

Gabby swiped a lock of hair behind her ear as she thought about everything he said. "You wouldn't have given someone a chance who lives in a rundown neighborhood, a prior arrest for possession when she was eighteen and had a husband who was so abusive he could've killed her?"

Dane finally removed the cork and poured them both a glass of the sweet red wine. "The prior arrest would have been enough for me to pass, and the fact she has no experience with what I needed her to do. But I can see how great of an employee she is. She works hard, doesn't complain when I do get snappy at her, because let's be honest, I can't help myself."

She smirked as he laughed and then continued. "It would never occur to me to give someone like her a chance. You've opened my eyes to see the world differently. I'm glad I'm able to help her out. She's a very nice woman, and she loves her son. It's good she got herself out of that relationship before something tragic happened."

She grabbed the offered glass of wine and took a sip. "It wasn't easy. Her husband isn't someone who's going to go away politely. He hasn't been around the office, has he? He will be in violation of the restraining order if he has been."

He leaned into her body, pressing her against the counter in an intimate embrace. "Nope. I've notified security, who has a picture of his face and a copy of the order. He'll be arrested immediately if he takes one step inside the building. I also made it known that Ms. Wallace is to be escorted to the bus stop and safely inside the bus before they leave her. She's safe while at work. It's the going home part that worries me."

"You're getting the hang of this helping people out just fine. She's a tough woman. Plus, she's taking defense classes, like I suggested to her. Everything is starting to look up for her."

He set his glass of wine on the counter, brushing a hand across her cheek. "You still look like you're a million miles away from me. I didn't mean what I said in a bad way. You like to help people, and that's great. I worry it puts too much on your shoulders. Are you sure you're okay?"

She pressed a kiss to his palm, smiling. "I had a small argument with Jaxson. I hate when that happens."

A muscle ticked in his cheek. "What was the argument about?"

"Do you really want to know?"

"No lies, remember?" He sighed as he frowned. "But by that question, I can take a good guess."

"You two don't seem to like each other. I don't understand why."

"I feel like I have to share you with him. I feel like sometimes I misjudged him. Maybe he likes you and not Mia. That's what worries me."

She set her glass to the side, running her hands through his silky hair. "Well, forget those worries because I want you. He's my best friend, but that's it. It will never be anything more than that. I only want you."

He gave her an adorable pout before kissing her. "I want to be your best friend as well."

She chuckled. "You really don't like sharing, do you?"

"No."

"Well, try. Because he's not going anywhere, Dane. Please try to be nicer to him."

Like he was born to do it, he scooped her into his arms with one fell swoop. "For you, I will."

"Where are you taking me? I thought you cooked me food," she asked as she wrapped her arms around his neck as he headed down the hallway.

"To the bedroom. The food can wait. I was trying to think of a nice dessert to make you when you walked in. I need time to think about that before we eat."

"So we're going to think about dessert, is that it?"

"Yep. I like dessert. Don't you?" he asked as he kicked the bedroom door closed.

Her response was muffled as he claimed her lips and laid her on the bed.

12

HE COULDN'T GET out of work fast enough. The week had been long and tiring, and it was finally over. He had to work late last night, as did Gabriella. Something he hated to think about because that meant she was with Jaxson instead of him.

But he promised he'd be nicer, give the guy a chance.

When he said he didn't like to share, he really didn't. His brother always took things from him, even now in adulthood. He despised the word "share." Because of the way his father always labeled it, "Share with your brother." Always turned into Champ taking and never returning it. That wasn't sharing. That was stealing.

He wouldn't have Jaxson stealing Gabriella from him.

"Hey, Dane, wait up."

He pushed the button for the elevator, praying it would open and close before his brother got near him—no such luck. Champ stopped right next to him before the elevator even opened.

"Leaving already? I'm shocked. This woman must have you under a spell."

"Is there something you needed, Champ?"

The elevator doors swished open. He walked in without waiting for an answer, hoping his brother took the hint to leave him the hell alone.

He didn't.

Champ entered the elevator as well.

"I thought I'd say hi to my brother."

His brow rose. "Give me a break."

"I can't say hi to my brother? I need a reason to speak to you?"

"Since when do you visit me without a reason?"

"Mom's birthday is coming up. Did you want to go in on a present?"

He chuckled, anger sifting through his veins like a volcano intent on erupting. "So, we get to the heart of it. You don't know what to get her and want to pawn off of my gift. The last time I fell for that, you wrapped it up and said it was only from you, and I looked like I forgot to buy her something. Go to hell."

Could this elevator go any slower?

"It won't happen this time. That was an accident."

"Nothing is an accident when it comes to you."

The door finally opened. He stepped out and walked away. Thankfully, his brother didn't follow him.

He knew Champ hadn't gotten the clue. He would nag him up until their mother's birthday finally got here. Well, news flash. He wasn't caving this time.

It had crossed his mind to have Gabriella help him pick out a present for his mother. Of course, first, he had to work up the nerve to ask her to join him this weekend at his parents' house to celebrate his mother's birthday. It wouldn't be a big affair—supper with his parents—and unfortunately, Champ.

He was also pushing his luck since the party was on Sunday. Two days from now.

He had never brought a woman to meet his parents. This was huge. His mother would probably find that as her birthday present. She was dying for one of her sons—him, specifically, since Champ was nowhere near settling down —to meet a nice woman and get married. Have grand-children.

He wasn't sure what Gabriella would say. Or think. Meeting one's parents was a huge step in a relationship. Were they ready for that step?

Although they had taken a huge step when they exchanged keys. Maybe she wouldn't find this request odd either. He should feel bad; they rarely went to his apartment. But he liked her place. She made it feel homey, and he felt more content than in his own home. Probably because he was rarely there anyway. Before Gabriella, he spent most of his time in the office. He had only used his apartment to sleep and shower. He didn't even eat supper there.

How sad.

Instead of going home first to change and freshen up, he went straight to Gabriella's. He had a few articles of clothing in her closet anyway, and he missed her. He hadn't seen her since Wednesday. Two days was too long. And with his thoughts venturing into dangerous territory, he had an intense need to see her. Hold her. Confirm she was his.

Just like she said, Jaxson and Mia had a habit of walking into her apartment without knocking, he did the same thing. If they could, so could he.

She never said he couldn't.

And he didn't like how Jaxson could and he couldn't, so he did it one day.

Ugh. Jaxson.

He promised to be nice.

He would be.

When he walked into the living room and saw Gabriella —his Gabriella—sitting next to Jaxson, laughing and smiling, he almost snapped. Yelled for him to get the hell away from her.

But he forced the impulse down and smiled.

Because he promised to be nicer.

"You okay? Bad day at work?"

Well, damn. His smile wasn't bright enough. Although Gabriella was very observant, especially about his moods. He had to give her credit for that.

"My brother stopped me on the way out. He always dampens my mood." He turned his gaze to Jaxson. *Play nice.* "Hello."

Unfortunately, his tone of voice didn't portray nice.

"Hi." Jaxson's voice sounded just as strained.

"Are we all eating in tonight?" There. That came out rather nicely if he did say so himself.

But by the stern look on Gabriella, he failed. Miserably.

"Mia's coming over, too. Is that okay? I know it's sudden, but I thought it'd be nice." Gabriella's lips split into a wide grin.

He could never resist her smiles. Although he wanted her to himself tonight, especially since he wanted to ask her to join him this weekend, he couldn't dampen her spirits. He refused to let her smile disappear.

"I don't mind." To his delight, her smile brightened even more, which told him he held no irritation in his tone. Finally, doing something right.

"Let me go check the supper. I'll be right back."

He almost followed her out of the living room. But enough was enough. He had to have a word with Jaxson.

Except the asshole beat him to it.

"I don't want to hate you, Dane, but I kind of do. You think I'm taking Gabby from you, and I think the same thing. If you two don't work out, I'll still be here." He stood up. "But, I'd rather see her happy than sad, so I want it to work out. How about we try to get along? For her sake?"

Well, he couldn't argue with any of that—especially the part where Jaxson would still be a part of her life if Gabriella decided to end it with him. He couldn't let that happen, which meant he needed to shape up his attitude toward one of her best friends.

But damn it.

He still didn't want to share.

Jaxson continued before he could think of something nice to say. Because everything swirling in his mind would have Gabriella washing his mouth out with soap. She had threatened that once when he said the wrong thing concerning Jaxson. Lesson noted. It had made him laugh— even though she hadn't been kidding—but he tucked it into his brain for future reference and promised to be nicer.

"You're hating the fact we're here tonight. I know you are, so don't even deny it. You haven't known her as long as I have." Jaxson's expression fell as he ran a hand down his face. "It was a bad night. Very bad. She likes to be surrounded by people when we have nights like this. She doesn't like to be alone. It bothers her. Not that she'd admit it, but I know it. I just thought I'd tell you why I'm here and why Mia is coming over."

His heart started to beat rapidly. Like he was standing on train tracks, his feet frozen, his legs immobile. A train heading straight for him. He hadn't gotten any kind of signal from her that she had a bad day.

That tore a hole in his heart that Jaxson knew, and he

hadn't picked up on the vibes. How pathetic. She could read him so well, but apparently, he couldn't read her.

What did that say about him?

"What happened?"

Jaxson looked away as his hand shook a little. "This guy killed his girlfriend—at least, we found promising evidence that he had. We knocked on the door just to have a chat, not necessarily going to arrest him yet. Instead of answering the door with a friendly hello, he answered by shooting."

His heart hammered in his chest. He swore it was going to jump right out of his body, it pounded so roughly.

Someone shot at Gabriella.

She could've died today.

He could've lost the woman—the woman he loved.

Jaxson turned his eyes back toward him. "She's fine. So am I. Neither of us was hit, but it was intense."

"And the guy?"

"Dead. We had to fire back." Jaxson shrugged. "I can't be sure who fired the shot that..." He blew out a deep breath. "Shit. I don't even want to be alone tonight. This is our job, Dane. If you can't handle it, you know where the door is. I'm not leaving. I'm always going to be here. She's not only my partner but one of my best friends. If you can't handle that, you know where the door is. She will be my best friend until the day I die. I would take a bullet for her. I would've today. If you can't handle that—"

"I know where the door is. I get the message." His jaw clenched.

Not because he wanted to spew nasty words at Jaxson.

Because he wanted to shout his rage at the fact he almost lost her today from a madman shooting at them.

He released a small breath and forced a smile out. "I

don't share well. You know my brother somewhat. He always took, took, took. I was always forced to give him whatever it was he wanted. Of course, I was told I was sharing, when really, he was just taking it. I don't want to share Gabriella." He sighed. "But she wasn't mine first."

Jaxson grinned. "She's not mine either. We're friends, Dane. We will always be just friends."

"I want to believe that."

"Then believe it." He swore, then laughed. "You were right. I like Mia. You have nothing to worry about when it comes to Gabby."

"You like me?"

Dane and Jaxson shifted their focus to the voice coming from the hallway. Mia stood with a shocked expression.

He glanced back at Jaxson, who looked like a deer caught in headlights. A small chuckle escaped. "I'll go see if Gabriella needs my help. Nice chat, Jaxson. Glad we had it."

He walked out, hoping things turned out in Jaxson's favor.

He really, really hoped so.

Because then he wouldn't have to worry so much he'd take Gabriella from him.

———

WARMTH SURROUNDED her as Dane's strong arms wrapped around her. She leaned her head back and savored his gentle touch.

A kiss hit the side of her head. "Jaxson told me about tonight. Are you okay? How can I help?"

She shivered as the memory flooded her mind. The bullets tearing through the door. The loud echoes of the gunshots. The feeling of her weapon firing back, jerking her in her spot. The blood that coated the floor around the suspect. Two bullets hit him. Maybe from her. Maybe from Jaxson. Maybe from both of them.

But a man died tonight. That's what mattered.

"Gabriella..." The way he whispered her name almost soothed the weariness coating her body.

His arms surrounding her did the trick better. She never wanted him to let her go. She could stay in his arms forever. What would he say if she blurted that out? That she wanted him in her life forever.

I love you.

The words floated out of her mind, willing him to hear her unspoken words of devotion.

His arms around her tightened, almost as if answering her silent plea of love.

"You don't have to talk about it. I didn't mean that when I brought it up. I only wanted you to know I'm here for you."

Or he was just still consoling her, and she was letting her crazy heart run away from her.

She turned around and rested her head against his chest and wrapped her arms around his waist. "Just being here is making me feel better. I've been a cop for a long time. I've never actually had to fire my weapon before. We're both on administrative leave while they investigate to make sure it was a good shooting, which it was. I had no choice."

Like Mia had no choice when she shot her father.

But she could already imagine rumors were flying around about her. That was also on her mind. Not that she fired the shot that killed Mia's father, but she was there. People would never forget that.

It was as if they were still trying to defend themselves.

That her father was this holy saint and could do no wrong, when in reality, he was the devil incarnate.

"I can take some time off of work. And I don't mean just this weekend."

She lifted her head, her mouth slid open from shock. That he even offered meant so much to her. She knew how important his work was to him. "I can't ask you to do that."

"You didn't. I offered. I want to be here for you."

"You're so busy right now. You have an important deal coming up. I can't let you."

"It's—"

She pressed her lips to his to silence any further argument. While she would love for him to take time off with her, she couldn't allow that to happen. He needed this deal to go through. He said so several times. She would not be the cause for it to fall through. Eventually, he would come to resent her if his work slid to the side, and he started to fail. She would never allow that to happen. Because if it happened, then she'd lose him forever and she wanted him forever.

The kiss ended too soon for her tastes, but he got the message. The argument was over. A tiny grin punctured his face.

What was with the grin? Would he take time off, regardless? She couldn't quite read his expression, and she'd been getting better at reading him well.

"So, Jaxson and Mia are chatting right now."

"I didn't even hear the door open. I had no idea Mia was here already."

He chuckled. "Yeah, we didn't hear the door open either."

Her brows puckered. "What does that mean? Were you two arguing?"

"We were having a friendly chat." He kissed her lightly on the lips. Probably to distract her, but it wouldn't work. She hated—simply hated—that they couldn't get along. "He might have told me he liked Mia and that I had nothing to worry about when it came to you."

"You don't." She smiled and snatched another kiss.

So, they managed to act like adults for once instead of two raging teenagers fighting over a silly crush.

"Mia heard it."

Her eyes bulged. "Oh, Jaxson. I should…"

He tightened his arms around her. "Let them talk it out. I wouldn't interfere yet. Maybe she likes him, too."

"I've never brought the subject up, even with knowing how he felt. I can't say for sure. But I do know Mia is very particular about men. I want to see them together; they'd be perfect for each other. But, as Jaxson told me his worries, I can see his point. He doesn't want to ruin the good friendship we all have. This might do that."

"Let's give them a few minutes."

A tender smile started to form until a loud slam echoed throughout the apartment.

Someone left.

Very unhappy.

Her heart started to pound. One of her friends was hurting. One was upset. And she had no idea what to do.

Everything was falling apart today. It all started with an asshole with a temper who killed his girlfriend, shooting at them.

Soft footsteps sounded in the kitchen. Gabby turned her eyes in that direction, as did Dane.

Jaxson stood with a morose expression. "She hates me." His eyes fell to the floor. "And I made her cry."

This would be a true test of how much Dane cared for

her. Because she needed him to stay with Jaxson and make him feel better, no matter how much he hated the man.

She had to check on Mia.

And change her mind about Jaxson. Because he was the perfect man for her.

13

GABBY OPENED the door to Mia's apartment and slammed the door for added effect. She wasn't mad or anything, but she knew she needed to be a bit lively to get through the emotions Mia was certainly trying to suppress and hide away.

She found her in the kitchen—of all places—sitting in the silence, her arms wrapped around her knees. Sitting down next to her, she slung an arm around her shoulders and squeezed.

"Why are you upset? This is a good thing."

"Nothing is good about this," Mia said as quiet tears slid down her face.

"Why not? Jaxson is a good guy."

Mia shuddered. "Exactly."

Jerking away, a brow rose. "What does that mean?"

Extracting herself, Mia stood up, wiping at her cheeks. "I want to be alone right now. Can you leave?"

For a moment, time stood still. The air in the apartment thickened like a dense fog, almost choking her to death.

Mia had never, not once, kicked her out. Told her to leave. Told her to mind her own business.

After the day she had today, shooting a man, she couldn't take this, too. Not from Mia.

Without a word, she walked out, closing the door as quiet as a mouse. As if she hadn't even entered in the first place.

She took her time heading back home. An hour later, when it should've only taken twenty minutes, she entered her apartment. Low voices could be heard from the living room. She found Dane and Jaxson sitting on the couch, one on each end, holding a beer with a baseball game on the television. Normally her eyes always sought out the score, hoping her team was winning. Not today.

Dane stood up immediately. He set his beer down on the coffee table in front of him and rounded the table. "What happened?"

He knew. She couldn't believe how well and how fast he read her mood, but he knew something was wrong. His arms settled around her.

She didn't know what to say. She didn't know how to explain that her best friend—for the first time ever—shut her out.

Tears gathered at the corner of her eyes, and her body shook as she tried to hold them in.

What was she doing?

Now was not the time to be breaking down, especially in front of Jaxson. Sure, Mia told her to leave, and she was hurt by that. But Jaxson was hurting, too. This wasn't about her right now. This was about him.

Inhaling, trying to regain her composure, she hugged Dane fiercely before letting him go. She felt him hesitate, but then he dropped his arms from around her and stepped to the side.

Jaxson looked at her from his position on the couch. He hadn't moved an inch. The sadness in his eyes when she left was still prominent. He looked like someone had driven over his puppy—several times.

She produced a smile she didn't feel like offering, but for Jaxson's sake, she forced one out. "She wouldn't talk to me. She kicked me out. But not before agreeing that you're a good guy."

At that, Jaxson stood up. "And?"

She shrugged, hating that she could feel the tears threatening once more. "And then before she'd tell me anything else, she told me to leave." Blowing out a deep breath, she tried to ignore the pain reflecting in his eyes. "What a shitty day. I'm sorry, Jaxson. I don't know what to say right now."

Dane clapped, the sudden noise making her and Jaxson jump. "I say we eat. The lasagna you had cooking is done. It smells delicious."

She knew he was trying to dispel the tension, and shift everyone's focus to something else, but she didn't feel like eating. She didn't even feel like socializing. As terrible as it sounded—because Jaxson needed her support right now— she wanted him to leave.

Her bottom lip trembled.

She wanted Dane to leave, too.

It didn't make her any better than Mia. She felt sick to her stomach at how she felt.

She wanted to be left alone. Cry in silence. In peace. Where no one could witness her breakdown. Her weakness.

Steeling her spine, she forced the tears back once more. Stopping the trembling of her lip. Smoothed her features into indifference. She couldn't fake happiness, but she could hide the sadness.

Maybe.

Dane's smile remained as he waited for her to say something in response.

Jaxson looked between both of them, yet silent.

"Look. I know you both had a terrible day. The night isn't turning out much better with what happened with Mia, and I'm sorry." Dane tipped his head toward Jaxson as if communicating something with him silently. She wondered what it could be. "We're all here. We all need to eat."

"I'm not hungry." She was surprised she could even speak. She barely had the energy to think right now. She wanted to curl up under her covers and bawl her eyes out.

His smile disappeared—a tortured kind of agony filtered into his gaze. "Maybe you want to be alone. I can respect that, Gabriella. I will respect that if you want me to leave." Then his expression hardened. "As long as Jaxson stays. But I won't leave you completely alone."

Warmth filled her heart, shattering a bit of her hurt away.

Wow. If she hadn't already decided she loved him, this would've sealed the deal.

He couldn't stand Jaxson. Barely tolerated him at times, his jealousy consumed him so much. Yet, he was willing to leave and let Jaxson console her. Hell, let her console Jaxson as well. They were both hurting from the day. One, from work. The other, from Mia.

Jaxson cleared his throat. "That...that's nice of you to offer, Dane, but I'll leave, and you stay."

Geez. Were these two about to argue who was going to stay and who was going to leave? She was in no mood to dispel an argument that would sound like two kindergarteners arguing over a box of crayons and who got to pick the first color.

As much as she appreciated Dane's gesture, she still wanted to be alone. She loved the man for his thoughtfulness, but she needed to break down in peace.

"How about you both leave? I'll be fine, and we all need time to ourselves."

Dane crossed his arms. His expression turned fierce and unyielding—the same look he'd given her when she gave him lip at work.

"I'm not leaving if Jaxson is leaving. I won't leave you alone."

She mimicked his expression, folding her arms and giving him a stern stare. "I want to be alone."

"Tough." He smirked, little devils dancing in his eyes. "You didn't say please."

Her eyes narrowed. She wanted to bash him over the head with the book laying on her coffee table for being so obstinate. But then she also had the urge to laugh at his teasing.

Before she could counter with her own witty remark, Jaxson rounded the coffee table and stood in front of her, shielding Dane from her view.

"Give the guy a break, Gabs. Let him stay. Don't push him away. Don't ruin this thing going on between you two."

Whoa. What a change in his attitude toward Dane.

"What happened to hating him?"

Jaxson rolled his eyes. "I never hated the guy...much. He just pissed me off too much." He sighed and squeezed her shoulder. "I'm sorry Mia wouldn't even talk to you. I know that has to hurt you right now. I'm sorry she heard what I said. This is why I never wanted her to know how I felt. It's my fault, and I'll make it right. But don't screw it up with Dane because of my mistake."

"Asking him to leave shouldn't screw anything up between us."

Jaxson grabbed her other shoulder and pulled her closer. "You did this with other guys, too. Not every guy you dated was a loser. You pushed them away when you needed them. You push a lot of people away when you need them. The only one you don't is Mia. Now, she pushed you away. As much as you think you want to be alone, you shouldn't be. Let Dane do his thing."

She laughed, more so because she hated how much Jaxson was right. It was better to laugh than scream in frustration.

"What thing is that?"

Jaxson shrugged and chuckled. "I don't know. You know I don't like the details between you two. But he makes you happy, so I imagine he can make the night turn for the better."

He grabbed a quick hug and stepped away to leave. She grabbed his hand to stop him.

"What about you? You shouldn't be alone either."

A tiny grin lit up his face. "I'll be fine." Then he looked at Dane and nodded.

Dane returned a similar gesture.

They both stood in their spot until they heard the front door click. Dane must've taken that as his cue to move. He entered her space, although he didn't pull her into his arms, almost as if unsure if he should. He was close enough where he could've. She wanted him to. But then again, she still also wanted him to leave.

The tears were threatening once more. Jaxson left. He'd be alone in his misery.

Processing the death of a suspect.

Dealing with a broken heart.

He shouldn't be alone either.

"I'm not leaving."

She shivered at the way his soft words hit her straight in the heart. The tenderness. The concern. The worry in three short words.

"Maybe I want to cry. Maybe I don't want you to see."

He reached out and took her hand. The minute his warm hand touched her icy cold fingers, a sense of rightness swarmed her system.

"I hated seeing you cry. It's not something I want to see again, but if you need to, then I'm here to hold you. To rub your back. To dry your eyes. Whatever you need from me." His loose hand reached up and caressed her cheek. "Just don't ask me to leave. I can't leave. I won't leave."

Damn Jaxson and pointing out why some of her relationships failed. Because she sucked at letting people in. Like, really inside her heart.

Here was this sweet, adoring man begging to be let in.

"I'm not hungry. I don't want to eat."

That wasn't what she had intended to say. Honestly, she didn't know what to say. She wouldn't make him leave, but she didn't know where to go from here.

He pulled her toward the couch and guided her to sit, snuggling her close to his side. "Then we won't eat."

While her eyes didn't focus on the game in front of them, she did focus on the softness of his touch—at the soothing way he rubbed his fingers up and down her arm. Nothing erotic. Nothing to get her blood pumping. Just a simple, soothing gesture indicating he was here, and he wasn't leaving.

They came suddenly and without warning.

The tears.

It erupted like a dormant volcano.

Dane said nothing. He shifted her into his chest as she poured out all her agony from the day.

DANE BLINKED A FEW TIMES, then his stomach grumbled.

Oh, damn. He was hungry. But he ignored it. Gabriella was in his arms, and the last thing he wanted was for her to wake up.

The night had not gone how he imagined.

She cried for so long on the couch, he'd been afraid she was going to make herself sick. He'd never heard a woman cry for so long. Could one even get sick from crying so hard? Well, she had developed a nasty headache once the tears abated. She'd said the lights hurt her eyes, and her head pounded.

That had been the moment he picked her up and transferred her to her bed without turning on the lights. He grabbed a glass of water, some pain mediation, and a cold washcloth. He didn't get many headaches, but a cold washcloth always helped him. He delivered the goods and helped her take the pills and laid the washcloth on her forehead. He had even helped her get undressed and put on a pair of pajamas.

It's as if all of her energy had been zapped from her body. Whether from the crying or from the events of the day, he wasn't sure.

He'd never seen anyone in so much pain before—not even one of his parents. He wasn't sure he was doing anything right, but she hadn't asked him to leave, so he figured he wasn't doing anything wrong.

She fell asleep shortly after moving to her bedroom with her head resting on his chest. He didn't move a muscle other than to slowly rub his hand up and down her back.

The evening faded into the dead of night. With a gentle twist of his head—because he didn't want the slightest movement to wake her up—he saw the clock on the nightstand read two am.

He must've fallen asleep at some point. He couldn't remember what time that might've been, he'd been so focused on making sure Gabriella was comfortable.

Although he didn't want to wake her, he couldn't resist placing a gentle kiss on her head. He ached to squeeze her tightly and hold her there for as long as he could.

He almost lost her today.

Some madman had shot at her.

He couldn't fathom his life without her. Thinking about it gave him the jitters. Strange, when a month ago the most he thought about was the next contract on his desk.

His worst fear earlier today had been asking her to join him at his parents this weekend. Which wasn't the best thing to bring up anymore. She was on administrative leave. How long? He wasn't sure because Jaxson didn't say. But her mind wouldn't be able to focus at his parents with something so heavy on her mind. And she'd need her full attention at his parents.

He always did.

His mother was a saint.

His father...

Could never get off his case.

Maybe he could bow out of the supper as well. Gabriella needed him.

And then his mother would disown him. He couldn't miss her birthday.

A warm hand hit his cheek, smoothing across the rough surface. "I can practically feel your thoughts. Your entire body is vibrating."

His eyes sought out Gabriella's. She was staring at him with what looked like contentment. No pain. No sadness. Just content. For the first time that night.

"I didn't mean to wake you up." He kissed her lips softly.

He truly didn't mean to wake her up. But damn, his thoughts about supper must've been heavier than he imagined, making him tremble with repressed anger. Dealing with his father always brought out his anger and irritation—sort of like dealing with Champ as well.

A wicked grin split across her lips. "I also heard your stomach speaking."

Thank heavens her curtain was open and the light from a nearby streetlamp allowed him to see her smile. He adored every single one of her smiles.

Before he could respond, her grin disappeared. "I'm sorry you couldn't even eat. I don't know why I got upset over something so si—"

"So important to you," he finished for her. He knew she didn't like it when people interrupted her, but he figured she was about to say "silly," and damn it, nothing was silly about last night. Her feelings weren't silly. She had every right to be upset and hurt. It never felt good when someone you loved pushed you away. So, Mia's actions hurt her.

A small smile reappeared. "Thank you, Dane. For everything. How can I ever make it up to you?"

His heart started to pound.

This could be his chance to ask.

But hadn't he already decided it wouldn't be the best time for her?

Yep, he had.

"A plate of your lasagna right about now would be great."

She giggled and sat up. "Now that you mention it I'm hungry myself. Let's go have a late-night snack."

He followed her out of the room. He wasn't about to pass on food. But he also wanted to continue to care for her, so when they entered the kitchen, he pointed toward the dining room.

"You sit. I'll get everything for us."

"You shouldn't spoil me so much." An appreciative smile adorned her sleepy face. But she didn't argue with him and walked back out.

It didn't take him long to grab two plates and heat up the lasagna. Even reheated, it smelled divine.

They ate in comfortable silence, obviously both very hungry. His fork clanged against the plate after he had scooped his last bite into his mouth.

Rubbing his hand over his stomach, he smiled in her direction. "Best lasagna I ever had."

"Oh, stop. I'm sure your mother makes better lasagna than me. I suck at cooking." Gabriella rolled her eyes as if she didn't believe him.

He chuckled. "My mom doesn't cook. But even Francis's lasagna is not this good. I swear."

She tilted her head, confusion littering her eyes. "Your mom doesn't cook? Who's Francis?"

Over the course of their short dating period, they'd kind of glossed over the family talk. At least, on his part. She already knew what she needed to know about his family. It was messed up.

She was a bit more forthcoming about her family life. He knew she had one younger brother who had followed in her footsteps and was a beat cop. Her parents were divorced.

Her father still lived in New York City, working as an accountant. Her mother had moved to Florida and worked at a beachside shop. She said her mother was sort of a free spirit and went wherever the wind took her. Before Florida, she lived in Connecticut, Georgia, and Alabama. She wouldn't be surprised if she somehow made her way to the west coast and started going up and down the states in that area.

"He's their cook. I've never seen my mom even pick up a pot and put it on the stove."

"I forget your dad owns the company you work for. It never occurred to me they'd have a cook." She leaned forward and put her hand under her chin and rested her elbow on the table. "What's your favorite meal by Francis?"

Yeah, his father could afford anything and everything he could want. Hell, Dane had enough money to live in luxury if he so chooses. Money was always there—it wasn't something he thought about. Since they had started dating, he hadn't displayed his wealth. They usually picked up takeout and brought it back to Gabriella's. Their night usually ended in bed. If they were feeling extra frisky, they didn't even make it to her bedroom before having the most intense sex of his life. Every. Single. Time.

He should be spoiling her more. It had never occurred to him, and now he felt like a cad.

"His chocolate chip cookies are the best. I usually devour way too many of them."

The most brilliant smile lit up her face. "You need to snatch some for me the next time you visit if he makes them. I love chocolate chip cookies."

Wow.

Another perfect opportunity for him to ask her to accompany him to supper this weekend.

"I definitely will."

And for some reason, he was still a chickenshit about it. He couldn't get the words out of his mouth.

"So..." Gabriella started.

"So..." he repeated, cocking a brow.

Her lips twisted into a mischievous smile. "What's next on your agenda of making me feel better?"

By the teasing glint in her eyes, he knew what she was asking for. Ignoring the mess on the table, deciding the dishes could wait, he stood up and pulled her to her feet as well. Then he swooped her into his arms, eliciting a delighted giggle from her.

"How about a massage?" He grinned wickedly. "Full body massage."

Her eyes heated with pleasure.

That was the look he wanted to see from her.

Not sadness.

Not pain.

Nothing but pure happiness and bliss.

Maybe those other emotions would pop back up tomorrow morning. But for now, his Gabriella—the fun-loving, joking woman he adored—was back.

He wasn't going to waste a minute of it.

Maybe when the sun woke up, he'd have the words to ask her to join him this weekend.

Just maybe.

14

"OH," a startled feminine voice said.

Dane glanced behind his shoulder. Mia stood in the doorway of the kitchen near the hallway. He hadn't even heard the front door open.

Damn.

Had they even locked it last night after Jaxson left? Obviously not, if Mia simply walked in this morning.

After their late-night snack and some delicious treats in the bed, they both slept like babies. Gabriella even woke up with a bright smile and exploratory fingers that still made his body tingle at her electrifying touch. She had decided to grab a shower, while he said he'd make breakfast.

Mia's appearance didn't bode well that the morning would continue in glorious bliss. He should've figured the entire day wouldn't be pretty.

"Gabriella's in the shower." His right hand still held the edge of the cupboard door. His fingers tightened as he thought of Gabriella's reaction.

His mind went blank. He wasn't completely sure how she'd react to Mia's visit.

Elation?

Anger?

More pain?

It was the pain that concerned him the most. He despised seeing a drop of water fall from her eyes.

Mia's eyes shifted down toward the floor. "Thank you. I won't be long."

She started to turn around, but her words sliced him like a knife to the gut.

"Don't." He couldn't keep the venom out of his tone.

Yeah, sure. He knew Mia was hurting as well. For whatever reason. Honestly, he wasn't sure why she was hurting. So what she found out Jaxson liked her. It shouldn't have been cause for such a serious uproar.

If she was about to make Gabriella cry once again, especially if she was planning on making her visit short, then nope. He wasn't going to stand around and do nothing about it.

She would not make Gabriella cry again. Not on his watch.

Mia stopped and twisted his way. "What?"

His eyes narrowed as his hand dropped from the cupboard. He folded his arms. His lips went into a tight line, and not an ounce of friendliness was displayed. It was the same look he developed whenever he dealt with his brother or a rival competitor trying to underhand him.

"I said, don't." His voice was low and harsh. "Don't you dare go in there, say some words, and then leave like you aren't causing anyone pain."

She shrank back as if he had slapped her across the face out of nowhere. Her bottom lip wobbled as if she were about to cry.

Why?

He didn't need another woman crying in front of him. But damn it, he wasn't about to let her waltz in here and cause Gabriella more pain.

"I didn't mean to hurt her last night. I needed some time to myself."

"Yeah, and what about what Gabriella needs? Do you ever stop to ask yourself that? Do you ever wonder that you take advantage of her friendship a little too much?"

"I do not," Mia objected, although her tone wasn't as strong as she probably meant it to sound.

"Really? So asking a friend to go undercover at your boyfriend's work to see if he's cheating is a normal thing people do?"

Mia steeled her shoulders back in a rigid stance. "She didn't mind."

"Well, I did." He hurled his words at her, hating how much she didn't see the pain she caused to her friend who was willing to do anything for her, no matter what.

Yet, Mia callously turned her back on Gabriella last night without a thought or care.

"Dane?"

He whipped his head to his left, surprised to see Gabriella standing in the other doorway to the kitchen. How long had she been standing there?

By the frown marring her beautiful face and the way her brows drooped low, she wasn't happy. Her hair was wet and still needed a good comb-through. Her skin looked a bit red around her shoulders as if she let the hot water beat down on her. Even a few droplets of water clung to her collarbone, indicating she missed a few spots—or maybe it was from her hair because it wasn't fully toweled dry. But it didn't matter how angry she looked and barely put together with no makeup; she was gorgeous.

But very angry.

Damn it. He had a feeling it was all directed toward him. As if sticking up for her was the wrong thing to do.

He wasn't about to apologize. Not for one word. At times, it still grated on his nerves what Gabriella had done. That she had lied. Yes, he had forgiven her. And yes, he realized he never would've met her in the first place if she hadn't done what she had. But when faced with Mia and her irrational behavior over something that shouldn't have had her shoving Gabriella out of the door—well, it pissed him off. That she lied. That she thought him a lying, cheating dirtbag. All because Mia had asked her to do it.

Her friend should show her more respect than she was giving.

"You should leave."

Gabriella's whispered words took that knife that Mia had first inserted and twisted it further into his gut.

He was defending her, and she wanted *him* to leave?

Well, this was his sign that he made the right decision not to ask her to join him at his parents for supper tomorrow.

Because when it came down to it, no matter what happened between her and Mia, Gabriella would always pick Mia over him.

He'd always be second best, and he hated being second best. That's all he ever was growing up. Just once, he wanted to be first in someone's life. Just once.

He nodded but didn't say anything else. He had nothing else to say. What could he say? What could he possibly use to argue with? They had a bond that could not be broken by anything.

Apparently, not even love.

He strolled past Gabriella. She didn't even look him in the eye.

Love? Ha!

She didn't love him. Not like he loved her. Foolishly.

Love was nothing but a foolish emotion.

He put on his shoes, grabbed his phone and wallet, and left the apartment without another word spoken to either woman.

This was why he made work his solace.

It never disappointed him.

———

GABRIELLA SHIVERED. Not from the fact she only had on a tank top and short pair of shorts. Usually, she didn't go around her apartment so bare. She liked wearing her old sweats and a comfy T-shirt most of the time.

No, she shivered from the soft click that echoed from the hallway. By the silent way Dane left. By the hurt in his eyes. By the fierce way he had fought for her.

But he didn't need to say what he had to Mia. He shouldn't have spoken to her like that. Mia had every right to ask her to leave last night. If she wanted to be alone, then fine.

Kind of like she wanted to be alone. Even though her heart had silently shouted at his back to not leave. *Stay! Don't go!*

Mia sighed from across the kitchen.

Gabriella lifted her head and met her troubled gaze. She didn't know what to say to her. While Mia had every right to kick her out last night—and she hadn't been rude about it, per se—it had still hurt. That pain filtered back in. All of

Dane's calm and soothing vanished as if he had done nothing to make her feel better.

"He's not wrong. That was selfish of me to ask you to do that," Mia said in a quiet, timid voice. Almost as if someone had forced the words out at gunpoint.

"I don't know why he brought that up. It makes me think he hasn't forgiven me, even though he said he had."

And he talks about despising liars. He was obviously lying to her. What was he doing with her if he still harbored hurt feelings about her little undercover stint?

Mia shrugged. "He was trying to make a point."

"I don't think so."

A tenderhearted smile spread across Mia's lips. The smile that always said, "You're so cute but completely dense."

"You're always there for me, Gabs. Always. No matter what I ask, you always come through." She shook her head, the shame hitting her eyes. "Sometimes, I shouldn't ask. He's right. I do take advantage of our friendship. I don't know why I never saw it before. I'm sorry." She let out another weary sigh. "I'm sorry I asked you to leave last night. I acted so silly."

"Your feelings aren't silly. I—"

"Neither are yours." Mia's tone was firm. Not harsh. Not cruel. But firm. Very, very firm. Mia rarely spoke that way to her.

"I was completely shocked by Jaxson's words last night. Like I got hit by a curveball. I reacted badly about it. I see that now. I didn't mean to upset you last night. I didn't, Gabs. I know..." Mia's voice hiccupped, almost as if she was about to cry. And damn it, if Mia started crying, then so would she.

"I know what happened yesterday with you and Jaxson.

The shooter and whatnot. I'm a terrible friend for not being there for you for once. I'm sorry. Forgive me?"

It had been a rough day yesterday. If not for the shooting, Gabby didn't think she would've reacted as badly to Mia, shutting her out as she had. But after dealing with death—a shooting that reminded her of Mia's dad—it had been too much.

She reacted badly as well.

"Of course, I forgive you. You don't even have to apologize."

"But I do."

Then they both started to giggle, knowing they'd go back and forth about who should be apologizing. The tension that had filled the room like a smoky parlor suddenly evaporated. They closed the distance and hugged, a mingling of laughter and cries. Yeah, a few more tears escaped.

Gabby swore in her head she wouldn't cry again for at least five more years. Crying took too much of her energy, and she had a full day ahead of her.

A full day of...

Well, shit. She wasn't sure now. Maybe hanging with Mia.

She had figured she'd hang out with Dane, but...that wasn't happening anymore. She had asked him to leave. And why? Because he saw what neither she nor Mia could see. Because, yeah, when she thought about it, she tended to drop whatever she was doing and be there for Mia no matter what. She couldn't help it. All she could hear in those moments were her cries of terror. *Help me, Gabby. I need you.*

Mia pulled away, wiping under eyes, clearing the evidence of her minor breakdown. Gabby wanted to punch

a wall, scream in frustration—hell, stomp her feet at how
Mia could shed a few tears and still look like a goddess. Her
face wasn't red and blotchy. Her mascara didn't run even a
millimeter down her face. She looked put together while
Gabby figured she looked like a horror show doll ready for a
massacre to begin.

"I didn't mean to cause problems between you and
Dane." Mia groaned and rolled her eyes. "Again. I'm always
screwing things up for you with him."

Gabby waved her off. "He shouldn't have said anything
to you. It's fine."

Mia tilted her head in that motherly way she could do
on occasion. "He had every right to say something to me.
You know what that means, right?"

Oh, God.

No, she had no idea what that meant.

"He loves you, you goof," Mia said with a chuckle.

"Don't be ridiculous." Gabby mock laughed and headed
for the pantry to grab a box of cereal.

She wasn't sure what Dane had been preparing, but she
only needed something light right now.

"Gabby—"

"Hey, we're not having this conversation," she said,
pointing the bright red cereal box at Mia with a stern
expression on her face as if that would stop Mia.

Then her eyes narrowed. Her mind processing everything Mia said since she arrived in lightyear speed.

"How did you know Jaxson and I were involved in a
shooting yesterday? I didn't tell you that over the phone
before you got here, and you left so fast, no one had time to
tell you then."

A light blush coated Mia's cheeks as she glanced away.
"Jaxson told me."

One hand propped to her hip as the other hand pointed the box of cereal at her once again. "When?"

Mia huffed. "Don't treat me like a suspect. Interrogating me with those beady eyes of yours."

"These beady eyes?" She narrowed them even further, purposely displaying a bit of her interrogation technique.

"Does that really work?" Mia giggled as she clapped a hand over her mouth.

Slamming the cereal box on the island between them, she smirked when Mia jumped a little. "Oh, I have a whole arsenal I can use on you. Or you can be the best friend that you are and just tell me."

"Admit Dane loves you."

"How in the hell would I know that? I can't read his mind. And trust me, I'm pretty good at reading his facial expressions, and I don't think he's anywhere near in love with me."

Mia narrowed her eyes this time. "So, you love him?"

Gabby started to open her mouth to deny it—which would've been a lie—when she pointed a finger at her. Hell, she was tempted to pick up the box of cereal and throw it at her. But then it might make a mess, and she didn't have the patience to pick up a bunch of tiny pieces of colorful cereal from the floor.

"You're deflecting from my original question, and I will not allow it. Now, spill. Before I tell Jimmy Calhoun that you really did have a crush on him in high school."

Mia's eyes bulged. "You wouldn't?"

The secret wouldn't amount to much, considering Jimmy was happily married with two kids. But the embarrassment would be plenty for Mia since she worked with his sister, who always loved to tease her that she liked Jimmy. She always had vehemently denied it. Although Gabby couldn't blame her. Jimmy—to this day—was a handsome guy. Star quarterback. Sweet. Full of manners. And smart. What woman could resist that? But he always only had eyes for Penny Smithson. Star cheerleader. Annoyingly sweet in her own way. Honestly, they were a cute couple. It sounded cliché, but neither had a mean bone in their body—the perfect, sweet power couple.

Mia crossed her arms. "Fine. A few hours after you left, Jaxson showed up. By that time, I had come to my senses how silly I acted, and I apologized for walking out on him. We made up, and he told me what had happened. I would've come over except he told me Dane was here and..." She shrugged, loosening her arms a bit. "Well, I figured you would've preferred his company over mine."

Gabby was about to deny that when her heart did a little pitter-patter as if hollering at her not to lie to her best friend. Because oh, boy, that would be a lie. She had enjoyed Dane's coddling last night. His sweet, tender comfort. She had preferred his company over Mia's.

That was a first.

But she refused to be sidetracked again by Mia. She knew what she was doing.

"So...there will be no you and Jaxson?"

Her eyes flashed a bit of pain, but then Mia smiled. "We're friends. It's better we stay friends."

Gabby had enough of her own problems than to try and tackle Mia's right now. But if she felt like lying to her for the moment, then so be it. Because it didn't seem to Gabby like Mia wanted to be just friends.

It felt like it was time to move on to a new subject. Because she didn't want to get into Dane and her feelings. Not in the mood for the love talk. And she knew Mia didn't want to direct her true feelings for Jaxson.

She lifted the cereal box. "Breakfast?"

Mia giggled. "One bowl, and then I have to get to the theater. You shouldn't spoil me with your cuisine."

"Only the best for my bestie."

15

Dane glanced to his right when the last person he wanted to see sat down.

"Gabby in the bathroom?" Jaxson asked as he signaled the bartender.

Cocking a brow, Dane smirked. "If I tell you no, will you not order a drink and leave?"

Jaxson's hand lowered. "What, she's not here?"

"Unless she snuck in through the backdoor and is hiding in there for some strange reason, no." Then he lifted his half-empty glass and took a sip.

"Why isn't Gabby here?"

"Why should she be here?"

A low chuckle floated his way. Dane wanted to smack the smile right off the asshole's face. Not that he was truly an asshole. But right now, he wanted to think of him as an asshole. Someone needed to feel his wrath. Since he didn't want bad service, he couldn't unleash it at the bartender, who had been treating him great since the moment he sat down this morning.

All day wasted. Sitting in a bar. Thinking of a woman he

wished he could forget for one moment. One peaceful moment.

"Umm...because she's your girlfriend." Another chuckle sounded. "And you're sitting at a bar around the corner from her apartment."

Dane shrugged. He didn't want to relay the story because no doubt, Jaxson would be on Mia's side.

Everyone always was.

Mia. Mia. Mia.

Hell, even his brother wanted good old precious Mia back.

He took another sip from his drink.

"Okay, I'm sensing something happened between you two," Jaxson muttered under his breath right before the bartender stopped in front of him. Jaxson pointed at him. "I'll have whatever he's having."

The brawny dude with tattoos up and down his arms standing behind the counter chuckled like Jaxson had delivered the world's funniest joke. He looked like he could grind you in a meat grinder with one hand tied behind his back. Yet, despite his menacing appearance, he was super nice.

Dane actually laughed. Because it was about to become funny.

Jaxson looked puzzled. "What?"

"He's been nursing a club soda on the rocks." The brawny guy—Dane thought he heard someone call him Brick, the name suited him—chuckled again.

Jaxson eyed him funny. "Seriously, man? How long have you been sitting here?"

Dane looked up, trying to remember the exact time he walked out of Gabriella's apartment. He had every intention of wiping the whole ordeal out of his mind and get some work done. Except it didn't happen as soon as he eyed the bar and noticed it was open. He'd been sitting in the same spot ever since.

"Well, don't know what time it is, but they have delicious breakfast burritos. You should try one. Simply superb."

Brick pulled a menu from below the bar. "We're on supper items now. The nachos are the shit." Then he put his fingers to his mouth and let them go as if gesturing they were delicious.

"Wow," Jaxson muttered. Then he smiled at Brick. "We'll take the nachos and two beers. If he's going to sit here and sulk, then he's going to do it the correct way."

"It's about damn time. First round's on the house," Brick said with a sly grin and pulled two beers out of thin air and set them on the counter in front of them.

Dane wanted to slap Jaxson's hand when he snatched his club soda away and replaced it with a beer. Instead, he grabbed the bottle and took a sip. The first swallow went down smoothly. The second, third, and fourth went down a little faster than he anticipated.

Damn it.

He had tried to avoid this.

Drown his sorrows.

And over a damn woman.

"Want to share what happened?" Jaxson asked, then took his own long swallow.

At this rate, they'd be on their second round before Brick had a chance to put in the nacho order.

"Mia happened."

Dane felt Jaxson stiffen next to him.

"What the hell does that mean?"

Dane sighed, tilting his head a little in his direction. "It means, Mia came, and nothing else mattered."

The rigidness in Jaxson's shoulders dissipated. He

slouched as he took another pull from his beer. "They have a tight bond. Not even I'm more important to Gabby."

This time, Dane stiffened. That made it sound like Jaxson wanted Gabby to give him more attention. But he saw the fallout of his confession last night. Did the damn asshole like both women?

Jaxson must've noticed the change in his demeanor because he turned. Then he suddenly clapped him on the back and smiled. "Dude, I like Mia. Only Mia. I'm just saying, as a good friend of Gabby's, she puts Mia over anyone, even me. I'm sorry."

Dane took another swig of his beer, nearly done with the bottle. "So, we're sulking together now?"

Jaxson eyed his bottle, running a finger up and down the label. "I went over to Mia's last night. She wasn't crying anymore, I was thankful for that. But we've decided it's better we stay friends and to forget I even said what I said."

"You both decided that?" Dane couldn't stop the laugh. Because that was some bullshit if he ever heard before.

"She decided that," Jaxson said with a clenched jaw. "But, I'll take her any way I can get her."

"Yeah, because she's Mia. Sweet, precious Mia."

He couldn't hide the disdain in his voice. Hell, if Jaxson wanted to sit with him and attempt to be chummy, then he'd have to deal with whatever came out of his mouth.

"What did she do to you?" Jaxson asked in a friendly voice, but Dane heard the gravel in his tone, the repressed violence just below the surface.

"She showed up this morning, and I asked her *nicely* not to hurt Gabriella again." Dane looked at him. "You don't like it when Mia cries. Well, it breaks my goddamn heart to see one tear in Gabriella's. I was not about to let that happen again." He shifted his attention back to his beer. "Gabriella didn't appreciate my support in the matter. She asked me to leave."

Brick appeared out of nowhere with two more bottles of beer. "Nachos will be done in five. Bottoms up, champs. Second round's on me, too."

"Champs?" Dane started to laugh. He finished off his first beer and grabbed the new one and downed half of that before more laughter started to escape.

Jaxson followed his actions, only a little slower. "I'm missing the joke."

"My brother, Champ. The bastard. He'll be the golden boy once again tomorrow." Dane wanted to smash the beer bottle against the counter. "Can't ever win against my brother. I guess it figures. I can't win the heart of the woman I love either."

Jaxson spewed beer over the counter. "Shit. You love Gabs?"

Damn it. He hadn't meant to let that slip.

He looked over at Brick and lifted his beer. "Round three, Brick. Pronto."

Brick winked, and Dane knew he was going to have a helluva hangover tomorrow.

Oh, what a birthday party it would be.

AFTER MIA LEFT, Gabby didn't know what to do with herself. The conversation she had with Mia went through her mind like a tape rewinding in a VCR. Then she popped in another tape and rewound the conversation between Mia and Dane.

So maybe he had been sticking up for her. But with Mia? It wasn't necessary.

But the more times she rewound and fast-forwarded,

trying to pinpoint one anomaly that could keep her in an irate state, she couldn't find one.

He had said what he did out of caring. Even Mia had agreed with what he had said to her.

With that knowledge in mind, she did what any normal person would do when they needed to apologize.

She took a shower.

Again.

Because she wasn't normal. She was messed up, imperfect, and made bad decisions all the time.

Right now, she felt like acting like a coward. Plus, the hot water felt so nice on her skin. As if it could cleanse all the hurt out of her body.

Her idiotic mistakes.

The fact she probably shot a man.

Of course, the man had killed his girlfriend and had tried to kill them. It was shoot or die themselves. They had no choice.

It still didn't make her feel better or erase the image of his bloodied body from her mind, lying half on his front porch, half inside the house.

They'd be on administrative leave no more than a week for the investigation to find they had just cause to shoot.

She had no idea what she'd do with herself in that week's timeframe. Suddenly—unlike last night when she only wanted to be alone in her misery—she wanted company.

She wanted Dane.

Talk about wishy-washy feelings.

Getting out of the shower for the second time that day, she got ready. Blew dry her hair. Styled with soft curls. Applied a tiny bit of makeup: mascara, eyeshadow, and a touch of red lipstick.

Yet, her foolish, scared pride still couldn't conjure the courage to call Dane. It was now nearing lunchtime. He hadn't called her yet, either.

Of course, why would he? She kicked him out. He wouldn't be calling anytime soon.

Trying to erase the pain she had witnessed in his eyes before he walked away, she decided to clean her apartment. Not that it was that messy. She usually picked up after herself right away rather than leave a mess to deal with once a week. But a blanket needed to be folded in the living room. The floor had to be vacuumed. Twice. Well, not really, but the noise filling the silent apartment soothed her somewhat.

She cleaned the kitchen, putting away a few pots and pans Dane had grabbed. No food littered the counter, so she couldn't be sure what he had planned to make for breakfast.

How did he learn to cook? It just occurred to her.

His mother didn't cook, so she didn't teach him.

Francis, his parents' cook? That seemed the likely answer to such a simple question. All she had to do was ask him. Pick up the phone and call.

An apology would be best first, then ask where he learned to cook.

She wiped down all the kitchen counters, even though they didn't need it, then organized the fridge because who likes an unorganized fridge. She even color-coded the items, so it looked like a rainbow when you opened the door. Everyone loved rainbows. Rainbows made a person smile.

She opened and closed the fridge a few times.

The colors captured her attention.

Like a pretty rainbow.

No smile appeared.

She slammed the door closed.

Because she was an idiot, finding the dumbest excuses to waste time instead of picking up the phone to apologize. It irritated her once again that another one of her friends was right. Jaxson said she liked to push guys away. Sure, she dated some full-on losers. But on occasion, she dated a nice guy or two. Like Greg. But it never amounted to much.

Because she pushed them away.

Kind of what she had done to Dane this morning. Instead of appreciating his kindness for sticking up for her, she told him to get the hell out, like he had done something wrong.

The past month had been one of the best months of her life. Full of fun, laughter, hot sex. Oh, boy, the sex was out of this world hot. Every time she saw Dane, her heart fell a little deeper in love.

It scared the shit out of her.

How could he love someone so brash, outspoken, and idiotic at times? Going undercover to see if your best friend's boyfriend was cheating on her was a very stupid thing to do. Grown adults didn't act like that. They had meaningful, truthful conversations. It would've been so much better if Mia would've just asked Champ if he was cheating.

Except Mia would've never done that, and Gabby couldn't say no to her.

It didn't make it right.

Ugh. She needed to clear her head. Everything kept going round and round in circles.

So, she took another shower. This time she turned the water even hotter, letting it scald her skin until almost every inch was beet red.

By the time she stepped out of the shower, she looked like a cooked crab waiting to be smashed open claw by claw.

Wiping the mirror clear of steam, she stared for a

moment at herself. She wasn't happy with the woman staring back.

And delaying the inevitable talk—because she'd have to face Dane at some point—only confirmed she was a coward. Damn it. She was no coward. Not in the face of anything. Armed suspect. Crazed, drunken asshole. Smart-mouthed teenager. Victim crying for the loss of a loved one. She faced anything and everything head-on. Every single time. She would with this, too.

She got ready for the third time that day. Same as the last time. Light makeup, cute hair. She pulled a nice shirt out of the closet. Not too fancy, but not too plain. She paired it with a set of black capris that always made her butt look fabulous.

Then she grabbed her phone.

And hesitated.

For a second.

Then hit dial and listened to the phone ring. And ring. And ring. Until the voicemail picked up.

Wow. All day worrying and wondering and going out of her mind with regret, and Dane didn't answer her call.

Well, that shit was unacceptable. She wanted to apologize. Not to mention, she might chicken out, so she had to do it now.

She grabbed her purse, locked the door, and headed for the place she figured he'd been since he walked out this morning.

Work.

Barry, the kindhearted security guy, who loved to show her pictures of his grandchildren, let her up to Dane's floor without even one word of begging. The floor was eerily quiet, the lights dim, only a few on. She took her time walking down the hallway, not because she was afraid someone would pop out of one of the offices and say boo, but because that weakness she fought with all morning was starting to creep back in. What would he say to her? Would he forgive her? Or would he finally say the relationship wasn't working? That she was too much work to deal with.

That thought made her laugh. He already had enough work to deal with.

His office door was closed when she stepped into her work area—well, now, Ms. Wallace's area. She couldn't have been happier when Dane gave her a chance. Sometimes all people needed was that one person to give them a chance. To show everyone they were more than a person with a record. A victim of a crime. A single mother trying to make ends meet.

Blowing out a breath, she steeled her spine. She could do this. Running her hands down her shirt to the top of her thighs, she exhaled another slow breath.

Yep. She got this.

Then she twisted the handle and opened the door.

To an empty office.

She walked inside, dumbfounded. Her eyes trailed to the gorgeous view of New York City behind his desk. She walked closer.

The sun was starting to slowly say goodbye for the day. The lights on the buildings weren't quite lit, but she imagined it looked wonderful from his office all lit up in its glory. She looked at lady liberty, mentally making a to-do list. She needed to go see the monument with Dane at some point. She wanted to see the relaxation in his eyes, in his posture as they took a leisurely ferry ride to the statue. She wanted to see the glee and excitement in his expression as they walked around—maybe even planned in advance to walk up to the top. Yes, she would go there someday—very soon —with him.

As soon as she apologized.

Turning away from the window, she glanced around his office again.

Empty.

She couldn't believe it. She swore this was where she would've found him. Sure, it was Saturday, but when he wasn't with her, he was working. Where could he be?

Well, she could always try his apartment.

She walked past his desk when another person entered his office.

Not a person she wanted to see.

"Well, well, well. What do we have here?" Champ said in a douchey, creepy tone.

Of course, anytime he spoke, his words sounded creepy. Because he was a creep. She had seen him a few times here and there when she visited Dane at work. He always had a few words to say, but she never did. Nothing nice would come out of her mouth anyway.

Right now, she had nothing to say to him, either. She headed in his direction because, unfortunately, he stood in her pathway to exit.

As she tried to sweep past him, he grabbed her arm, stopping her with a strength that surprised her. She twisted her head, eyeing him, then his hand on her arm—the audacity—like he had a right to touch her.

"He's playing with you." Champ leaned closer, his mouth getting way too close to her mouth for comfort. "He'll never love you. You're a little toy to my brother." His eyes lowered to her mouth. "I play better than him. I can show you."

Her entire body shivered at his insinuation. She thought

he was an asshole before for cheating on Mia. He was worse than that. She couldn't even find the right word. Despicable. Downright disgusting.

She twisted more of her body, so she was face to face with him. His hand still held her arm like a tight vice. A slow, wicked smile emerged on his face. Like he was going to get what he wanted.

Oh, how wrong he was.

She produced her own sweet, wicked smile.

Then she brought her knee up as hard as she could into his family jewels. His hand fell from her arm as he dropped to the floor with a bellowing moan.

"You bitch," he whispered in agony.

"And don't you forget it." She winked. "Champ."

Then she walked out of the office with her goal still well in hand.

To find Dane.

And damn his brother for planting more seeds of doubt in her head.

He'll never love you.

Sadly, she had to agree with that. While Dane gave her his attention, his affection, his devotion while they were together, sometimes she felt like she had to pry him away from his work. It was disheartening. And she didn't think she'd ever be able to fully compete with his job.

He would never love her like he loved his work.

16

DANE HALF-SNORTED at Jaxson's latest tale. Probably a very disturbing story if he wasn't so drunk. Hearing about Gabriella chasing suspects and walking into danger wasn't that funny. Except Jaxson had a way of weaving the story to make him laugh. How Gabriella could take down a brute suspect with her dainty little fingers and not even break a sweat. He could picture it. She had such a fierceness about her.

Yet, such tenderness and vulnerability that she tried to hide.

Like last night when she wanted him to leave and break down in silence and cry tears that she didn't want anyone to see.

Damn it. He wanted to dry those tears. He wanted to be the one to comfort her and tell her everything would be okay, even though he had no idea if it would be. He wanted to share in her vulnerability and show her his when it scared him to death to show anyone any kind of weakness.

Jaxson paused with his beer close to his lips, but not

touching. "You okay? You went from laughing to looking like your mother died."

Dane twisted the bottle in his hands. His fifth...sixth. Hell, he lost count after bottle number three and the two shots that followed. Something Jaxson insisted on.

He didn't argue. They were both wallowing in their pain. Why not wallow together? Kind of odd, considering they had disliked each other the day before. But it didn't feel awkward.

"Dude?" Jaxson nudged his shoulder.

Looking at him, he shrugged. "It occurred to me how dangerous her job is. She could've died yesterday. You, too."

They stared at each other for a second before Jaxson averted his eyes first.

"It's not something I think about. I can't; otherwise, it'd be hard to walk out the door. I love my job, though. So does Gabby. We both have our reasons why we do it." Jaxson inhaled and looked back at him. "Just like I'm sure you have your reasons for working at your dad's company when you could own your own."

A strangled chuckle escaped. "Gabriella tell you that?"

"We work long hours together, Dane. We talk about a lot of things." Jaxson chuckled, then shivered as his features twisted into disgust as if he saw someone throw up on his shoes. "But not everything. I don't like to hear everything... like sex and shit."

"Well, if you ever need any pointers, I have a lot of moves that—"

"La, la, la, la," Jaxson started to sing loudly as he covered his ears. "We're not going there. I have my own moves that work perfectly fine."

Hearty laughter bellowed out. Dane took another swig

of his beer after he settled down. His belly hurt from laughing so hard.

"Thanks. I needed that, Jax."

One shoulder tilted up in a careless gesture. "Hell, what are friends for?" Jaxson started to mirror his earlier melancholy as he twisted his bottle. "I never thought I'd be sitting here with you over a couple of beers like we were old friends." Then he clapped him on the shoulder. "But I like to think we've turned a corner and I can call you a friend instead of an enemy."

Dane released a heavy breath. "Yeah, you can. As long as Gabriella hasn't officially kicked me out of her life."

Jaxson squeezed his shoulder, smiled, and picked his beer up again. "She gets pissed all the time at me. She'll get over it. You two are...I've never seen her...your relationship..."

"It's clearly hard for you to describe." Dane laughed, yet nothing was funny about that.

But Jaxson's tripped up words made sense.

He had a hard time himself figuring out their relationship. The past month had been wonderful. Spending time with her. Enjoying laughter. Delicious time between the sheets. Growing closer.

He had also been neglecting his work. Well, not necessarily neglecting it, but his mind wasn't focused on it, and that was not normal for him. He was waiting for a mistake to pop up and bite him in the ass. Show him how truly distracting Gabriella was in his life.

But he liked her distraction.

Because he loved her.

Yet, would love be enough? It wasn't in his family. Sure, his parents were cordial to each other. But he didn't see an undying love in their eyes when they looked at each other.

At this point in their lives, he figured they stayed together because it was comfortable and too much work to split. That wasn't love. That was avoiding disaster.

"You're perfect for each other. You balance each other out. There. That's how I would describe it."

He soaked up Jaxson's words. Thinking hard on them.

Balanced each other out.

In a way, sure, they did.

He worked too much, and she made sure he stopped to smell the roses. Sometimes, literally.

When she needed emotional support, something he could tell she struggled with excepting, he provided it, refusing to let her push him away.

Except for today.

He walked away a little too easily. He upset their balance.

"So, you think you'll ever start your own company? Gabs is always saying how well you'd excel at it. That it would make you happier."

He tilted his head, his brows puckering low as he shared a look with Jaxson. Odd. She had never told him that. Was that what she thought? That he wasn't happy at his job.

He loved his work.

Hmm.

But he didn't necessarily love his job. Love how Champ would always burst into his office without knocking. How he'd steal clients right out from underneath his nose just because he was the owner of the company. The clients thought that meant they'd get better service. Oh, how wrong they were.

"I'm not unhappy." Which was bordering on a slight lie.

Jaxson laughed. "Yeah, but it also doesn't sound like you're completely happy either."

He shrugged, hating where this conversation was turning. He'd rather dissect his relationship with Gabriella than his relationship with a company that honestly made him unhappy.

"Aren't we supposed to end this night of debauchery with laughter and lots of drinks?" Dane tipped his bottle toward him, as if to cheers to more fun on the way. "Not this serious tone."

"Is debauchery the right word you're looking for?" Jaxson eyed him funnily. "Because we're not surrounded by beautiful women right now, nor are we leaving this bar with women that aren't Gabby and—" His eyes rounded as he realized he was about to say "Mia" as if she were his. "Well, you're not leaving this bar with someone else."

"You know what I meant." Dane clicked with his bottle even though he didn't follow through on his own. "Sorry about Mia."

Jaxson shrugged. "Me, too." Then he pulled out his wallet and threw his card on the bar, signaling to Brick.

Well, Dane took that as a sign the night was over for them. But he wasn't done drinking and wallowing in his misery. Because tomorrow morning, when he had to get up and find his mother a gift and celebrate her birthday, he would not wallow ever again in misery. Not for any woman. Even Gabriella.

"I got both tabs," Jaxson said as Brick took his card.

"I'm not leaving."

Jaxson clapped him on the back. Hard.

"You are. You have some debauchery to do."

Dane looked at him with his mouth twisted in confusion. "I'm not hooking up with some random woman. Is this some sort of test? Are we suddenly becoming enemies? You trying to trip me up?"

Jaxson leaned in closer. "I meant Gabby, dumbass. Go to her." His expression softened with pain. "One of us should at least end the night happy."

"And if she slams the door in my face?"

Because Dane saw it as a possibility. The look of heartache and hurt in her eyes this morning couldn't be forgotten.

"Then I got a nice bottle of whiskey at home that I don't mind sharing."

Well, Dane preferred Gabriella over whiskey. But at least he had something to fall back on if she pushed him away once again.

GABBY UNLOCKED her apartment door and slammed it.

Whoops!

She slammed it a bit too hard. Mrs. Stenson might come to check on her like she had the one time she dropped her crockpot, and it made the loudest noise imaginable. Not to mention, it broke into pieces. It had made her sad she had to buy a new one because that one had worked like a charm. Sure, she had to use a specific outlet to get it to work, the machine was a finicky one. The dial was stuck on low, so no matter what meal she wanted to cook, she had to adjust the time to a low setting. It didn't matter. She had loved the crockpot, and the new one didn't cook the same with all its fancy features.

She waited for a beat or two. When no knock sounded on the door with concern from her elderly neighbor who liked to worry about everyone on their floor, she flipped the lock and headed for the kitchen.

She had two choices.

Drink herself into oblivion.

Or try calling Dane one more time.

She had called him before she left her apartment.

No answer.

His office had been devoid of him except for his slimy brother. Before she caught a cab to his apartment, she tried calling him again.

No answer.

When she arrived at his apartment, she knew before she even unlocked the door, he wasn't inside. Despite the ache that stretched across her heart, she tried calling him again.

No answer.

Her eyes glided to her wine rack. Then her eyes trailed to her purse hanging loosely in her hand where her phone was hidden inside.

Decisions, decisions.

She didn't want to end the night without clearing the air between her and Dane. It didn't feel right. That age-old saying "don't go to bed mad" rang true to her right now. It wasn't something she thought about before.

But could she handle another ringing rejection with him not answering his phone?

She'd cried enough last night. She didn't know if her body could handle any more tears.

And it'd be nice to thank Dane while she apologized for her behavior. Because her mind had been more focused on him rather than the shooting she had been involved in. She was thankful for that. She didn't like to see that man's soulless eyes staring back at her—no life in them. No hatred. Nothing but emptiness. Because she had killed him.

She eyed the wine rack again.

Getting drunk didn't sound appealing, even though it

would help erase painful memories. But only for the night. She didn't want it for just one night.

She wanted Dane. She wanted his warm arms around her, soothing her. Comforting her. He made the painful memories not seem as bad. As close to her.

She dumped the contents of her purse onto the counter, too lazy to dig for her phone. It slid out and stopped a few inches from landing off the counter.

She'd try calling him one more time. If he didn't answer, then...then...

Then she didn't know what to do. Or what to think.

Grabbing her phone, she dialed before she chickened out because she didn't want to hear only ringing once again.

When the first ring echoed in her ear, she tensed. Another went by with no low timbre voice answering. By the third ring, her heart swelled with disappointment. He was still ignoring her.

Making her way out of the kitchen with the phone clutched to her ear, hoping against hope he'd answer before the last ring, she paused in her living room.

A soft tone echoed down her hallway at the same time another ring sang in her ear. She started down the hallway toward her bedroom.

One ring in her ear.

One muted tone down the hallway.

At the same time.

His voicemail popped up. She ended the call without leaving a message as she entered her bedroom.

Dane lay sprawled on her bed, almost in the middle, but slightly more on his side than hers. He was snoring, and his phone sat on the nightstand he always used.

Glancing at the clock that read it was a little past eight o'clock, then at Dane, she blinked a few times, confused.

He was here. In her apartment. In her bed. Asleep.

She set her phone down next to his, then ran a hand across his forehead. He barely stirred. When she leaned closer, the strong odor of alcohol wafted her way.

No wonder he was snoring—something she hadn't heard from him before—the man was drunk.

They had shared drinks together. But they had never gotten wasted before. If he was already passed out this early in the evening, he must've had quite a bit.

And instead of going home, he came to her.

A sweet smile spread across her face as she started to undress down to only panties. Grabbing a light tank top from the top of her dresser, she put it on and then crawled under the covers on her side of the bed. It took a bit of finagling with the unconscious—ridiculously adorable— man to get under the covers with her. She decided trying to wrestle his shirt off would be too much of a struggle. He had already taken off his pants, so she didn't have to worry about that.

She snuggled closer, and to her surprise, he wrapped his arms around her as a low contented sigh escaped from his lips. Although he didn't wake up, it's as if he instinctively needed to hold her.

Then his light snores continued.

She chuckled and kissed his forehead.

"I love you, Dane," she whispered against his forehead.

Then she fell asleep with him, hoping everything was as perfect as this moment in the morning.

Peace. And a feeling of rightness in his arms.

17

Dane groaned, shoving a hand over his eyes as the sun streamed through the window. The warm body snuggled against him shifted.

Gabriella.

Oh, damn.

Well, she hadn't kicked him out of her bed last night, so that was a plus. Although his memory was shaky, he couldn't quite remember climbing into her bed. He vaguely remembered leaving the bar with Jaxson's arm around his shoulder. He sort of recalled shuffling Gabby's key between his fingers and getting the door unlocked after multiple attempts. It was embarrassing even to think about it. His memory kind of came to him as he closed her door and stumbled to her room. His shoes came off. His pants next. He even pulled out his phone. Probably to call Gabby to find out where she was.

Then nothing but blackness. He obviously had passed out.

Oh, he was never drinking that much again.

His heart started to pound in tune with the hammering

going on inside his head. He had no idea what to say to Gabriella. Why he showed up drunk and passed out sprawled across her bed.

Maybe he could lay here all day pretending to be asleep, and he could avoid all talk. Except he couldn't. It was his mother's birthday. He still needed to buy her a present and mentally prepare himself to see his father and brother.

She shifted again, moving closer. One leg even stretched across his.

He lowered his hand and nearly groaned again. This time in agony from the gorgeous sight in front of him.

The covers were half off her, exposing her lithe, luscious backside that he wanted to cup with his hands and then position her over the top of him. He could snap her black panties off with little effort and then plunge deep inside.

God, how badly he wanted—needed—to be inside her. To be as close as humanly possible. To know he hadn't completely screwed everything up with her.

He couldn't resist. His hand glided down her back and smoothed over her ass before tickling lightly down her leg.

She trembled at his touch. He felt her smile against his chest.

Well, that had to be a good sign. Perhaps she wasn't totally mad at him still.

Her eyes opened. She blinked a few times to remove the sleep.

"Good morning." He figured starting with small talk would be best.

Of course, an apology might be better. Except he wasn't that sorry for speaking to Mia the way he had.

When she didn't say anything right away, he feared that's what she was waiting for. An apology he couldn't give.

He wouldn't lie to her. And saying sorry would be a complete lie.

Then she sighed, brushed a hand across his unshaved cheek, and deepened her smile. "Morning. You snore. It was quite adorable."

"I doubt that."

"Oh, mister, you probably woke up Mrs. Stenson two doors down."

His mouth opened in shock. There was no way he snored that loud. Or at all. He did not snore.

"Well, you drool," he countered.

Then they both burst out laughing. As soon as the laughter died down, an icky tension filled the space. A tension he knew would linger until they talked about it.

"I'm sorry for showing up...drunk." There was no other way to put it.

Her hand slid down his chest. "About that...why were you drinking?"

"Honestly? I blame Jaxson. I was content with my club sodas."

She jerked and lifted her head. "You were with Jaxson yesterday. I looked everywhere for you, and that is the last place I would've thought to look."

Pure happiness settled in his chest. She had looked for him. That had to mean something good in his favor.

"You looked for me?"

She lightly slapped his chest. "I even called you, you big dummy. You never answered."

"I'm sorry." He kissed her forehead—a small gesture to show how sorry he was. "I ignored all calls after my brother wouldn't stop calling. I had enough."

"Why was he calling so much?"

He glanced away, not wanting to venture into that

conversation. Right now didn't seem like the best time to ask her to join him at his parents tonight. Although, yesterday didn't seem like a good time either. Nor the night before that. Would there ever be a good time?

"Dane..." she whispered as she cupped his cheek and forced him to turn his head back in her direction. "I over-reacted yesterday. I never should've asked you to leave. I hope you're not still mad at me for what I did, going undercover at your work. I am sorry, but I'm not sorry I met you."

He grasped the back of her head and kissed her. Hard. He couldn't stand to hear the torment in her voice.

He pulled away and rested his forehead against hers. God, she probably didn't want to kiss him when he had terrible alcohol breath. Yet, she hadn't shoved him away when he locked lips with her, nor was she pushing him away now.

"I'm not mad. It's in the past. I was only..." He swallowed and strengthened his grip on the back of her head. "I was trying to protect you from more tears."

"I know," she whispered.

He placed another kiss upon her lips—this time, light and tender.

"So...you and Jaxson. A night on the town, huh?" She giggled as she rested her head back on his chest as he laid back down to his pillow.

"It wasn't planned if that's what you're asking. I had every intention of heading to the office when I left here and found myself at The Corner Bar instead. Aptly named, by the way. They have delicious breakfast burritos, too." He grinned, pulling her closer when she chuckled.

"I'll have to ask Rick to make me one."

"Who's Rick?" She couldn't be talking about Brick.

Because he had even called him Brick and he didn't say a word.

"He's the owner of the bar. Big brawny dude with tattoos up and down his arms."

Sounded like Brick.

Well, shit. He heard the guy's name wrong, used it to his face, and he had the kindness not to correct him. He felt like a complete dumbshit.

"Why do you look like you just threw up that breakfast burrito?" she asked with a tender smile and a smooth brush against his cheek.

"I thought his name was Brick. I swear even Jaxson called him that."

Dane didn't even care she started laughing at him and his idiocy because anytime she smiled, it filled his heart with joy.

"Jaxson should know better."

"Yeah, well, we were both mending broken hearts and —" And he did not mean for it to come out of his mouth like that.

Broken hearts?

Would she see how much he loved her with that simple statement? How much it had gutted him she had asked him to leave?

"And his mind was preoccupied." Gabriella sighed. "I wish Mia would've never overheard him saying that. She's content staying friends, and I know that hurts him so much." Then she removed the frown from her face and grinned. "Continue with your story. I need details."

He laughed, but only to loosen more of the tension that appeared when he mentioned Mia. "He found me sitting at the bar and wouldn't leave. We had a drink, which turned into two, then three, then some shots, and somehow, I found my way here. Because that's where I wanted to be from the beginning."

The most gorgeous smile lit up her face. He wanted to bottle that smile so he'd have it for always. For the days he'd upset her, and she looked at him with nothing more than a frown or stern glare. For the days she came home from work with the pain etched into her irises. For the days...when he might not even have her in his life.

"Let's have a better day. We could start by trying breakfast over like we meant to yesterday. Then a trip to see the Statue of Liberty."

Gabriella always managed to surprise him. While he'd love to spend the day acting like a tourist and catching in the wonderful sites of the city, he couldn't.

She bit her bottom lip and shrugged. "Or not. I suppose you need to get work done since that's where you were headed yesterday before you got sidetracked by delicious breakfast burritos, bricks, and whatnot."

She produced a grin with her lame attempt at laughter. The last thing he wanted was to make her feel bad.

No.

His every intention yesterday was to make her feel better. To make her forget about shooting a man.

"I would love nothing more than to spend the day with you. Except I can't."

Her smile fell into a frown and her eyes shadowed with pain.

Right now was a prime example of why he wanted her smile bottled for his to release.

"Unless you don't mind joining me at my parents for supper. It's my mother's birthday."

There.

Done.

He finally asked.

"I would love that."

The beautiful smile on her face lit up his heart with joy. Filled his soul with contentment. Made him think life was perfect.

Until he realized he might never see her again once she met his father.

SHE SQUEEZED Dane's hand and attempted to keep a serene smile on her face. A forlorn frown wanted to take its place with ferocity. Because the tension emanating for Dane was almost unbearable. And she had no idea why.

It started right after they got out of the shower—together. Best shower she had all weekend. But that's when the phone calls started from his brother. By the third one, Dane shut off his phone.

Not that she didn't believe him—because she had—but she didn't doubt him when he said he stopped looking at his phone when his brother wouldn't stop bothering him.

The question she burned to ask was, why? For some strange reason she couldn't explain, she didn't dig deeper. She didn't ask any questions about why he was ignoring his brother. She figured she would, too—the disgusting pig.

Ugh. She still couldn't get his smarmy smile out of her mind and the way he tried to come onto her as if she'd fall for his lame ass charm.

She should tell Dane about the encounter. Except they barely had time for small talk. There was never a right time to tell him.

After grabbing a quick breakfast burrito at The Corner Bar—where Dane apologized to Rick for mistakenly calling him Brick, who laughed and said he liked the nickname—they went shopping.

What an experience.

Dane did not like shopping.

Nor did he know what to get his mother for her birthday.

She suggested flowers. When they first met, their first trip down the elevator to grab a coffee, he had asked her what kind of flowers to get his mother.

All he said in response was, "Not good enough. We can get flowers, but I need something else, too."

They did stop at a floral shop and bought her a bouquet of white lilies. After that, they went from shop to shop, browsing, perusing, and passing on everything. He couldn't make up his mind.

When she asked if his mother was particular about her gifts, he eyed her funnily and said, "Of course not. She'll love whatever I get her."

Which further confused her. Why was he having such a hard time picking a gift if she'd love whatever he gave her? Since she didn't want to add to the tension already vibrating off him in waves, she followed him with a supportive smile on her face.

They finally found a gift at the most peculiar store that had things from antiques to some very naughty sexual items. The tension switched from icky, I'm-about-to-have-a-mental-breakdown to let's-get-it-on very quickly. Dane even delivered the most intense kiss in the back of the store surrounded by dildos, whips, and edible delights.

They didn't buy any of the items, though. Because as soon as he eyed the perfect present for his mother, the bad tension returned full force.

From there, they went their separate ways to get ready. He said to dress nice.

She had no idea what nice meant. Casual nice. Formal nice. Nice nice. Like, *nice* could mean so many different things. That time, she did ask her question because she didn't want to dress the wrong way. His parents did have a lot of money. She figured it'd be more on the formal nice side of things.

"Just something nice. No matter what you wear, you'll be beautiful."

She had nodded and kissed him goodbye. Because that had not been helpful at all.

Half of her closet was still strewn across her bed from trying to find that one *nice* outfit. She settled with a white dress that went to just her knees. Not tight to her slender frame, but a bit flowy. Not too flowy where she could twirl and look like an expert dancer, but flowy enough where it wouldn't be considered skintight. The top was overlaid with lace, which gave it a formal look, but not too formal.

All in all, she thought it looked nice. Like he'd asked.

When he picked her up, he was dressed in tan slacks and a pink dress shirt. No tie. The pink surprised her. She had never seen him wear anything other than white or gray shirts with a black suit. On the weekends, he did dress down with polo shirts, even T-shirts on occasion, but no pink.

Now, here they stood outside his car in front of his parents' house—a very large house. Not something she'd classify as a mansion, but it was huge. It screamed money. And her pretty white dress suddenly felt not nice enough to even step inside.

He had helped her out of the car, closed her door, yet made no other movements. No step forward. No quick kiss. Nothing.

"Should we go inside?"

His head shook as if shaking himself out of whatever trance he had been in. He looked at her. "We should. Thanks for coming with."

"Of course." She patted his chest, running her hand down in a slow, smooth gesture, hoping to relax him a bit. "You look so handsome. I love this pink on you."

For the first time since he picked her up, he smiled. It lit up his features, personified every sexy inch of him, from his perfectly styled hair to his deep brown eyes that sparkled with desire. To his five o'clock shadow that made her itch to brush her hand across his jaw, then replace it with a sweep of her lips.

"Thank you. I don't wear pink often. It's only for special occasions."

With that, he pulled her toward the front door.

By the slight devilish twinkle in his eye when he said the last part, she didn't think he meant special occasion in a pleasant way.

He let go of her hand to knock on the door since he held the beautiful bouquet of lilies in his other.

The door swung open a few seconds later to an older woman with beautiful blonde hair swept up in a simple coif. She had on a light layer of makeup that brought out her gorgeous features. She wore a light white blouse that went all the way to her wrists and black slacks that fit her perfectly. Gabby always had a hard time finding slacks that fit her hips and butt just right.

By the way her eyes lit up—that were the same deep brown as Dane's—she assumed this was his mother.

"You made it," she said brightly, hugging Dane with a tenderness that had her a bit envious. Her mother never hugged her like that. More like, patted her cheek with a goofy grin, like she was high or something.

His mother took the flowers from his proffered hand, then switched her attention to her. "You brought a guest. How wonderful."

"I told you I was bringing Gabriella, Mom." Dane sounded as if he was about to lose the deal of a lifetime. The despair and anguish in his tone made her heart beat a little faster.

Was she not welcome? Did his mother not want her here?

"Oh, I know, I...this is wonderful." Then his mother pulled her into a sudden hug and squeezed. Tightly. "You have no idea how wonderful it is you're here. He's never invited anyone here."

His mother whispered the last part in her ear, low enough where Gabby figured she didn't want Dane to hear.

By the fierce hug and delight in her tone, Gabby's heart settled back down. His mother didn't mind she came. Yet, it had sounded like she didn't believe she'd actually show up. How odd.

"Come. Your father and brother are in the living room. The meal is almost ready. I'm going to put these beautiful flowers in a vase. How thoughtful of you, Dane." She caressed his cheek in a way only a mother could do, then wandered off down the hallway.

"Are you okay?" she whispered, in case anyone was nearby. She wasn't even sure why Dane still seemed so tense. She knew he didn't get along well with his brother. And his father wasn't always supportive as he should be, but the odd way he was acting concerned her.

Maybe Dane didn't want her to come with. Maybe he felt obligated to ask her.

But that didn't sound right either.

His mother whispered she was the first to ever be invited.

She didn't know what to think. All she knew was Dane's behavior had her nervous.

He suddenly produced a smile. Not a real smile. Not the kind that reached his eyes and enhanced his handsome features. And in the past month, he had smiled more than she figured he used to.

"I'm fine." Then he leaned down and kissed her. "I'm fine."

For the first time, she knew Dane just lied to her.

Because he was not fine at all.

18

DANE STEELED his spine and stepped into the living room with Gabriella by his side. Her presence helped the tension weaving its way through his veins to not warp his body as if he just received the worst beat down. But it all worried him.

Would his father act appropriately? He didn't expect much from Champ, and Gabriella already knew the kind of man his brother was. But he didn't want his father to act like he always did. Not in front of her.

"Hello, Father." He managed a slight grin for him. When his gaze landed on Champ, he dropped all pretenses. "Champ."

"You finally made it. Your mother's been worrying like crazy. I don't know why you couldn't be here early," his father scolded. "Like your brother."

And there it was. Already. The first words out of his mouth.

No hello.

No how are you?

No nice to see you.

Just simple berating and "why can't you act like your

brother?" Shit never changed. And if it wasn't for his mother, he wouldn't even come around. Why should he when he dealt with this kind of treatment every single time?

Instead of responding with a sarcastic comment, an automatic response usually when he dealt with his father, he smiled.

A big, wide smile that had his father frowning. Not an unusual look for him. He usually frowned when Dane was around.

"This is Gabriella. My girlfriend." He pulled her closer to his side and looked down at her. She returned his smile with a sweet one of her own. That smile managed to uncoil one knot of tension sitting deep in the pit of his stomach. "Gabriella, this is my father, Bryan Holloway." He inclined his head toward his father. "And you know Champ."

"Mr. Holloway, it's a pleasure to meet you." Gabriella stepped forward and held out her hand in greeting.

Dane should've known Gabriella wouldn't cower in his father's presence. Most people did. Not his Gabriella. She was the most fierce, most courageous, most confident woman he had ever met.

His father shook her hand, yet no smile appeared. If anything, he narrowed his eyes some.

"I hear you worked at the company."

Her smile faltered, but only for a second. "Yes, temporarily. To help Dane out."

Champ coughed. More like a laugh, but he had to cover it up with a fake cough. Dane figured Champ was the one to tell their father Gabriella worked at the company for only a week. Because he sure in hell didn't say anything. Of course, he knew Champ didn't tell their father the real reason she had because then he'd have to admit he cheated on a woman. And

Champ never let their father see his many failures. Either that or his father was blind when it came to him.

"Yes, well, that doesn't surprise me. Dane usually needs help. He's not like his brother at all." His father turned toward Champ with a proud smile that made Dane want to puke.

Gabriella chuckled. She made it sound like the kind of giggle a woman would give a man she was trying to please. "Oh, yes, Dane is *nothing* like his brother."

Then she grabbed his hand and snuggled into his side while looking up at him with adoring eyes. Oh, how he could drown in her eyes until the end of time.

This beautiful woman had no idea how much her presence meant to him. He thought this supper might be a night of hell. But not with her by his side. Her witty retorts. Her secret sarcastic comments. Her standing tall and proud by his side. Giving her support.

"Well, Dane isn't dating a useless woman for once. How nice." Then his father started to head out of the room as if he hadn't insulted Gabriella. "Let's head to the dining room before your mother comes looking for us."

Her mouth opened a bit in surprise, yet she didn't say a word.

Champ chuckled and followed his father.

Dane stood there.

She brushed a soft hand across his cheek and then swept it through his hair. He closed his eyes, picturing the two of them alone in her apartment. In bed. Her tender hands moving to other parts of his body, soothing him. Making all the painful moments disappear.

"He's never even met anyone you've dated, has he?"

His eyes opened. Her understanding gaze gutted him for

some reason. It's as if she could see straight to his soul—all of his dirty little secrets.

How could she read him so well with one look?

"No, he hasn't." A wry grin twisted on his lips. "He always believes what Champ tells him."

"And what about what you tell him about Champ?"

Dane laughed. "I don't say shit to my father about Champ." Then he lifted her hand and kissed the back of it. "He wouldn't believe a word I say anyway."

They made their way to the dining room where a large table that could seat ten people was set up as if they were at a formal dinner party.

He took the seat across from his mother. Gabriella sat next to him. Champ sat across from her, and his father sat at the head of the table. He almost wished his mother would've wanted them to eat out on the patio where the table wasn't as large and didn't feel as imposing. It was also a circular table where no one could sit at the end. His father always acted like he was some sort of king when he sat at the head of the table.

The first plate was set in front of them. A delicious Cobb salad that he always devoured. Francis was the best chef on the planet. There were times he wanted to steal him from his parents. Except he was never home to eat an actual meal there. It would be pointless to steal him.

The mundane conversation started. His mother was doing most of the talking, asking Gabriella questions about herself. What did she do for a living? Was she from New York? Her favorite things to do? Things a mother would want to ask the woman dating her son.

Dane found most of the questions harmless. Gabriella seemed at ease and didn't mind answering.

The main meal was delivered—roast beef, with carrots

and potatoes, and a nice portion of asparagus. Francis had also delivered a warm bowl of handmade rolls. Simply delicious. Every bite.

It wasn't until the dessert was set before them—a slice of tiramisu pie, his mother's favorite—when his father started asking some questions.

"So, Gabriella, tell me, why did you become a cop? Such an odd profession for a woman."

He tensed, scrunching the napkin in his lap. Gabriella must've sensed his immediate tension because she slid her hand under the tablecloth and grabbed his hand, squeezing. Then she smiled at his father.

"I like to help people. Being a cop is a great way to help people."

"But homicide?" His father frowned in that disapproving way. "It's so morbid."

"Someone has to do it. I like it."

Champ scoffed. "You like looking at dead bodies? Blood, guts, and gory shit?"

His mother cleared her throat, throwing Champ a scolding look. "Language, young man. And must you say such things while we're eating?"

Champ's lips thinned in a tight line as he looked at him, raising his brows. As if saying, "See, she's always on my case and not on yours." He didn't respond even with a silent gesture because fair was fair. Their father never got off his case.

"I'm curious, though. How did you meet Dane and know he needed help at the company?" The question surprised him. Why was his father stuck on that?

"Why does it matter, Mr. Holloway?" Gabriella countered. She smiled as if she received an endearing compliment. It always amazed him how she could smile in such tense moments. She even had when she worked for him that short week, and he had a short temper.

"Because it's my company, and I'd like to know."

"I don't work there anymore, so it's not relevant any longer."

"But you were once employed, so I want to know." His father's voice echoed throughout the room. The very authoritative voice that said no one would disobey him. Even Champ never tried to test his father when he used that tone.

"Well, quite frankly, Mr. Holloway, it's none of your damn business." Gabriella increased her smile. She even looked at Dane and giggled. "Remind me to add a quarter to my swear jar when we get home. How silly of me to let that slip."

"Excuse me, Ms. Stileano," his father started to say.

"Yes, Mr. Holloway?"

Dane wanted to kiss her breathless and say thank you in the most pleasurable ways for the way she was not bowing down to his father. Why couldn't his father stop and drop the conversation?

"How dare you talk to me that way."

His beautiful Gabriella cocked a brow. "How dare you talk to Dane the way you do. If you must know, my friend asked me to see if Champ—who she was dating at the time —was cheating on her."

"He'd never treat a woman like that." His father tilted his head in Dane's direction with the disgust on his lips and the devil dancing in his eye, as if daring her to say something like that again. "Dane, on the other hand, it wouldn't surprise me."

"Bryan," his mother whispered as if shocked he'd say such a thing.

Gabriella grasped his hand tightly, somehow knowing he needed all of her support right now. Because shit was truly hitting the fan like he'd never seen before.

"You're either very obtuse or pretend to ignore the kind of man Champ really is. I found out he was. Screwing the secretary right there on his desk with the door wide open."

"The damn door wasn't wide open," Champ spouted as he threw his napkin on the table.

Dane lifted Gabriella's hand and kissed it. He had never seen anyone stand up to his father like that. Not even he had.

His father couldn't deny it happened when Champ just openly admitted to it.

Dane couldn't hold in his laughter. "Wide open. That's still all you focus on. Not the fact you cheated on a good woman."

His father made an odd sound. Not quite clearing his throat. Not quite a scoff—just an odd muffled sound that drifted from his throat.

"This woman wasn't good enough. Champ wouldn't cheat on a good woman." His father's words reverberated around the room.

Wow.

His damn brother still could do no wrong in his father's eyes even when he truly did wrong.

Gabriella exhaled slowly as her hand slipped from his.

He looked at her, almost feeling the invisible thread holding them together snap. Breaking the bond they had with one quick snip.

Then she stood up and looked at his mother. "Thank you so much, Mrs. Holloway, for a delicious meal. Happy birthday. I'm afraid it's time for me to leave."

"Oh, please, don't. I'd love to have a glass of wine with

you on the back patio while the boys do whatever boys do."
His mother stood up as well, rounding the table quite fast.

She hooked her arm through Gabriella's and gave each
of them a pointed stare.

"I expect this table to be cleared and the dishes taken
care of. It is my birthday, after all."

Then the two women walked out of the room.

"You heard your mother." His father left as well.

Dane sat there staring at the mess, wondering what the
hell happened. It felt like he lost Gabriella. Not to his mother's company. But lost her for good. That once they left, he'd
never see her again.

Because she had a good picture of his family, and it
wasn't a pretty sight.

Not to mention, his father insulted Mia, and that was one of
the worst things he could've done. Nobody hurt her best friend.

"Why didn't you answer my calls? I've been calling you
all weekend," Champ snapped as he stood up, almost
knocking his chair over from standing so fast.

"I didn't see you call."

Champ rolled his eyes, not believing the blatant lie.

"What did you get Mom?"

"What did you get her?" Dane countered.

By the look in Champ's eyes, he didn't get anything,
which was why he had bothered him all weekend. He
wanted to hoard in on his gift like he always did, instead of
going out and buying something himself.

"Add my name to the damn card."

Then Champ walked out of the room as well.

Dane sat at the table, surrounded by a mess, and a
massive hole in his heart.

Screw his brother.

Damn his father.

But bless his mother. For she was the only one trying to stop Gabriella from leaving him with an empty heart.

GABBY TOOK A SIP OF WINE, even though her feet itched to jump up out of the—very nice—plush patio chair. But it was Mrs. Holloway's birthday, and it felt wrong to leave her in the lurch when she asked her to join her outside.

Of course, she also knew why she asked her to join her. To dispel the icky tension. Maybe even warn her away from Dane.

It was quite transparent that his father and brother did not like her. His brother, Champ, sure, she understood. She ruined his chances with Mia by discovering his lecherous behavior.

But his father...

She couldn't fathom why he didn't seem to like her. Probably had something to do with Champ as well.

The weather was beautiful. Not too cold, especially with a light breeze. The sun was going down, leaving a gorgeous hue of colors during its descent—a mixture of pink, purple, and orange. Blending so well, she imagined it as a painting. One hanging in Dane's outer office. It would fit nicely next to the one that held the splashes of paint. She didn't know why she thought that or why her mind even went there, but it would look perfect together.

"Dane cares for you." His mother took a small sip of wine. "The best birthday present I received today was him bringing you as a guest."

Gabby wanted to snort as if saying, "give me a break."

How could him bringing a woman to supper be considered the best present ever? Especially at this supper table.

His mother continued. "Bryan's not a cruel man, even if he displayed some very unsavory behavior inside. He can be hard on Dane. I will admit that. And Champ," she laughed in a motherly sort of way, "he's the youngest. What can I say other than he was coddled a bit too much as a baby, and it just...continued. He had a heart defect as a baby. It was scary for a moment we'd lose him. Bryan gets very protective of him because of that."

Interesting. Gabby wondered if Dane knew that piece of information. He hadn't mentioned it. Besides the one night he shared about his brother, he didn't talk much about his family. She could see why. Of course, just because Champ might've had poor health as a baby, it didn't give him—or his father—a right to act the way they did.

"I imagine that was a stressful time in your life."

His mother looked at her as she reached out a hand and gently settled it on her arm, a wistful smile on her face. "So stressful. I pray when—or if—you ever have kids, you don't have to go through something like that. It can put a strain on your marriage. It can affect your job. It's...hard." Her hand drifted away. "But, he's healthy as an ox now. A bit too spoiled, I'm afraid. I apologize for any hurt he may have caused you or your friend."

"It's not your apology to give, Mrs. Holloway." She smiled. "But I thank you for it."

She turned her direction to the sinking sun once more. Any more talk like this and she might burst into tears. And why? She wasn't prone to tears that often, even though she had in the past month a little too much.

But it had been a helluva weekend so far. Her emotions had been put through the wringer, and she honestly didn't know how much more she could endure. She wanted to leave.

"I've never seen him so happy."

Gabby shifted on her seat and looked back at Mrs. Holloway. "What?"

"Dane. I've never seen him so happy before. You make him happy. You make him focus on more than work." Mrs. Holloway smiled. A bright, beautiful smile that lit up her features. Her eyes crinkling with slight wrinkles. But they did nothing but enhance her beauty, not deter it.

"He doesn't work as much anymore. Bryan's noticed. Dane tended to do most of the work. I knew this. Bryan knew it. But he thinks it's better Champ doesn't exert himself too much, in case, you know, with his health. But with Dane not working every weekend and late into the night recently, Bryan's seeing how much work he was doing for Champ."

Oh, here it comes. The part where she warned Gabby off. To stay the hell away from her son. All because poor Champ had to pick up his pretty little fingers and put them to use other than pleasuring a woman.

Gabby refused to look away. If this woman wanted to scare her off and tell her to stay away from Dane, she could look her in the eye.

"Thank you, Gabriella." She turned her gaze to the setting sun, nearly put to bed for the night. "Thank you for showing my son what life should be about. You're perfect for him. He probably doesn't even realize how much."

Huh?

Well, maybe she wasn't mad about her taking Dane away from work.

But she knew his father was. She feared what his father would do to break them apart.

They finished their glasses of wine, talking about the upcoming wine festival that she and Mia loved to attend every year. They had the best Strawberry wine. She could usually devour an entire bottle at the event itself. Plus, she usually bought a case before she left because it was the best. She could never find it in stores, so buying it in bulk until the next year rolled around for the festival had to do.

Dane joined them. He gave his mother the present he had painstakingly shopped for. A simple gold necklace with a pendant shaped like a penguin. Apparently, his mother loved penguins. She had stuffed animal penguins. Pictures of penguins. She even had a few garden statues of penguins lingering in her roses.

She, of course, loved it. Considering he didn't have a card and had pulled the tiny box out of his pocket, she knew it only came from Dane. Gabby saw a moment of pain echo in her eyes when Champ came out on the porch with no gift.

Gabby didn't feel an ounce of remorse when Champ's cheeks flushed a light shade of red when he said he accidentally left her present on his kitchen counter. But he said he'd deliver it straight away tomorrow morning. His mother cooed with happiness as if she believed the bald-faced lie.

The man sure had a way with words.

Dane insisted they leave shortly after. Gabby didn't argue one bit.

The ride back to her apartment was silent. She didn't know what to say. Obviously, Dane had no idea either.

She liked his mother. She could mention that, but then it'd bring the topic of she didn't like his father and brother. Awkward.

He walked her up to her apartment and followed her inside. He even locked the door behind him. When they got to the living room, she turned around and looked at him. He stared back.

Still, neither said anything.

The silence stretched.

"This isn't going to work."

Her voice held finality to it.

She couldn't even believe the words came out of her mouth. They were a mistake. Except she didn't take them back. She didn't say she was wrong and hadn't meant to say that. She simply waited for him to argue the fact.

He sighed and nodded.

He. Nodded.

Oh, shit. He actually agreed.

So, she didn't protest; she hadn't meant to say it.

"Thank you for coming with me tonight. It was more bearable with you there."

Then he turned around and walked out. The soft click of the door confirmed his departure.

The best relationship of her life and it was over.

And she had no one to blame but herself.

19

A KNOCK SOUNDED on his door. He thought about ignoring it, but he told himself—forced himself—to be more vigilant about how he acted toward others. Just because he was unhappy and miserable, didn't mean he should make the people around him unhappy and miserable.

"Come in."

His voice held nothing but indifference. No happy tone whatsoever. Sure, he wouldn't ignore the knock, but he couldn't muster about any bright emotion in his tone.

Ms. Wallace opened the door and stepped inside. "It's time to leave. I thought you might want to walk down with me." The kindness and understanding in her eyes made him so appreciative he had such a wonderful secretary. Truly, a heart of gold.

"I'm not quite ready. But Barry will see you to the bus stop. Have a good night."

Her eyes portrayed she wanted to argue, but she nodded and closed the door, leaving him once again to his misery.

It had been two weeks.

Two, long agonizing weeks without Gabriella in his life.

He hadn't tried to call.

He hadn't tried to visit.

Sadly, she hadn't tried either option either.

He vowed he'd smell the roses more often, not let work consume him. He wouldn't let this breakup change him back into the man he used to be. But it only lasted one day. He'd been working late into the night every other night.

He had nowhere to go. No good reason not to work. His apartment wasn't appealing. It was a place he slept and showered. Nothing more. It wasn't a home. The home that felt like a home—Gabriella's apartment—wasn't his home. Not anymore.

Not after she kicked him out of her life.

Could he blame her? Nope. Not after the disastrous supper with his family.

His mother—God, he loved his mother—she had called once asking about Gabriella. He had to confess they weren't seeing each other any longer. He heard the disappointment in her voice, which he knew he'd hear. But he couldn't lie. Not to his mother.

As if an unasked prayer from heaven, his brother hadn't ventured into his domain once. Probably because things were back to the normal status quo. He was doing all the work again.

Well, the last laugh would be on Champ. He couldn't wait to see his expression when he found out.

Hell, the bastard wouldn't even care. Nor his father.

He stared at the open folder, wondering why he was still in the office. Why didn't he go down with Ms. Wallace? He should've. It was Friday. He could do so many other things.

This folder. This piece of paper, and the ones below it, meant nothing to him anymore.

He closed it and stood up. Grabbing his jacket from the

back of his chair, he slung it on and left the office. He didn't even glance back.

A moment of terror entered his system, almost pitching him to the floor in agony, but he managed to stay upright and at a fluid pace.

The trip down the elevator felt cathartic. Sad and disheartening, yet quite uplifting and exhilarating.

Another slice of terror hit him when he stepped out of the building. He stood there a moment, frozen. His body immobile, his insides twisting with dread and unease.

"Move it, man. You're in the way," some random guy said, bumping his shoulder.

That jolted him out of his stupor.

He walked away from the building and hailed a cab. When he knew he couldn't see the building any longer, a weight lifted from his shoulders. A heavy weight that had held him down for far too long—way longer than he should've allowed.

He paid the cabbie when he arrived at his destination, almost hesitating to tell the driver to take him home instead.

Hell, no. Tonight was for him. He'd end it how he wanted to.

He strolled into The Corner Bar and took a seat at the end of the bar away from the other patrons. He'd never been here on a Friday night, so he didn't know how busy it would get, but for now, it wasn't too full, and this area was free of other people.

Brick—or Rick—stopped in front of him with a beer ready for him. "This looks like this one might be on the house."

Dane grabbed it and inclined his head in thanks. "Why didn't you correct me and tell me your name is Rick?"

He still felt like an idiot getting his name wrong.

Brick shrugged. "It didn't seem right at the time. A few others heard you call me Brick, and I can't seem to get people to stop. It's growing on me." Brick leaned against the bar and crossed his tattooed arms, his sleeves halfway rolled up, eyeing him. As if weighing whether to inquire about his problems.

Wasn't that what people did with bartenders? They acted like therapists, people spilling their whoa-is-me problems without a thought or care who they were telling their issues to.

"I quit my job."

Brick's brow rose.

Wow. How did he do it? Dane confessed the monumental way his life just altered courses, and Brick didn't even ask him to confess. Yet, a part of Dane felt even lighter than before. More of that nasty weight shifted away by telling someone.

"Any particular reason why?"

Dane rubbed the label on the beer. He barely knew this guy, other than he was a fabulous bartender who deserved the best tip on the planet.

"I was sick of working under my brother, who doesn't do shit. I can do better on my own." A wistful smile touched his lips. "At least, I was told I could by someone...important to me."

"You don't strike me as the type to quit on the spot."

Dane exhaled, letting the air escape on its own due time. "Well, for my mother's sake—it's a family business—I should've given two weeks' notice. But to hell with my father and brother. I didn't tell them anything. I did tell my office manager, so he won't be put on the lurch. My father will think I'm making the worst mistake of my life when he finds out."

Tom was a good man. He had promised to keep the information to himself. A few minutes before Ms. Wallace had knocked on his door to tell him the day was over, he had sent his father an email, cc'd his brother. It wasn't an elaborate and long explanation—a few simple words to get his point across.

I quit. With regards, your least favorite son.

He hadn't received a call yet from his father, so he could only assume he hadn't seen the email. Or maybe he didn't care.

"Are you?"

Dane didn't even need to ponder that question. "Hell, no. I've only made one mistake in my life, and it would never involve my brother."

"Well, I sure in hell hope the mistake you're referring to is leaving Gabby, you dumbass." Jaxson appeared out of nowhere, settling on a barstool right next to him.

"Umm..." Dane cocked a brow, completely confused by Jaxson's irate manner. "Gabby broke up with me."

"Yeah, because that's what she does best. Pushes people away. She loves to help people, but when it comes to herself, she doesn't let anyone in. She pushes and pushes and pushes people out, and you let her." Jaxson slammed his hand hard on the bar top. "You walked away without a fight. I thought you loved her. You said so yourself."

"Yep, I heard it, too," Brick said as he produced another beer it seemed out of thin air and set it in front of Jaxson.

"You didn't...you didn't say I said that to her, did you?" Because if Jaxson had, then Gabriella didn't love him back. She would've come to him if she knew he loved her.

He hadn't heard a peep from her in the past two weeks.

"It's not my place to tell her." Jaxson leaned closer. "It's yours. We might not have gotten along in the beginning, but

I can see how perfect you're together. She's perfect for you, and you're perfect for her. And only an idiot would walk away from something so damn perfect."

"Hold this conversation." Brick walked away to the other end of the bar. It appeared two patrons were giving the woman bartender—Dane didn't know her name—some grief. A few words from Brick, with a menacing glare, and they stopped whatever attitude they had.

Jaxson and Dane watched the entire scene, oddly enough, waiting for Brick to start the conversation back up.

"Okay, continue," Brick said as he leaned back against the bar once again with his arms crossed. "Does she know you up and quit your job?"

"You what?" Jaxson asked as the surprise slid across his features.

Dane shrugged, hating to get into his family affair once more. "It was time. I'm starting up my own company. I already have a secretary. I just need to find some clients."

He had enough money to start his own company. Money was something he never worried about. Plus, he rarely spent it, and he knew how to invest wisely. He even found a modest space to rent for the time being until he built his company up to something amazing. And he would. If nothing more than to spite his father and show him who was the better son at architecture and making the business thrive.

"Gabby would love to hear that. In fact," Jaxson said with the sarcasm lacing his tone, "she'd love to hear anything from you. She's a mess, dude. She won't admit it, but it's been hell working with her. She misses you. She needs you."

But did she? She survived much worse without him in her life. Was he really that important to her? She didn't even last after one supper with his family.

Not that he blamed her. It had been a brutal affair. He barely survived the meals himself. It took a strong mental strength to deal with his father and brother.

"Do you love her still?" Brick asked as if they were talking about going to a baseball game and how good of seats he got.

He stared at the label on the beer and started to pick at it. "I love her so much it hurts she told me it wasn't going to work between us. She could be right."

"She's dead ass wrong. And she lied." Jaxson leaned even closer. "She lied to you."

Dane looked at him. "What?"

"You know what I'm talking about."

Damn it. Dane knew Jaxson was baiting him. Gabriella swore she'd never lie to him, and he believed her. Yet, maybe she had lied when she said it wasn't going to work between them. He should've asked her why. Why would she say that? Why would she think that? Why would she lie and say words she didn't mean?

Or maybe he was a fool for trusting her. Maybe she believed they wouldn't work out in the long run.

"Get off your ass and go to her."

That sounded like an order from Jaxson. The fierce look from Brick said he'd kick him out of the bar using the muscles stretched across his chest and arms.

Fine.

He'd go to her.

And beg her to give them a chance.

Because Jaxson was right.

She was perfect for him.

GABBY CURLED her legs underneath her and stared at the TV. She had no idea what was even on. She had flipped the switch, yet her eyes hadn't processed anything.

It had been a long week of work with barely processing much. She had a short temper, little patience, and she didn't even organize the two filing cabinets the idiots at work purposely messed up.

Just to get her out of her funk.

It didn't work.

Nothing seemed to make her feel better. Not Jaxson's comforting presence. Not Mia's consoling words. Mia didn't pry as much as Jaxson had. He wanted to know what happened. She refused to talk about it. To explain why she ended it.

She knew Jaxson figured that out on his own. He was smart, plus a damn good detective. And one of her best friends who happened to read her very, very well.

But it was for the best.

Dane needed someone stronger in his life. Someone who could let things slide and choke back their words when his father and brother were being complete assholes. For Dane's sake. For his mother's.

She was not that kind of person. She still wanted to issue more slurring words in their direction for their callous remarks and behavior. Not for the things they said about Mia, but the way they treated Dane.

Okay, fine. Poor Champ and his health problems as a baby. But he was a grown-ass man now who made conscious decisions to cheat on women. To treat his brother like an asshole. To act like his shit didn't stink. He wasn't some helpless child who needed coddling. He was an adult who needed a good ass-kicking.

She was more than happy to apply for the job.

Since that wouldn't be wise to beat his ass within an inch of his life, she did the only thing she could.

She had to let Dane go.

It had gutted her. To her very core. Right down to her soul.

It had been one long week of roaming her apartment, with visits from Jaxson and Mia, while they waited for the shooting investigation to be complete. Then another long week of working, of trying to get back into a normal routine.

She didn't even want to see what next week would bring. More short tempers, little patience, and a lack of care for the disorganization going on. Who knew how long she'd act this way? She didn't want to act like a pitiful woman like she was the scorned one. She wasn't. She left him. But her battered heart felt like she was the victim. Like she'd never recover.

Well, the break up did bring one good thing in her life.

A distraction from the shooting.

Her mind had been on Dane more than it had been on the investigation. She didn't like to think about the fact she had to shoot a man even though he had shot first.

She heard her front door open and close.

Odd.

She swore she had locked her door because she didn't want anyone to bother her. She had wanted to wallow in her self-pity for the entire weekend, and by the end, maybe she'd be ready to get back to some sort of normalcy.

Her entire body jerked when Dane stepped into view. He looked handsome yet sad. His hair, although not long enough to mess up, stood slightly on its end, as if he had been running his hand through his hair a little too much. Deep shadows rimmed his brown eyes. Wrinkles manned his forehead as a severe frown marred his lips. But his clothes looked pristine, as always.

She stood up.

He continued to stare at her.

Neither said a word.

Then he held his hand out, palm up. Her apartment key rested in the middle. She knew she had locked her door. He let himself in. Her damn fault for not getting her key back. It had slipped her mind.

"Do you want it?"

She eyed the key, then glanced at him. No, she didn't want it. She wanted him.

Instead of answering with the words that ached to escape, she stepped closer and took the key. That was about all she could answer with.

It felt warm in her palm. As sad and pathetic as it seemed, she squeezed the key tighter as if she could soak up the warmth from his touch. Pretend he was touching her and not the tiny key.

"I had a lot of different things I thought I'd say to you, but now..." he shrugged.

Now, what?

What sorts of things?

By his sudden silence, she didn't think she'd be hearing any of it.

Of course, she wasn't acting much better. Her silence was grating on her own nerves. But she couldn't seem to find her voice. Because once she spoke, she might beg him not to leave. To give her one more chance. She didn't deserve another chance.

"Jaxson said you lied to me. Let's start there." His jaw clenched, a few muscles ticking in his cheek.

She flinched. "When did you talk to Jaxson?"

"Answer my question first."

She didn't want to. Mostly because it wouldn't help her already strung emotions.

"Gabriella—" he started to say as he took a step forward. But he stopped when she took a step back.

Enough was enough. She had to put her big girl panties on and tell him the truth—kind of. Then kick him out of her life once again before she broke down in tears.

"I haven't lied to you."

At least, not really. When she told him things wouldn't work between them, she hadn't lied. She didn't things would work between them—unless they fought hard to make them work.

And he didn't fight. He walked out instead. So, she didn't fight either. She didn't want to be the cause of even more tension between him and his father and brother. She made the best decision for both of them.

A slow grin emerged. "I didn't think you did. You promised you wouldn't."

"You should go."

Please stay.

"Okay. I'll go."

He still wasn't going to fight. Damn her for putting all the fighting onto his shoulders. It was selfish, and she knew it. She should scream out that she loved him. That she missed him. That she wanted—needed—him in her life. For always.

Dane started to turn around, then stopped.

"Before I go, I thought I'd share that I quit."

She frowned. "Quit...your job?"

An enigmatic smile popped up. Not just on his lips, but in his whiskey-colored eyes. "About an hour ago. Via email. I thought my dad would get a kick out of that. No notice, either. It felt liberating. He never cares how he treats me, so..." Dane shrugged. "I know I should take the higher ground and act like an adult, but I couldn't help myself. Ms. Wallace is coming with me. The only employee on my payroll right now."

"With you?"

He nodded, the excitement suddenly gleaming in his eyes. "I'm starting my own company. This beautiful woman once told me I would do amazing with my own company. I've decided to take a leap of faith and see if she's right."

A tentative smile slowly appeared. She couldn't have stopped it if she tried. "She sounds super smart. I'm glad you took her advice."

He took a step toward her. This time she didn't take a step back.

"Yeah, she also told me—a lot of times," he chuckled, "that I needed to not work so much. To have some fun."

"Everyone needs downtime." Her heart started to pound.

Another step forward.

"She made me see how much I was missing out on things."

Another step.

"She showed me what love was."

One more step. He stood so close, all he had to do was bend slightly to kiss her.

"And that I can't live without that love."

Whoa. Not at all what she was expecting.

Then he grabbed her hand that didn't hold the key and interlocked his fingers with her. His lips touched hers. Softly, and oh so tenderly, she wanted to burst into tears.

She was so sick of crying, but she couldn't help the intense emotion filling her up. Like a bathtub filling until the water hit the rim and well, where was the water supposed to go but over the side. That's how she felt with her tears building.

"I love you, Gabriella. I love every fierce, strong, exciting thing about you." His mouth stayed close to hers as he whispered with a yearning that had her heart beating even harder. "You said you don't think things will work between us. Well, I call bullshit. The last two weeks have been two long weeks of hell. If things weren't going to work, then it wouldn't feel like my heart was ripped out of its chest and stomped on repeatedly."

"But your father—"

"Can go to hell."

Although her heart wanted to sing with delight and happiness, she couldn't. "I won't be the cause of more tension between you two. He doesn't like me."

"He doesn't like anyone unless they adore Champ. And you don't cause anything. He does." He squeezed her hand. "That supper wasn't great. I know. I'm sorry he offended you. But it was the first supper that wasn't as bad as they usually are."

"Seriously?" Her brow slid up incredulously.

"Because you were by my side. You make things better. You make me better. You're perfect for me, and I'm sorry I even walked away two weeks ago. I should've fought for us." His expression turned stern. "But I'm fighting now."

It's as if he read her thoughts from earlier. As if he knew she needed him to fight for her.

She was always fighting. Fighting for the victims she met daily. Fighting for Mia—in all aspects of her life. Fighting to survive in a world that wasn't always pretty. She was so tired of always being the one to fight.

But not today.

Not with Dane.

"Tell me you love me."

Her lips twisted into an instant smile as she chuckled. "That sounded like a demand."

A sly, sinful grin slid across his lips. "Please."

Oh, how could she resist that?

She slid her hand that held the key into his pocket and dropped it.

"I love you, Dane."

"That's all I needed to hear."

Then he kissed her. Hard and passionate. Letting loose all the other unspoken words he had filled in his heart. She heard them in every twist of his lips. From the stroke of his tongue. At the way he pulled her tighter into his embrace. She heard each and every delicate word of his love.

She might have gotten the wrong brother in her original mission, but it was the best mistake she ever made.

EPILOGUE

Two months later

"Yo, Brick, can you turn up the TV?" Jaxson yelled over the loud crowd filling The Corner Bar on a Saturday night.

Dane wanted to groan out loud and slap Jaxson on the back of the head.

Brick did the job for him—figuratively speaking. He sent a menacing glare, crossed his arms—something he often did—and stared at Jaxson until Jaxson caught on.

Perhaps that was the last time he confessed to Jaxson his plans. He knew he planned to propose to Gabriella tonight, but he didn't want to have to fight for her attention if they turned the volume up to the baseball game. She sure loved her baseball, getting lost in a game quite easily.

Not that he minded most nights. She watched her baseball—he peeked a few times—while he worked relentlessly next to her on the couch.

It hadn't been easy, but his company was coming along. New clients came easily. Probably because he wasn't new to the game and people knew his name in the architect world.

His father's company was still doing well, but barely. Champ was somehow managing to keep it going with few hiccups. Tom, his old office manager, gave him updates since his father and brother haven't spoken to him since he quit.

It didn't bother him one bit. Except for the times he talked to his mother and knew how much the discord between them hurt her.

But Gabriella was his rock through it all. He knew he'd never want anyone else by his side but her. No matter the issue.

Which was why, even though they'd only been dating three months, he decided it was time to ask her to marry him. Why wait? He knew she was the one. And when he wanted something, he went for it.

He hadn't meant to tell Jaxson and Brick, but a few nights ago, while they were waiting for Gabriella and Mia to arrive, it slipped out. Brick had a way about him where he always felt compelled to confess his deep, dark secrets. The man probably knew more about him than his brother. It was scary how one look had him spilling the oddest things.

While they both suggested he propose at home or even at a quiet restaurant, he thought Gabriella would like it more if her friends were in attendance. Her family.

His family.

These people who had only entered his life three short months ago felt more like his family than his real one. And yes, he wanted them here, too. He wanted their support, their happiness to surround both of them.

If only he could find the nerve to ask her.

Since they arrived an hour ago, all he'd been doing was twisting the tiny box in his pocket over and over, his heart pounding, sweating with intense nerves.

She might say no.

Just because they said I love yous and moved in together —her apartment—over a month ago, didn't mean she'd say yes to marriage.

But he wouldn't know if he didn't try. Just like he never knew he could run his own company. Build it from scratch all on his own. Unless he tried. And he was knocking it out of the park.

That didn't mean it was easy. He worked late nights on occasion. Sometimes even on the weekends.

Except he owned the company.

He worked from home. With the woman he loved by his side.

"Do it already," Jaxson whispered.

He sat next to Jaxson with Gabriella on his other side so she couldn't hear him whispering like a jackass. It's as if he was trying to ruin the moment.

"She's not going to say no. Just do it." Jaxson rolled his eyes. "Please."

That garnered a chuckle he couldn't stop.

"You really want that TV turned up." He couldn't help but needle Jaxson a bit. Plus, it was working to settle his nerves a bit.

"It is a good game, and we're winning."

Suddenly the crowd erupted in cheers as their team hit it out of the park. Gabriella grabbed him by the shoulder and squealed excitedly.

"Five run lead. Take that." Then she kissed him soundly on the lips.

"God, you're so beautiful." He wrapped his free hand around her neck and deepened the kiss.

He told her with each sweep of his tongue how much he loved her.

"Oh, you two, enough with the kissing." Mia said it jokingly, yet Dane heard the underlying tension.

Oh, and that tension was usually there when Mia and Jaxson were in the same room together. They both said they talked about Jaxson's confession. They both said they were going to remain friends.

They both royally lied and refused to admit it.

Dane slowed the kiss, then lessened his hold on Gabriella. She turned around and stuck her tongue out at Mia. He took the opportunity to pull the box out of his pocket.

He couldn't keep delaying it. He was acting like a chickenshit and for no apparent reason. He knew it down to the bottom of his soul; she wouldn't say no.

Because they were perfect for each other.

He set the box on the counter and opened it.

Gabriella shifted her attention back to him. Her eyes rounded in shock when she noticed the jewelry box and the large sparkling diamond sitting there.

Damn it.

That was all wrong. He should've gotten down on his knee.

Too late now.

"Will you marry me?" Then before she could dodge his question with her witty sarcasm. He added, "Please."

"I thought you'd never ask." She grasped his shirt into a fistful and pulled him closer. "Yes." Her lips met his in a kiss once again.

"She said yes!" Brick shouted out to the bar as if the entire bar had known his secret all along. "Next round's on me."

The entire place roared with more cheers.

Dane would pay for the round, no matter what Brick said. But it was a nice gesture.

Thank goodness for good friends.

And for the beautiful woman in his arms. Life wouldn't be as happy and carefree without her.

WANT TO READ JAXSON AND MIA'S STORY? CHECK OUT
THE RIGHT TIME!

FOR JAXSON & MIA'S STORY
THE RIGHT TIME
A PERFECT FOR YOU NOVEL, #2

The plan: Organize an epic birthday party without spilling the massive secret—that has nothing to do with the party.
Time Frame: Two weeks.

Plan a party? Check.
Try not to think about the man she can't have? Check.
Suddenly accept said man's proposal. Check.

Wait...what did Mia Carter do? There was no way she could marry Jaxson Brandt. It would never last. Nothing in her life ever does. They weren't even dating. They couldn't go from just friends to marriage. She'll just have to tell him she changed her mind. If only he'd give her a chance to do so. But between planning a birthday party and trying to keep her bestie from finding out they're getting hitched, she can't seem to find the right time. He's making it his mission to show her what love is truly about—something she'd never had before. She's just not sure it'll be enough to convince her.

For Brick & Jezebelle's story

The Easy Part

A Perfect for You Novel, #3

The Agreement: Pretend to be her fake fiancé to placate her overbearing, selfish mother.
Timeframe: Five days.

Brick likes things carefree and simple, especially after the falling out with his brother. The moment Jezebelle walks into his bar looking sad and troubled, he's determined to do anything to turn her frown upside down. Even if that requires posing as her fake fiancé to get her bossy mother off her back. Pretending to love her will be the easy part—because he does. Walking away will be futile. But he doesn't see a way he can keep Jezebelle for real, not when her mother's diabolical ways prove she can make his life more than just complicated, but downright impossible.

Jezebelle can't believe her luck when Brick hatches this crazy plan. One, because she's always had a secret crush on him, and any reason to get closer to him makes her heart stutter with anticipation. Two, because it might actually work to keep her mother at bay. Of course, her mother isn't a woman who takes no for an answer. She'll do everything in her power to get her way. The last thing she wants is for Brick to get hurt. The best thing she can do is walk away and forget he ever held her heart. If only it were that easy.

FOR COREY & GENEVIEVE'S STORY
THE HARD CHOICE
A PERFECT FOR YOU NOVEL, #4

The Goal: Start taking responsibility for his actions—one in particular: taking care of the baby that landed in his arms.
Time Frame: Forever.

Life's always been hard for him. Cruel father. Losing his mom. Falling prey to drugs. Getting clean and fighting to stay on the straight and narrow. Now, raising a little girl with no help from her mother. It's nothing new, and he's determined to give his baby girl what he never had—a loving father in a good home. In order to do so, he has to stay away from his old life—too much drugs and a whole lotta sex. Which means no women...until she walks into his life.

She's always had it easy. Loving parents. Protective and supportive brothers. Decent job. A best friend...until her bestie isn't there anymore. She feels the walls closing in and her world looking not so perfect. She failed her best friend and she vows to make everything right. To do that, she has to tangle with a man she should stay far away from. He's nothing but bad news. Except she's finding it hard to resist him and his sweet charm. Of course, she loves his little girl. But loving him...it'd be the wrong choice.

ABOUT THE AUTHOR

I'm a *USA Today* Bestselling Author that loves to write contemporary romance and romantic suspense novels, although I am partial to romantic suspense. I even dabble in paranormal. Honestly, I love anything that has to do with romance. As long as there's a happy ending, I'm a happy camper. And insta-love...yes, please! I love baseball (Go Twins!) and creating awesome crafts. I graduated with a Bachelor's Degree in Criminal Justice, working in that field for several years before I became a stay-at-home mom. I have a few more amazing stories in the works. If you would like to learn more about me and my books, head to my website by scanning the QR code. Thanks for reading!

Scan me